THE RELUCTANT COMPANION

13 KINGDOMS #1

H.L DAY

Copyright

All Rights Reserved:

This literary work may not be reproduced or transmitted in any form or by any means including electronic or photographic reproduction, in whole or in part, without express written permission.

The Reluctant Companion is a work of fiction. Names, characters, places, and incidents either are the product of the author's imagination or are used fictitiously, and any resemblance to actual persons, living or dead, business establishments, events, or locales is entirely coincidental.

Warning

Intended for an 18+ audience. This book contains material that may be offensive to some and is intended for a mature, adult audience. It contains graphic language, explicit sexual content, and adult situations.

Cover Art by Sheri-Lynn Marean at SLM creations

Editing by Alyson Roy - Royal Editing Services

The Reluctant Companion © 2022 H.L Day

OTHER BOOKS BY THE SAME AUTHOR

EagerBoyz series
Eager To Try (#0.5)
Eager For You (#1)
Eager For More (#2)

Too Far series
A Dance too Far (#1)
A Step too Far (#2)

Temporary series
A Temporary Situation (Tristan and Dom #1)
A Christmas Situation (Tristan and Dom #1.5)
Temporary Insanity (Paul and Indy #1)

Fight for Survival series
Refuge
Rebellion

Standalones
Time for a Change
Kept in the Dark
Taking Love's Lead
Edge of Living
Christmas Riches

Exposed
The Longest Night
Not So Silent Night

H.L Day's alter ego H.L Night

<u>Twisted Web series</u>
Shai (Twisted Web #1)
Elijah Twisted Web #2)

BLURB

Sebastian might have the power to summon animals, but winning Jack over? Far more difficult.

As first encounters go, Jack and Sebastian's isn't ideal, leaving Jack nursing a grudge he's not about to let go of in a hurry. Yet, if Jack is to find his missing sister, and Sebastian is to rescue his captured prince, they'll need to set their differences aside and work as a team.

Jack is stubborn and somewhat volatile. Sebastian is vain and clearly in love with himself. But as the unlikely companions face all manner of dangers together, they grow closer. Rescuing the prince should be easy. Rescuing him from an impenetrable tower guarded by dragon-shifting knights? Okay, that part is harder.

But once the adventure is over, letting Sebastian go might be the hardest thing Jack has ever had to do.

The Reluctant Companion is an 85k MM enemies to lovers story featuring murderous orcs, deadly creatures, and marauding bandits. Opposites attract in this light-hearted fantasy romance which mixes humor with action and adventure. Meet a whole cast of colorful characters in the first book of the 13 kingdoms series.

Maps

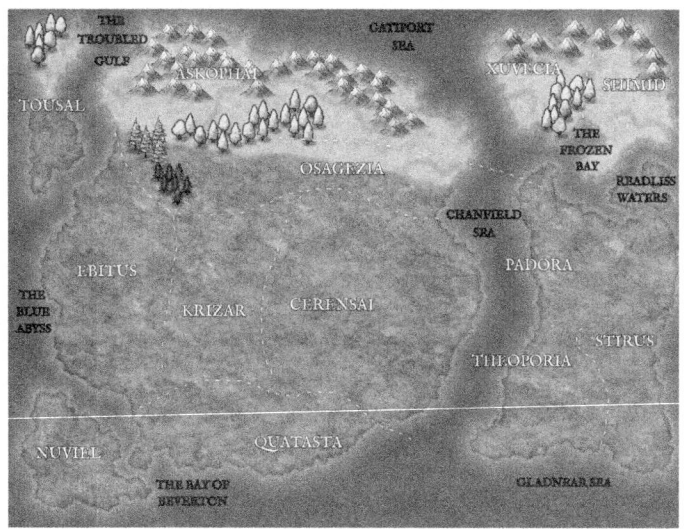

The 13 Kingdoms

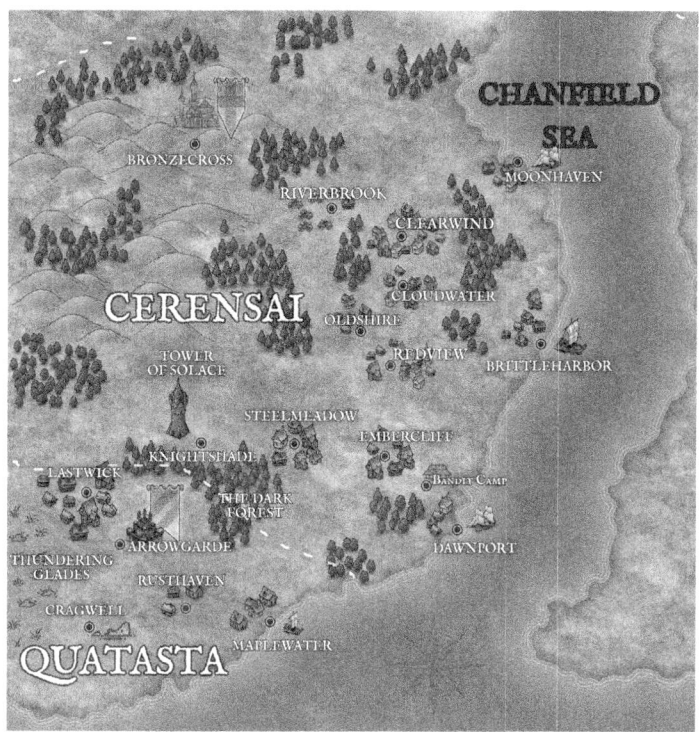

The Kingdom of Cerensai

FOREWORD

When I wrote this book, I had no idea that I'd subconsciously picked up the pet name that Sebastian calls Jack from The Princess Bride. I agonized over whether to change it or not during revisions, but in the end decided not to, so it stayed. So thank you, The Princess Bride for unwittingly placing that in my head. I've erm.... borrowed it.

Also, I wanted to say a huge thank you to my beta readers Barbara, Jill, and Sherry whose comments made this story better.

CHAPTER ONE

JACK

I lifted my head to peer across the tavern. Did that elf have a tail? For a moment there, I could have sworn there was something long, black, and curly waving in the air behind him. When the elf turned to look my way, I quickly averted my gaze, realizing too late that there was no tail and all I was doing was staring at his ass. The last few days had been difficult enough without getting into a fight.

It had all seemed so simple when I'd left my farm in Riverbrook a week ago to track down my missing sister. I'd travel to the neighboring villages. I'd enquire about a woman with distinctive red hair, which was such a rarity in this kingdom that she'd stand out like a sore thumb, and I'd find her in no time. She'd return home with me, and everything would go back to the way it had been before, where everyone was happy.

Except... Annabelle had disappeared into thin air. No one had seen her. No one had heard of her. No one even knew who she was. I was no closer to finding her than when I'd first set out. It was painful to recall how upset my mother had been about Annabelle's disappearance. She did her best to hide it, but constant crying took its toll, both on her and those around her.

It had been decided that someone needed to go and find her, and despite being the youngest of my siblings at twenty-six, I'd volunteered. My mother had said that it was a bad idea, that she wasn't willing to risk losing two of her children, but I'd seen the hope shining in her eyes when she'd said it. Deep down, she'd wanted me to go. We'd scraped together what money we could as a family, and here I was.

I pulled my gaze away from the murky depths of my tankard of ale to the leather pouch on the table. It had contained considerably more gold coins at the start of the week than it did now. I'd been careful. I really had. But food and drink cost money. As did having a roof over my head at night.

At my current rate of spending, I had about another week, and then it would be all gone. I rubbed a weary hand over my face while I contemplated my options. The obvious solution would be to return home, to admit defeat. But then I'd have nothing to show for it, and we would be right back at square one, no wiser as to where my sister had disappeared to. And it wasn't as if I only wanted to find Annabelle for my mother's sake. I wanted to find her for me too. I was just as worried. We all were.

I lifted my head to stare around the tavern, its occupants strangely fascinating to someone who had rarely left their village before. Riverbrook might attract the occasional stranger passing through, either by intent or because they'd gotten lost, but that was nothing in comparison to the cluster of citizens that had come together under this roof. It was like someone had raked a hand through the people of the surrounding kingdoms, given them a good shake, and then tipped them into the tavern.

There were dwarves, and wizards, and elves. And in the corner was a lady whose skin shimmered in the light. I wasn't sure what she was. It didn't matter who I asked, though, the story was always the same. No one had caught a glimpse of a girl with red hair. Had she headed in a different direction, or was she covering her hair? And if so, why? Had she suspected that one of us might come after her? Those questions paled in significance, though, compared to why she'd left in the first place.

Annabelle had always been a free spirit. Most women in Riverbrook were married and had children by twenty-eight, but she'd never seemed interested.

There'd been dalliances. There'd even been men who'd competed for her attention and would quite happily have married her should she have shown even the slightest bit of interest. But Annabelle had laughed and moved on.

And then one day she'd been gone.

No goodbye. No note. No explanation. Just gone. If it hadn't been for the fact that there was no sign of a struggle, and that all of her things were gone too, we might have feared some sort of abduction. But what sort of abductor took clothes as well? Her disappearance was a complete mystery. One that at the beginning of this week I'd expected to solve relatively easily.

Movement on the other side of the tavern caught my attention. A flash of something furry. There one minute. Gone the next. I leaned forward to peer into the dark shadows, but just like the previous time there was nothing to see. Lifting the tankard to my mouth, I lowered it again without taking a drink. How many had I had? If I was starting to see things that weren't there, it was probably time to lay off the ale. I shook my head and returned to pondering the decision I needed to make. Go home and break the bad news, or continue searching for my sister for a few more days?

I reared back as something dropped onto the table from above, and I found myself staring at black eyes and sharp canine teeth. A monkey. *What in the name of all that is holy!* It opened its mouth and chattered, the sound almost indignant, as if it was chastising me for being in the wrong place rather than the other way round. Looking around, I expected to see faces as surprised as my own at this rather strange turn of events. But no one seemed interested. They either hadn't noticed or didn't care that there was a monkey loose in the tavern.

What did you do with an uninvited monkey? Did you ask it politely to leave, or were there other measures you were meant to take? There were no monkeys in Riverbrook. In fact, I hadn't thought there were any in the kingdom of Cerensai at all, which made its presence all the more absurd. Was it someone's pet? Where had it come from? If I could capture it, perhaps I could sell it. That would not only get rid of the monkey but also solve my financial problems at the same time.

As if reading my mind, the monkey leapt from the table in a black and white blur to streak across the floor in the direction of the door. Shaking my head ruefully, I lifted my tankard to my mouth once more. At least now that I knew I hadn't been hallucinating, I could drink again.

I didn't get that far, freezing in place as I registered the blank space on the table where moments before my money pouch had sat. Had it fallen off when the monkey landed on the table? Leaning to one side, I craned my neck to look under the table.

Nothing. There was only one possible explanation. The monkey had stolen my money. Furry little bastard. I looked up just in time to see the tip of the monkey's tail disappear out of the door. I stood up, the ale from my tankard sloshing over the table. "Stop that monkey!"

There was a titter of embarrassed laughter, heads turning my way and people staring at me like I'd taken complete leave of my senses. I waved a hand at the door. "There was a monkey. It stole my money."

The barmaid crossed the room to stand in front of my table with her hands on her hips. There was a sympathetic smile on her face as she dipped her chin in the direction of my tankard. "I think you've had enough, sweetheart. It's probably time to call it a night. There aren't any monkeys in Cerensai."

The dwarf at the next table lifted his tankard in a toast. "No monkeys to be found until you reach Theoporia... and I'll drink to that. They're sneaky little fuckers. They probably would steal your money if there were any around here, but there aren't. They like a warmer climate."

It was clear that there was no help to be had around here. And every second I spent trying to appeal to the good nature of strangers was another second that the monkey was getting away. Abandoning the rest of my ale and grabbing my bow, I darted to the door and out into the street. Where was it? If I could catch it, I could get my money back. The alternative didn't bear thinking about. It would leave me stranded, three days' journey away from Riverbrook, and with no means of paying for anything. I could sleep rough, but I couldn't survive on nothing but air.

There. A flash of tail. The little bastard had climbed to the roof and was making his way along the street above my head. Keeping my eyes trained on it, I followed. It would have to come down eventually. The monkey was fast enough that I was forced to break into a jog. Without slowing, I plucked an arrow from the quiver on my back and notched it in my bow. I blew out a frustrated breath. Even as good a shot as I was, and I was one of the best, the monkey was too small a target and too nimble for me to stand a chance of taking it down. I needed to be patient and bide my time.

Bumping into someone, I almost pushed them out of the way in my haste not to lose sight of the monkey. Curse words were shouted after me, but I ignored them. Could they not see that I was in pursuit of a thief? It was almost like the monkey was invisible to anyone except me. I drew closer, close enough to be able to see my money pouch in the monkey's mouth, a rush of excitement at being proved correct giving me an extra burst of speed. And then the monkey ran out of roof. Ha! Now what was it going to do?

It began to shimmy down the side of the building, its nimble paws making the descent look easy. Once it reached the ground, it took off on all fours at breakneck speed to the other side of the street. It was imperative that I reach it before it found its way off the ground again. I was so intent on my prey that I didn't see the man until he was right in front of me.

I skidded to a halt, my gaze fixed on a pair of black boots. I let my eyes drift slowly up. Tight trousers almost plastered to muscular thighs. A rather generous bulge. *Holy shit! Those trousers really were tight.* Blushing furiously, I yanked my gaze away, taking in the rest in one glance as he leaned casually against the wall with his arms crossed. Shirtless. Arms and chest just as nicely defined as the thighs. Long blond hair with a slight wave to it. The bluest eyes I'd ever seen perfectly framed by long blond lashes. A well-shaped nose and jaw. The man was absolutely breathtaking. And the knowing smirk on his face said he was all too aware of that fact.

"Sorry, I..." I stopped. I'd been so intent on drooling over the man's many positive attributes that I'd failed to notice the monkey perched on his shoulder, its tail hanging loosely over his chest, the curl at the end framing one brown nipple like it was a piece of art.

A wave of rage coalesced inside me, and I saw red. "Your monkey stole my money. Give it back."

"What monkey?"

The man had a cultured voice, the letters perfectly enunciated. I stared at him. The monkey and its annoying owner both stared back. I lifted a hand to point, too far gone down the path of righteous anger to be able to control the slight tremor in my fingers. "That monkey."

Gold sparks shimmered in the air. I blinked, and when I opened my eyes, the monkey was gone. Magic. It figured that this... peacock of a man who was clearly in love with himself and had already been blessed with good looks and a good physique, would also have access to magic. When I'd been a boy, magic had been a rarity in this kingdom—something that only royalty possessed—but in recent years, it had become more commonplace.

The monkey was a summon: an animal that existed only to do its master's bidding. Which meant that the monkey was no more to blame for stealing my money than the tree that lay to my right was. No, the fault lay entirely with the man. He'd summoned an animal for the express purpose of robbing someone in the tavern, and I'd been the one to fall victim to his machinations.

"As I said, what monkey?"

My mouth fell open at the sheer audacity of the man. "You... you..." I was so enraged I couldn't get the words out. If I couldn't manage words, then I'd take matters into my own hands. I was on him in a split second, seeking out possible hiding places for my money pouch in his clothes. As there weren't many clothes to search, I was forced to concentrate on his trousers, the pockets revealing nothing of note as I patted them down. Where had he put it? I ran my hands down his thighs, swallowing when there was nothing but hard muscle beneath my fingertips. There was of course one prominent bulge, but I wasn't going there. Not until I'd exhausted every other possible avenue first.

"I normally insist on dinner first before I let someone grope me to their heart's content."

"I doubt that."

He laughed. It was a throaty laugh that under other circumstances I might have found decidedly sexy. "You're right. Why waste time with dinner when there are far more interesting things to do. I'd claim that I normally insist on knowing a person's name, but that wouldn't be true either. Speaking of names, I'm Sebastian, by the way. Sebastian Beau. My friends call me Bass."

A pretentious name for a pretentious person. I paused in my search to give him my most venomous glare. "Why would I have even the slightest interest in your name? Once I've got my money, I have no intention of ever seeing you again. If I saw you walking in my direction, I'd turn and walk the other way."

"That's a bit harsh...?"

The pause and the way his voice went up at the end in a question was clearly designed to encourage me to give my name. Well, that wasn't going to happen. "Where is it? Give it to me." I was breathing hard, my chest rising and falling rapidly. I couldn't remember the last time I'd felt this much fury. I wasn't sure it had ever happened. Riverbrook was blessedly free of men like this. Forcing myself to take a step back, I scanned the street.

"What are you looking for?"

Sebastian sounded both amused and slightly curious. What did he think I was looking for? Wasn't it obvious? "The authorities. So that they can arrest you and I can get my money back."

He nodded sagely. "Ah! Then I'm afraid I have bad news for you. There are no authorities in Clearwind today."

"None?" Did he really think I was going to take his word for it?

He shook his head, his blond hair swishing gently around his shoulders in a golden cloud. "I'm afraid there's been an incident in Cloudwater that they've had to deal with. Something to do with escaped pigs and a fruit stall, or so I heard."

I narrowed my eyes at him. "Was it something to do with you?"

He clasped a hand to his chest in mock offense. "Now why would you go and throw out accusations like that when we've only just met?"

"Oh, I don't know. Maybe because you stole my money. And it doesn't take a genius to work out that such a crime would be far easier when the authorities are conveniently missing."

He raised his chin. "Where's your proof that I stole your money?"

I'd had enough, rage subsiding enough for me to be able to think a little more clearly. Retrieving my bow from the ground where I'd dropped it, I notched an arrow and aimed it at the center of his chest. "Give me my money."

He raised his hands in the air, blue eyes going wide. "Or what? You'll kill me? Now, who's gaining an advantage from there being no authorities around. Perhaps *you* had something to do with the pigs escaping and going on a rampage." I pulled the bow string back, the action seeming to shock him into realizing I was serious.

"Okay. Okay. Fine. He slid a hand into his boot, a familiar money pouch dangling from his fingers when he withdrew his hand. His boot. Of course. Why hadn't I thought to look there? He gave the money pouch a quick toss in the air, his expression thoughtful. "It doesn't feel like there's much in it. Would you really kill a man over this amount of money?"

I smiled. Although, it was probably more teeth and less actual smile. "Not usually, but I'd make an exception for you."

Sebastian's eyebrows shot up. "You're a feisty one, aren't you? Good job I like feisty."

"I don't need you to like me." I put the arrow back in its quiver and made a grab for the pouch. Sebastian was too quick, though, the money pouch yanked away before my fingertips could so much as brush it. "Give. It. To. Me."

"I'm sure we can come to some sort of mutually beneficial agreement."

I frowned. "Like what?"

"Like..." He thought for a while, his face brightening after a few seconds. "I've got it." He gave the money pouch a little shake, the coins giving an obliging little tinkle. "I could provide a service, and this could be payment for that service."

"A service? What sort of service?" I couldn't think of anything this man could provide that would be remotely useful to me. Not unless he could locate missing sisters.

Sebastian lowered his eyelashes in a flirtatious fashion. "What do you want? I can be very accommodating. You only need to ask."

For a moment, I could do nothing but stare at him. He couldn't mean... Shit! He did mean that. "Are you insinuating that I might want to pay you to sleep with me?"

Sebastian winked. "There won't be a lot of sleeping going on, but yes, that's about the long and short of it." He gave the pouch another shake. "There's probably enough to cover one night. So, what do you say? Do we have a deal?"

I counted very slowly to ten. And then I added another five just for good measure. It seemed to work, my voice surprisingly calm when I finally spoke. "I wouldn't touch you if you were the last man left in all the thirteen kingdoms, and you were hand delivered to my door. The money in that pouch would be far too much even if I were buying you for the rest of my life, which, just for the record, I wouldn't do unless I'd had some sort of terrible accident which had given me the mental faculties of a turnip. And even then, I would like to think that I might have turned my sexual interests to farmyard animals rather than you."

"Are you saying you would rather have sex with a goat?"

I nodded. "That's exactly what I'm saying."

"Huh!" Sebastian seemed momentarily thrown by my rejection of his charms. He probably wasn't used to it. I imagined that most women—and men—were easily won over by the muscles and blond hair. It was lucky that I was made of stronger stuff. He smiled. "I could find you a goat. For a price." I made another swipe for the pouch, but he was too fast again. "Listen, I need this. I have a very important quest to carry out, one that needs capital to get it off the ground. What do you say we go to the tavern and talk about this?"

"No."

"Please."

"No."

Either Sebastian's ears were just for decoration, or he simply wasn't used to people saying no to him. Unfortunately, while I was still pondering which it was, Sebastian took my arm and steered me back the way I'd come. And as he still had my money, I let him.

CHAPTER TWO

SEBASTIAN

Several heads turned our way as we entered the tavern. Used to attracting attention, I didn't think much of it. Keeping tight hold of my new friend's arm, I steered him toward the table in the corner. I wasn't worried about him running off. It was clear he had no intention of going anywhere until we'd reached a compromise over the money that had come to be in my possession. However, those arrows of his did look quite sharp, so anything that kept his hands away from his bow was a bonus in my eyes.

He sat down with all the easy acceptance of a dog shoved into a cage, plotting its escape. The barmaid arrived a few moments later. She planted her hands on the table and leaned forward, a position designed to accentuate the heaving bosom only barely constrained in her corset. I looked. It would have been rude not to when she'd gone to all that trouble. She giggled and curled a tendril of dark hair around her finger, peering at me coquettishly from beneath her lashes. "What can I get you?"

"Two ales."

Her gaze strayed across to my reluctant companion. "I can get one for you, but he's had enough."

I turned to face him, his expression sour enough to curdle milk. "Have you? I didn't realize you were deep in your cups. Although"—I waved a hand at the bow resting on the seat next to him—"it would go some way toward explaining your aggression."

His eyebrows shot up. "My aggression!" I watched with fascination as his nostrils flared and his cheeks grew slowly redder. He definitely had anger issues. His fingers curled around the table as he leaned forward. "I barely drank anything. The people in this tavern are, however, concerned that I was seeing monkeys."

I stared at him for a moment and then I threw my head back and laughed, dimly aware of him still speaking.

"...perhaps you could explain that said monkey was real, or at least looked real."

I sat back in my chair and shared a conspiratorial look with the barmaid. "Sorry, I can't help. I haven't seen any monkeys." Ignoring the frenzied muttering that met my announcement from the surly man at my side, I gestured for the barmaid to come closer. She came with an eagerness that, had she leaned just a little bit more forward, would have had her in my lap. Perhaps that had been the plan. I gave her a wink. "Listen, I'll look after him." I tapped my nose. "You know, keep him safe from the monkeys."

She gave another giggle. "Two ales coming right up." She put on a special sashay for my benefit as she returned to the bar.

"How are you going to pay for that ale?"

I tore my eyes away from the retreating barmaid and back to my new friend. He was far more interesting to look at anyway, a lock of his dark hair having fallen over his forehead to offset his green eyes beautifully. He had good bone structure as well. And as for his lips, well, let's just say that I was far from averse to finding out what they'd feel like against my own. He might have claimed that he'd rather sleep with a goat, but I'd seen the way he'd checked me out in the moments before he'd realized where the monkey had come from. He'd definitely been interested. Could interest die that quickly just because of one little misunderstanding? I didn't think so. I lifted the money pouch. "With my money."

"*My* money."

At least he didn't try and make a grab for it this time. That was progress. The barmaid returned with two tankards of ale, the kiss I blew her turning her cheeks scarlet. "*Our* money."

A furrow appeared on my companion's brow. "'*Our*' money?"

I scooted around to face him. "What if I told you that I could take this money and give you double the amount back?"

I took the opportunity during the long pause that followed to take a gulp of my ale. At least a minute ticked by before he rested his elbows on the table and let out a sigh. "I'm listening. How?"

I smiled. "There's a price for that information."

His snort was tinged with a great deal of irritation. "I can't give you any money. You already have all of it."

I leaned in. "There are more important things in life than money."

"Clearly not self-respect and human decency. Not for you, anyway."

He certainly had a sharp tongue. I liked it. It made a refreshing change from being fawned all over. "All I want is your name. Is that too much to ask?"

Green eyes narrowed suspiciously. "My name?"

"Your name." I propped my chin on my hand and waited. It wouldn't be something exotic. It would be something straightforward, like him. A strong name. A name that couldn't be shortened, that couldn't be anything except what it was.

His expression said he was being forced to provide the information under duress. "Jack."

"Jack, what?"

"Jack Shaw. Now, tell me how you're going to double my money?"

I smiled in triumph. "There's a big tournament in Cloudwater tomorrow. You've probably heard about it. It's an annual event. In order to take part, I need a stake. That's where... your... *our* money comes into it. I take that money and I turn it into far more money." I sat back, satisfied that the problem was solved.

He held my gaze. "That's it. That's your plan. Gambling? And what happens when instead of doubling it, you lose it all instead. Where does that leave me?"

I shook my head. "I don't lose. You need to trust me. By tomorrow night, I can give you your money back and a bit extra for your troubles."

Jack's grimace demonstrated what he thought of that idea. "You expect me to trust a man who robbed me?"

"I didn't rob you. I borrowed some money from you."

"Against my will and without asking me first. And it wasn't even you, it was a monkey controlled by you. I didn't hear him asking if he could *borrow* some money either. Unless that was what he was saying when he was chittering at me. I wouldn't know. I can't speak monkey."

I shrugged. I could already tell that Jack was one of those people who saw things in black and white—a straight arrow. I scooched along the seat and slung a friendly arm around his shoulders. He went so still that I may as well have threatened him with grievous bodily harm. I ignored it. Jack was clearly just a little uptight. He'd loosen up in time, once he got to know me. "Sometimes great things come of unlikely circumstances." That was good. It made me sound like I was full of wisdom. I'd have to remember that and use it again.

Jack didn't seem quite as impressed by it, if the way he ducked under my arm was any indication. I was left with no option but to let him go. Shame. He'd felt good there. All lean and muscled and warm.

He narrowed his eyes. "Why aren't you wearing a shirt?"

Strange question. There I was, cutting him in on a deal that would double his money, and that's what he wanted to talk about. "It's hot."

He lowered his chin, the following words muttered into his chest so that I had to strain to hear them. "Not that hot."

I took another gulp of ale. "Do you have a room? We're going to need somewhere to stay."

"We!" Jack looked utterly horrified by the concept.

"I assumed you wouldn't want to let me out of your sight? You know, in case I forgot the money was ours and thought it was just mine."

A multitude of emotions crossed his face, the last of which could only have been described as resignation. "One room?"

I ran a hand through my hair and offered him a dazzling smile. "One room."

The room had already been prepared for us by the time we got there, probably by the barmaid who had made it more than clear that if I wanted a bit of company I only had to ask, and she'd be up there like a shot. I had no idea what she expected Jack to do during our interlude, whether he was supposed to watch or join in. Actually, that last idea had some merit, but based on his announcement that he'd rather screw a goat than have sexual relations with me, I didn't think he'd be up for it.

Lanterns had been lit, the bed turned down, and a steaming bath had been placed in front of the roaring fire in the hearth. I wasted no time in stripping off and easing myself into the water, my knees pulled up to my chin. Jack didn't seem to know what to do with himself. He'd spent most of the time since we'd entered the room staring at the bed. I'd assumed his fascination with it had been a determination not to look my way while I'd been naked. Except, I was safely ensconced beneath the water, and he was still staring at it.

"Does it not meet with your approval?"

Jack flicked a glance my way. "I'm not sharing a bed with you."

I began to soap my arms and chest, Jack averting his gaze once more. "You don't have to."

"No?"

"No, of course not." I waved a wet hand at the space next to the bed. "You can sleep on the floor."

He whirled around, that same red flush appearing on his cheeks as earlier. "Why do I have to be the one to sleep on the floor?"

"Because..." I lifted a leg out of the bath to soap that too, my toes pointed toward the ceiling. "I'm not the one who has a problem with sharing the bed."

"I bet you don't."

I hid a smile behind my hand and did my best to sound indignant. "What's that supposed to mean?"

"That you're clearly up for sexual relations with anything that moves."

"Huh!" I lowered my leg back into the bath and repeated the process with the other. "And yet, I wasn't the one talking about having sex with a goat. That was you."

Jack came and stood in front of the bath, forcing me to look up at him. "Has anyone ever told you that you're completely insufferable?"

I pretended to take a moment to consider it. "No... I don't think they have. Not to my face anyway." Capitalizing on his close proximity, I rose from the bath in one fluid move, enjoying every iota of shock on Jack's face as I stood unabashedly naked in front of him. I smiled sweetly at him. "Your turn."

His gaze dropped, lingering on my cock for a split second before he seemed to register what he was doing and turned away. "For the love of... Put some clothes on."

"Most people tell me to take them off."

"I'm not most people."

"Clearly." Not willing to try and pull clothes on over wet skin, I settled for seating myself on the bed and pulling a corner of the blanket over my lap instead. I waved a hand at the bath. "Go on. I didn't take that long. Water is still hot."

Indecision was written all over Jack's face. It was obvious he wanted to bathe, but from what I knew about him so far, he was certainly stubborn enough to cut off his own nose to spite his face. Well, I was nothing if not generous. I knew just what to say to make that decision far easier for him. "You paid for it. It would be a shame not to reap the benefits of it before it gets cold."

Jack's smile was wry. "That's right, I did pay for it." Jack pulled his boots off before coming to a stop. "You need to look away."

I let out a long-suffering sigh. "Really?"

"Yes. Really."

I lifted my hand to cover my eyes. "How's that?"

"Close your eyes as well."

I lifted my hand momentarily to show that my eyes were closed before lowering it again. I listened to the rustling of clothes being removed and gave it about thirty seconds before opening my eyes and splaying my fingers slightly. I was just in time to witness Jack dropping his trousers with his back to me, a throb of arousal taking hold as I viewed him in all his glory. And the sight *was* glorious. He might not have the same build as me, but there wasn't an ounce of fat on him, and everything was put together perfectly. It was all I could do not to groan at his beautifully rounded ass as he stepped into the water.

"Okay. I'm in. You can look again."

I obediently pulled my hand away from my eyes. "Where are you from, Jack Shaw?"

There was a long beat where I didn't think he was going to bother to answer. "Riverbrook. I doubt you've been there."

I shook my head. "That's farming land, isn't it?"

He nodded.

"So what are you doing here? People could take advantage of an unworldly farm boy."

Jack shifted slightly in the bath, steam billowing around his head. "I guess I learned that today."

A stab of something that might have been guilt bloomed in my stomach. I refused to succumb to it. "So why are you here?"

"My sister has gone missing. I'm trying to find her."

"Missing?"

"We woke up one day and she was just... gone."

"Had someone taken her?"

Jack shook his head. "There were no signs of it having been against her will. From what we can see, she left of her own accord."

"And where do you think she's gone?"

Jack's sigh carried a world of weariness that gave away how long he'd spent asking himself the exact same question. "I don't know. I don't understand why she'd want to leave in the first place."

I thought about it for a moment. "Perhaps she wanted more out of life. It's not a crime to want to see more of the world. Haven't you ever wanted that?"

"No."

There was a note of something in Jack's voice, though. Something less than convincing that told me he was either lying or not too sure himself. I couldn't help trying to get a rise out him. "You're probably right. A *boy* like you should probably stick to what he knows. Wheat and barley. And goats. Your sister will come home once she's had enough excitement."

It was a testament to how concerned Jack was about his sister that he didn't so much as blink at me calling him a boy, or at me getting yet another jibe in about goats. His forehead creased. "What if she doesn't? What if something has happened to her?"

Silence hung between us. I didn't need to point out that there were plenty of people across the thirteen kingdoms who would be only too happy to take advantage of a lone woman without protection. It didn't need putting into words. Not when we were both aware of it. For the next few minutes, there was no sound apart from the occasional slosh of water as Jack soaped himself. He was the first to break the silence. "I've finished. Close your eyes again."

I told myself that I wouldn't peek this time. My resolve lasted all of a few seconds. I was rewarded by the front view this time. It seemed that Jack had been blessed in that department. If he hadn't been so uptight—and hung up on the fact that I'd borrowed money from him—we could have had a lot of fun together before going our separate ways.

CHAPTER THREE

JACK

Reality had dawned along with the cold light of day as we'd started the long trek to Cloudwater, a journey which would take us the best part of two hours. I was putting trust in a man who had done absolutely nothing to earn it. In fact, quite the opposite. What if he had nefarious connections in Cloudwater? What if he was luring me there for some other purpose than the one he'd stated? There was nothing I could do but go along with it, though. Not when I needed my money back.

I risked a glance across to my companion, the twist of my neck doing nothing to ease muscles that had been stiff since waking. I lifted a hand to massage my shoulder, digging my fingers in in an attempt to soothe the ache.

Sebastian's gaze met mine before dropping to the hand on my shoulder. His lips quirked up in a knowing smile. "I warned you what would happen if you insisted on sleeping on the floor."

He had. Several times. He'd detailed every scenario short of me being devoured by rats. "It's got nothing to do with the floor."

Sebastian snorted. "Yeah, right. So you slept well, did you?"

"I slept absolutely fine." It was a blatant lie. What with the cold and the hardness of the floor, I'd woken numerous times during the night, the upshot being that I'd spent more of it awake than asleep. Then there was the small matter of my companion's strange habit, which had woken me more than once. "Although... I would have slept far better if I'd been sharing a room with someone who didn't talk in their sleep."

Sebastian's brow furrowed. "I don't talk in my sleep."

"So who was talking, then?"

He shrugged. "You were probably hearing things."

"I don't think so. You were definitely talking. Constantly and incessantly." I raised my hand and moved my fingers in a pincer movement. "Blah, blah, blah, blah, blah."

"That's not true."

I raised an eyebrow.

Sebastian slowed before turning to look at me with a curious expression on his face. "What was I talking about?"

"Ale and pies. And someone called Leofric. Who's Leofric?"

His eyes narrowed. "What was I saying about him?"

"Who is he?"

"A friend. What was I saying?"

I shrugged. "That would be telling." In truth, most of it had been too jumbled to derive much sense from. But it felt good to turn the tables on him, and if nothing else it had succeeded in distracting Sebastian from talking about my decision to sleep on the floor. I'd already questioned that decision myself numerous times before the sun had risen. After all, what was it I'd thought might happen? Sebastian might be a posturing poser who expected men to fall at his feet, but I doubted he'd have forced himself on me. Therefore, my stubbornness had achieved nothing but to leave me aching and sore, and not in a good way.

Or was it myself I hadn't been able to trust? Had I been concerned that with all that bare golden skin so close, I might have been tempted to forget who he was and how we'd met and give in to the fact that beneath all my bluster, I did find him attractive? Very attractive.

Sebastian's voice broke into my thoughts. "Have you been to Cloudwater before, farm boy?"

"No." I paused, my brow wrinkling. "And don't call me that. I have a name."

"So do I, but you don't use it."

Was that true? Probably. "I didn't realize you were so easily offended, *Sebastian.*"

"Bass."

"You said your friends call you, Bass. *We* are not friends." The announcement gave me a smug sense of satisfaction, particularly when his face fell. It seemed that Sebastian Beau was surprisingly sensitive when it came to the possibility of people not liking him. It was a strange trait for a man who went around robbing others to have. He was obviously used to batting his eyelashes and tossing that impressive hair of his and having that person forgive him. Well, I was made of stronger stuff and immune to his physical attributes. Mostly.

"Have it your own way, farm boy."

"I asked you not to call me that."

And I asked you to call me Bass."

"That is *not* the same thing."

Sebastian smirked. "That's the deal. Take it or leave it."

I sniffed and looked away, fastening my gaze on a tall tree instead. I wouldn't be blackmailed over something as simple as a name. "Fine. Call me whatever you want. I really don't care. In a few hours, you won't need to call me anything because you'll have given me my money back. With interest. And we'll have gone our separate ways."

Sebastian apparently didn't have an answer to that, and we spent the rest of the journey in silence, a state of affairs I was only too happy with. I was distinctly weary by the time Cloudwater came into sight. The settlement was a hive of activity, the streets bustling with traders of every description, people jostling each other wherever I looked. For someone who didn't spend that much time around lots of people, the cacophony of noise and movement was a lot to take in.

I followed Sebastian as he navigated the throngs of people, my eyes fixed on his back so I didn't get separated from him. No Sebastian meant no money. I had to raise my voice to be heard over the shouts and chatter. "Why are all these people here?"

The look on Sebastian's face as he glanced over his shoulder said I'd asked a stupid question. "For the tournament."

I scanned the street, narrowly avoiding tripping over a chicken that had come out of nowhere. "All of these people are here to play a stupid game?"

Sebastian tutted. "That 'stupid game' is only held once a year, and it's incredibly popular. People come from miles around for a chance at winning the jackpot. And of course, they're not all here for that, but where there's lots of people"—he waved a hand at the nearest stall festooned with bright necklaces and bracelets—"there's money to be made."

"The jackpot?"

Sebastian either hadn't heard me or chose not to answer. I suspected the latter.

I tried another question. "How can so many people play it at the same time?"

Sebastian took a sharp right which took us down a narrow alley blessedly devoid of people and therefore much quicker and quieter to traverse. "They can't. They have to get through the qualification rounds before they get a chance at winning the money."

I stopped dead. "Hang on. You made it sound like this would be easy. That it was just a case of turning up and the money would be yours."

Sebastian turned to face me with a shrug. "It will be easy. There are just a few obstacles to get past first. Trust me."

I was getting sick of hearing those two words. That was the problem. I didn't trust him. Not one little bit. Yet, when he started walking again, I followed him without hesitation.

The alley led out into a large, open square, Sebastian ploughing across it. Here, it wasn't just stalls, there was entertainment too: jugglers and fire-eaters, acrobats and dancers. Someone thrust a tankard at Sebastian as we passed, but he ignored it, his steps taking us to a large building on the other side of the square, which according to the placard dangling from its roof with a large picture of a grinning black cat, was The Thin Cat tavern.

I barely had time to take in any details of the building before Sebastian ducked inside. If I'd thought the street was busy, I was forced to revise that opinion as I was met with a wall of noise and people. The tavern had been set up with an almost empty space at its middle except for a few tables. Chairs had been placed around the edges of the large room to form a ring, and where there weren't chairs available, people stood behind to form a second row. All the tables at the center were occupied, games already going on. "Did we miss the start?"

Sebastian shook his head. "These are the qualification rounds. They'll go on all day, and then the top eight"—he pointed across the room at a large board which was apparently some sort of scoreboard—"will compete to become the champion." As I studied the board, a small officious-looking man with a clipboard stepped forward to rub a name off the bottom of it. An orc stood up from one of the tables and let loose a string of expletives so colorful that I was convinced he'd invented at least half of them.

"There's always next year, Golag," someone shouted from the audience in an effort to be helpful. Golag gave them the finger and left the tavern in a cloud of stormy indignation.

"Player or observer?"

I hadn't even noticed the blue-haired woman sitting at the table with a ledger in

front of her. She lowered her glasses to peer over the rims as she waited for Sebastian's answer. "Player." He inclined his head toward me. "He's watching."

She leaned forward to make a note in the ledger and then held out a hand, the bored expression on her face that of someone who'd had the same conversation a million times and would have it a million more. "That will be six gold coins. Five to take part in the game and one for your friend to watch."

"I'm not his friend." It had to be said, but I was left feeling distinctly put-out when neither the woman nor Sebastian so much as glanced my way. Apparently, I'd achieved invisibility.

Sebastian dipped his hand into the money pouch—*my* money pouch—to withdraw the coins and hand them over. After paying for food and board the previous night, the money was disappearing quickly. If Sebastian didn't win, there would be virtually nothing left. And how could he win if all these people were competing?

Three more people had left the game while we'd been standing here, none of them looking any happier than the orc had. Their places at the tables had been filled immediately by new players. Games seemed to be won and lost at a rate of knots, the audience seeming to understand what was going on if their shouts of encouragement and jeers were anything to go by. And they definitely had their favorites, a heavyset troll with skin the color of grass proving particularly popular as he won a game.

The blue-haired woman handed a ticket to Sebastian, announcing in a monotone. "Don't lose this. Your number will be called when it's your turn. If you miss your turn, there's no refund. You need to win three games in order to make it through to the next round. There are five rounds. You're allowed one loss per round. Another loss after that and you're out. No arguments. No second chances. No refund. Do you understand?"

I turned my attention back to the ongoing games as Sebastian gave his acknowledgement that he did. We were finally free to enter, Sebastian nudging me as we did. "A lot of people here today have come from far and wide."

"Yeah, so you said." Did he expect me to be impressed? He'd be waiting a very long time if that was the case.

Sebastian headed straight to the bar. I followed reluctantly, waiting while he ordered two ales. Only once he'd taken a sip did he finish his earlier thought. "It's the perfect opportunity for us to ask people about your sister."

I blinked at him, fighting down the rush of emotion that threatened to transform itself into gratitude at the thoughtfulness of the gesture. In a bid to hide it, I seized onto the word so at odds with the rest of the sentence. "Us?"

Sebastian gave an enthusiastic nod. "I can help. There's going to be a lot of waiting around between rounds." He gestured at the circle of people. "And the audience will come and go throughout the day." Blue eyes bored into me, and I had to force myself not to squirm beneath the disconcerting scrutiny. "Does she have any distinguishing features?"

I cleared my throat, still battling with an uncharacteristic wave of emotion. Did he really give a damn about my sister? It seemed he did. "Red hair. Very red. And it's long. Down to her waist."

Sebastian frowned. "So she'd stand out?" I nodded. "Yet, no one's seen her at all?"

I gave another nod, silently begging him not to put his thoughts into words. "Huh! I see."

When that was all he had to say, I was grateful. I had enough worst-case scenarios in my head. I didn't need anyone adding more.

The door suddenly swung open, and an orc who had to be at least seven-foot tall strode in, a hush descending across the tavern. I shot Sebastian a quizzical look and he leaned in, close enough that a lock of his hair brushed my cheek as he whispered in my ear. "That's Ulgan. He's been unbeaten in this tournament for the last five years."

Oh, that was just great. "And you think you can beat him?"

Sebastian's smile was nothing short of cocky. "I know I can."

It was noticeable that Ulgan didn't need a ticket as he stomped past the blue-haired official without sparing her so much as a glance. It seemed he didn't need to wait either, taking the first empty seat at one of the tables that became available, his opponent turning a little green around the gills at finding themselves faced with him.

Sebastian, meanwhile, kept his word, and as I worked my way around the room one way, he went in the opposite direction. We met back at the bar and I raised an inquisitive eyebrow. "Well?"

He shook his head. "Nothing. You?"

"No. Same old story."

He looked like he was going to say something, but then a shout rang out across the tavern from the man with a clipboard. "Number three hundred and three."

Sebastian held up his ticket and gave me a blinding smile. "That's me!" He waggled his eyebrows. "How about a kiss for good luck?"

I stared at him. "I'd rather—"

"Kiss a goat, I know."

The woman next to us chuckled. "I'll give you a kiss, sweetheart."

Sebastian spun around, dipping her over his arm and depositing a noisy and somewhat lingering kiss on her lips. Her cheeks were bright scarlet when he eventually eased her back to standing.

My lip curled at the unnecessary display. Mind, it was probably for the best. He might have been kind enough to offer help in finding my sister, but it reminded me what sort of man he really was. One whose company I would only have to suffer for a few more hours. Maybe even less if he got knocked out in the first round. Although obviously I hoped that didn't happen. For my sake. Ulgan had already won his three games and was holding court on the other side of the tavern, so at least Sebastian didn't have to go up against him.

Sebastian's first opponent was a goblin, the man barely tall enough to see over the edge of the table, even with the help of a cushion. The game itself seemed overly complicated, consisting of cards, counters, and dice. Although, from what I could tell the cards seemed to carry a much heavier weighting when it came to deciding the winner. I couldn't say I understood what was going on, and I found myself having to rely on the audience's reaction as an indicator of how the game was going.

My heart sank as Sebastian lost the first game. One more and he was out. As he got up and changed tables to take on a new opponent, I gave serious thought to how I was going to get home without any money. I had my bow. If there was woodland nearby, I could hunt for animals and sell them. Or failing that I could eat them and sleep rough. It wouldn't be pleasant, and there would be a danger of falling foul to larger animals, or roving bandits, but it would only be for a few days until I got back to Riverbrook.

I lifted my gaze back to Sebastian in time for something strange to catch my eye. Sparks of light underneath the table? I squeezed my eyes shut and when I opened them there was nothing to see. Scrutiny of the audience seemed to suggest that no one else had noticed anything amiss. Was I imagining things? Given the poor night's sleep and the fact that I'd already drunk a tankard full of ale, it was entirely possible. If I did manage to leave this place with any money at all, I'd find a comfortable tavern and allow myself the luxury of sleeping the day away. At least it gave me something to look forward to.

Sebastian won the next game, and the two after that, arriving back at my side with a huge grin on his face a few moments later. I had the absurd urge to smile back but managed to quell it beneath a withering glance. "That's just the first round. Don't get too cocky."

Sebastian's smile grew wider, his eyes glittering. "Me?"

I rolled my eyes. "Yes, you. The world doesn't revolve around you, no matter how much you try to convince yourself it does."

He propped himself up against the bar, his gaze warm on my face. "You barely know me."

I let out a noisy breath. "And for that, I am eternally grateful."

"You'll change your mind."

"Hardly. I'm only here until you win or lose. Then you won't see me for dust."

He flicked a lock of blond hair behind his shoulder. "We'll see."

It was exactly that sort of smug self-confidence which made him so infuriating. The end of the day couldn't come quickly enough.

CHAPTER FOUR

JACK

The rest of the afternoon passed in something of a blur, Sebastian and I continuing to question the influx of people about the whereabouts of my sister in between his games—his winning streak continued. The story remained the same, with no one having heard her name or having seen her. I was beginning to feel like Annabelle's existence was all in my head.

We ate a hearty meal of meat pie, potatoes, and vegetables in a somewhat companionable silence, interspersed with the occasional snipe on my part. Mainly about how much Sebastian was drinking when he had an important game coming up. He waved my concerns away as if they were nothing, even going so far as to drain his tankard of ale and order another just to spite me.

The tavern was absolutely heaving by the time the tournament rolled toward its climax. I had to fight for space to even be able to see as Sebastian swaggered to the closest of four tables, the competition down to just eight people. There was Sebastian, Baknok—a dwarf with a long red beard and a hooked nose—a woman called Susan whose long dark hair was tied back in a plait, and who to my thinking looked completely out of place, two elves who seemed to know each other and might even have been related, and two men with no real distinguishing features. And lastly, Ulgan, the orc who had apparently reigned supreme for the last five years.

Sebastian had already informed me that the final round operated on a sudden death basis: one game, where the winner progressed and the loser was left with nothing. That meant three games again, with the person left standing proclaimed as the champion. To add to the hype, they'd brought a host in for the evening, the man standing on a small dais at the center of the four tables. He introduced himself as Steve Bash before giving a quick rundown on the eight remaining contestants to the cheering audience. And then the games started, Sebastian paired with Susan.

"I saw you with the blond man." I turned to find a tall, dark-haired man on my right, his brown eyes warm on my face. After a short appraisal, I had to admit that he was extremely good-looking. Maybe not in an obvious Sebastian way, but he certainly had a lot of features which all came together in a rather pleasant way. I returned his smile. It had been a long time since anyone had made a move on me. Riverbrook, for all its good features, had a definite shortage of men who swung that way.

He held out his hand. "Name's Dan."

I took it, his palm warm as we shook. "Jack."

He inclined his head toward Sebastian. "Are you with him?"

I puffed out my chest. How sweet. He wanted to check that he wasn't stepping on Sebastian's toes. "No. We're not together."

His smile in response to my words had a frisson of something working its way up my spine. I was already revising my earlier plan to hole up in a tavern and sleep the night away in favor of getting to know Dan better. It would be the perfect way to let off some steam before I was forced to return home with nothing to show for it.

"So he's"—Dan leaned forward in a conspiratorial way, his eyes gleaming—"available?"

Reality slammed into my chest, the rush of bitterness accompanying it snagging in my throat. Dan had never been interested in me. Of course, he hadn't. Like ninety-five percent of this tavern, he only had eyes for the preening blond fool, who had managed to wear a shirt today, but seemed to demonstrate the passing of time by undoing an extra button every hour. He was down to the last one now as he leaned over the table with an intense look of concentration on his face. I let out a small sigh, Dan still waiting on my answer. "Yeah, he's available… if you like that sort of thing."

Dan's brow furrowed. "What do you mean?"

I pondered my words and then said them anyway. "He robbed me yesterday. Him and his monkey." I realized too late that bringing the monkey into it had been a mistake. So far, there wasn't anyone who hadn't looked at me like I was insane when I'd mentioned the monkey, and Dan was no exception. I suspected that if we hadn't been so tightly squeezed together, he would have taken a step back. I added somewhat maliciously, "And he's probably diseased."

Dan's eyebrows shot up. "What sort of disease?"

"Sexual."

Dan laughed as if I'd made some sort of joke. "I'll take the risk. I'm sure he'll be worth it."

I pulled a face, tamping down on the urge to tell him that he clearly had no taste. "It's your funeral."

He laughed again. "Can you introduce us?"

Oh, great, so now I was apparently meant to offer some sort of matchmaking service as well. I gave a shrug that I hoped came across as casual. "Sure."

Dan beamed at me before switching his attention to Sebastian, his expression turning dreamy. "I think it's the blond hair that does it."

"Probably a wig. You should give it a yank. I bet it'll come off."

"Or the muscles."

"They'll probably disappear once the spell wears off."

"He has really blue eyes as well."

He said it like Sebastian had battled an army to the death and earned them rather than just being blessed with good genetics. I stayed silent.

Dan grabbed my arm, the expression on his face grave. "And can you make sure he knows that I was interested in him from the moment I saw him. I mean... imagine if he wins. He's going to think I'm only interested in him for his money."

"I sincerely doubt that."

Dan carried on as if I hadn't spoken. "And I really don't want our relationship to start off with a misunderstanding like that."

I blinked at him. "Relationship!"

"...although I suppose it's a good story to tell our children one day."

Steve Bash's voice rang out across the tavern, and I was glad for the interruption. Much more of that and I probably would have laughed in Dan's face. Sebastian have a long-term relationship that included children? As if. "And we have our first semi-finalist." I lifted my gaze to find Steve Bash holding Sebastian's arm aloft, Susan beating a hasty retreat with a scowl on her face.

I let out a surprised "huh" at the same moment that Dan released a soft sigh, possibly because the last button on Sebastian's shirt had given up the fight and his shirt hung open to reveal his bare chest. Both elves went out within minutes of each other, one losing to Baknok, and the other to Ulgan. That only left one match to be decided, Steve Bash making a meal out of it once one of the men had emerged victorious.

There was a short break before the semi-final match-ups were announced, Sebastian drawing Baknok, and the man, whose name I now knew to be Rowan, looking none too pleased to get Ulgan. And then we were off again for more of the same, with Steve Bash working himself up into a state of total apoplexy. "... did you see that, ladies and gentlemen? Ulgan just played his ace card, and yes, it was an actual ace." He paused and waited for laughter before continuing, the audience only too happy to provide it. "And what's that? Is it my imagination or does Sebastian not look too happy with the cards he's been dealt in this round? Is his luck finally starting to run out? But wait... what's that he's just played? A red king. It's almost like he knew Baknok didn't have any red cards left. Is Baknok going to be able to come back from that? Place your bets now."

There was a scurry to do exactly that, as if people had needed permission before doing it. Ulgan made short work of his opponent in the next round, Rowan reacting with a sheepish shrug and telling Steve Bash that he'd be back next year. That left Sebastian and Baknok to battle it out for the right to face Ulgan in the final. Could Sebastian actually win this thing? I was beginning to think it might be possible.

The noise in the tavern had grown exponentially louder, Dan having to lean forward to shout in my ear. "He's amazing, isn't he?"

"He's something, alright."

Dan nodded enthusiastically, my sarcasm going over his head. I'd hoped he'd go away once I'd agreed to introduce him to Sebastian, but it seemed he was going to stick to me like glue just in case I decided to renege on the deal. I wasn't sure how much more simpering over Sebastian I could take. It was funny how quickly an attractive man could lose their shine. Drooling over another man and robbing you with a monkey, two examples that immediately sprang to mind.

There was some sort of commotion going on, numerous members of the audience tilting their heads back to peer up into the rafters. Rather than asking Dan, because that would have meant speaking to him, I turned to my other side where a short woman with long blonde hair stood. "What's going on?"

She pointed to the roof, her announcement of "pigeon" coming at the same time as I heard the fluttering of wings. I looked up to find there was indeed a pigeon, perched directly above the table where Sebastian and Baknok still played.

Steve Bash finally caught wind of it, his gaze lifting to the ceiling too. "Well, would you look at that. I know that this is the place to be tonight, but I had no idea that the local wildlife shared that view. But here we have one of our feathered friends determined to get the best seat in the house, a definite bird's eye view. Perhaps he, or she... who knows how you tell a pigeon's gender... not me, that's for sure, is checking out the competition before they take part next year."

The crowd parted slowly to allow a man holding a broomstick through. I assumed he was the tavern owner, and that someone had decided that as it was his tavern, it was his problem. Steve Bash of course turned it into a big drama. I was beginning to think the man could get excited about a falling leaf. "Here comes Reginald to the rescue. He might not be your archetypal knight in shining armor, but what he lacks in stature he makes up for in possessing a very long broomstick. And that is not a euphemism, ladies. Have you seen the handle on the broomstick? That pigeon doesn't stand a chance."

As it turned out, the pigeon did stand a chance, easily evading being prodded by the end of the broomstick by fluttering from one rafter to the next and then back again, its indignant shrieks making it clear that it took umbrage at being continually poked. How Sebastian was managing to ignore all the fuss, I had no idea, but he'd barely lifted his gaze from his cards. If he did lose, at least he'd tried.

As if he could sense my scrutiny, he turned his head my way. Our gazes met. And then the bastard winked, just before he laid down a card and the audience went wild.

Steve Bash was in there like a shot, raising Sebastian's arm in triumph once more. "And we have our second finalist, Sebastian Beau! Who will prevail in the final round? Will Ulgan walk away with the crown once more, or will Sebastian waltz in and steal it away from right under his nose?"

There was a five-minute break before the final round got underway. During the break, all the other tables were cleared away to leave just the one right in the center. Steve Bash gave it the usual spiel before they took their seats, Sebastian milking the crowd's applause for all it was worth. He offered his hand to Ulgan, but the orc was having none of it.

I was surprised by how rapidly my heart was beating, and the slight sweatiness of my palms, when it wasn't as if it was life or death. Either the tense atmosphere of the crowd had gotten to me, or there'd been something wrong with the meat pie I'd eaten earlier. I preferred to think that it was food poisoning.

The game should have been underway by now, but Ulgan kept gesturing up at the rafters, the occasional feather floating down to remind everyone of the pigeon's presence. It seemed Ulgan wasn't prepared to start until the pigeon had been dealt with. And despite Sebastian's jibes about how his concentration was much better and a bird couldn't put him off, Ulgan refused to back down.

What followed was a comedy of errors where the tavern owner was joined by three more men, the four of them eventually succeeding in corralling the disgruntled pigeon out of the door.

Despite my lack of understanding of the game, it quickly became clear that Sebastian was losing, even with the bulk of the crowd supporting him. I wanted to believe that it was because he was the underdog, or because they were ready for a new winner, but it was far more likely that they liked him for the same reasons Dan liked him. Whereas even in the dimmest of lights, Ulgan could never be described as pretty, unless you had a fetish for green skin and protruding canines. Was Sebastian really going to come this far, only to lose at the final hurdle? The possibility tasted bitter in my throat.

Heads turned as the tavern door suddenly swung open, a latecomer framed in the doorway. The crowd cheered as the pigeon flew in over his head to take up its previous perch in the rafters. It was certainly determined; you had to give it that. Ulgan lifted his head to glare at it but seemed to know he had absolutely no chance of getting the game stopped in the middle of it. Steve Bash, of course, made out like it was the most exciting event that had ever happened in the history of the thirteen kingdoms. I was beginning to think that if I ever heard his voice again after tonight, it would be too soon.

The tension thickened as Sebastian began to fight back, and then before I knew it, he was announced as the winner, the crowd going wild and surging forward to congratulate him. Or to have an excuse to touch him. One or the other. I let the victory sink in. He'd actually done it. He'd won. I'd doubled my money and I was going to get to sleep comfortably and return home with more money than I'd started with. That, and I supposed I had an interesting story to tell as well.

I couldn't see Sebastian, but I could hear Steve Bash. "… and in one of the biggest comebacks we've ever seen in the history of the tournament, we have a brand-new champion! And as the champion, he gets to take home with him *two hundred* gold pieces. What are you going to do with the money, Sebastian?"

I stopped listening. Two hundred! What the hell. My money pouch had contained ten gold pieces when Sebastian had stolen it. The deal we'd struck was for Sebastian to give me twenty. Yet, he was going to walk away with one hundred and eighty more. The bastard had failed to mention what the prize was, and in my naivety, I hadn't bothered to ask.

And suddenly there he was in front of me, his arms outstretched and his lips pulled into a wide grin. "How would you like to hug a celebrity, Jack?"

I side-stepped him. "Point me toward a celebrity, and depending on who they are, I'll have a think about it. Or if you mean *you*, I'll pass, thanks."

Sebastian's grin drooped slightly. "I won. I thought you'd be happy."

Grabbing his arm, I dragged him into a corner of the tavern, the crowds already starting to thin now that the excitement was over. Sebastian looked slightly startled as I pushed him back against the wall and moved closer to him. He quirked an eyebrow, his voice dropping low. "Oh, Jack, I didn't know crowds did it for you."

I ignored him, anger sizzling its way along my veins. "Two hundred gold coins! The prize is two hundred gold coins."

Sebastian gave a slow nod, a slight furrow appearing between his eyebrows. "That's right."

I poked him in the ribs. "And you never thought to mention that?"

"You never asked."

I stared at him incredulously. "You knew I didn't know anything about this tournament. So... therefore, you also knew that I would think it was a good deal. Except... it's not a good deal is it, Sebastian? It's a shitty deal. For me, anyway. I get twenty and you get one hundred and eighty. How is that fair?"

He looked slightly perplexed at the force of my fury. "You get double your money."

I poked him in the ribs again, harder this time. "My money that was stolen, so I guess I only have myself to blame for expecting anything more. You're a con man, an absolute..." I paused while I searchetai for a word that would sum him up adequately. "A chancer. Someone who sees nothing but an opportunity to make money."

I went in for a third poke, but it was curtailed as my hand was grabbed and held in a firm grip, Sebastian's eyebrows shooting up. "You need to stop doing that."

"Why?"

"Because it hurts."

"Try fastening your shirt sometimes. That might help."

"My shirt." He looked down, his frown growing more pronounced. "What's this obsession you have with my shirt?"

"Obsession!" I almost spat the word at him. "You wish I had an obsession with your shirt. I was simply pointing out that an extra barrier might help."

"Or..." Sebastian dragged the word out. "You could just stop poking me."

I regarded him stonily. "You should be glad it's my finger and not an arrow."

Sebastian let go of my hand and crossed his arms over his chest. "Do you want your money or not?"

I dragged in a calming breath. It hadn't occurred to me until that moment that Sebastian could refuse to give me anything at all. We had a gentleman's agreement, but as he was a long way from being a gentleman, that amounted to nothing when all was said and done. Therefore, it would be wise to stop provoking him, take the money, and run. "Yes, I want my money." I held my hand out and waited.

Sebastian took his time in counting out the golden coins before handing my money pouch back. I sniffed. "So... I guess this is it."

Sebastian nodded. "I guess it is. What will you do now?"

"Go home."

An awkward silence hung between us. I opened my mouth to say something without having any idea what it was going to be, but I didn't get that far, a polite throat clearing coming from behind me. I turned to find Dan standing there with a big smile on his face. Right, Dan. I'd forgotten all about him. I sighed. "Sebastian, this is Dan. He's a huge fan of yours, and he's been chomping at the bit to meet you." Dan coughed, and with an eyeroll I added the extra bit. "And that was before you won any money, so he is not after your money at all, which is probably just as well, as we both know the chances of you giving him any are slim to none. You're far more likely to take his money and…"

I trailed off. Neither man was listening to me. Dan had stepped close to Sebastian and was whispering something in his ear, and Sebastian was nodding and smiling. I waited for a beat. "I guess I'll go then."

When neither man looked my way, I backed away a few steps. I threw one last glance at Sebastian, taking in Dan's hand which was now pressed to Sebastian's bare chest before turning on my heel and walking away. It wasn't until I stepped out into the cold night air that I realized how warm it had been in the tavern with the crush of bodies.

I stood there for a moment, feeling at a complete loss as to what I was supposed to do now. Which was stupid. I had my money and I'd already planned this earlier. I was going to find another tavern, eat and sleep well, and put the last twenty-four hours behind me. Only, the idea no longer seemed so attractive. It seemed almost… lonely.

"Jack?"

I turned to find Sebastian behind me, a spark of something I didn't want to think about settling in my stomach. "What do you want?"

"I'm not just going to let you wander off into the night."

"No?"

"No. There's"—he gestured vaguely down the street—"dangerous and unknown things out there."

"Like what?"

"If I knew, they'd be known things, wouldn't they? Anyway..." He rested a hand on his hip and cocked his head to one side. "You're not really just going to return home, are you?"

I shrugged. The idea had definitely lost its shine. "What would I do instead?"

"Keep looking for your sister. Just because no one's seen her here, doesn't mean no one has in other places. There's a whole world out there where she could be."

I sighed. "That's a nice idea but my money won't last forever."

Sebastian's lips twitched. "You should make a friend who's just come into a large sum of money. He might be able to help."

I didn't even bother to try and hide my disdain. "Are you offering to give me my fair share?"

The twitching morphed into a smile. "Of course not. But... I'm a generous man. I often cover the cost for my traveling companions."

"'Your... traveling companions?'" My mouth dropped open as I got what he meant. "Me and you?"

"Yeah, why not?"

"Because I'd probably kill you within a week."

"Or... I'd grow on you and you'd realize that some of these strange ideas you've got about me are wrong."

"I think it would be the first."

"I think it would be the second."

I laughed. "And that's why we couldn't travel together. We'd drive each other crazy. We haven't agreed on a single thing so far."

Sebastian shrugged. "Who needs to agree? There's nothing wrong with a bit of healthy debate."

I regarded him coolly. "Why are you pushing this? Do you want to rob me again, is that it?"

Sebastian spat on his palm and held it out, the look in his eyes sincere. "I do solemnly promise that I will never rob you again for as long as we both shall live. I will say that I don't regret it, though. If I hadn't robbed you, we'd never have met."

I stared at the hand. "I don't want to touch your spit."

"Oh, come on, farm boy. You've touched worse. Spit on yours and take my hand."

"Don't call me that."

"Do what I say, and I'll stop."

"No, you won't."

A grin broke out on Sebastian's face. "No, I won't."

I sighed. I could either stand here and argue about it, or I could just get it over with. Although, I'd lost track of what I was agreeing to. Was I agreeing not to be robbed? Or was I agreeing to travel with him? And if it was the latter, why on earth would I do that when he was the most insufferable man I'd ever met?

Except, I couldn't deny that there was a part of me that did want to see more of the world, to experience more. I might have spent most of the last twenty-four hours sniping at him, but there'd been a certain amount of enjoyment in it, and I'd felt more alive than I had for years. Would it be so terrible to at least give it a try? I spat on my palm and pressed it to his, his fingers closing around mine. "I'm not going to be nice to you."

Sebastian's lips curled into what was rapidly becoming a familiar smile. "I'm counting on it." He crooked his elbow in a strangely gentlemanly gesture, as if I was a lady he wanted to escort to the ball. "What do you say to me and you finding a nice tavern? I'm sure there's a floor with your name on it."

I pointedly ignored his arm because I wasn't a lady and there was no ball to go to. "What happened to Dan?"

"Dan?"

"Dan. He was already sold on the relationship you two were going to have. I reckon he'd already picked out the names for your kids."

"Not my type."

I let out a snort. "He was breathing, wasn't he?"

"True." Sebastian started to make his way down the street, and I fell into step beside him. He turned his head to look at me. "Let's just say I had more important things to sort out."

I rolled my eyes, even though given how dark it was, it was probably a wasted gesture. I could see Sebastian's grin, though, his teeth flashing white as he grabbed my arm. "You can pay for the room tonight."

"Like hell I can. You've got one hundred and eighty gold coins and I've got twenty. You're paying for it."

"I'll toss you for it."

"You're paying."

"How about some sort of wager?"

"How about you pay."

"You're no fun."

"Yet, you want me to travel with you."

"I might have changed my mind."

It was my turn to smile. "Too late."

We came to a stop outside a tavern, this one far smaller than the one that had housed the tournament, the painted sign proclaiming it as 'The Dancing Monkey.'

I narrowed my eyes at the sign but didn't say anything.

Sebastian paused by the door. "By the way, what did you tell Dan about me? He kept asking if I had rashes in certain places."

My lips twitched, but I quickly schooled my face into an expression of innocence. "I don't know. I can't remember. Poor man must have gotten confused about something." I pointedly dropped my gaze to his crotch. "Maybe he thought your trousers might chafe. You know, on account of them being so tight."

"Tight? What do you mean?"

But I'd already breezed past him, the question asked to my back.

CHAPTER FIVE

SEBASTIAN

I watched Jack with growing amusement as he stomped around our makeshift camp. "I did tell you that it was a long way to the next village."

Narrowed green eyes turned my way in a scathing look that Jack had honed to perfection. "I thought that meant we'd only just reach it before nightfall. Not that we'd find ourselves stuck in the middle of nowhere."

"I would have thought that a farm boy like you would have embraced the outdoors."

"The known outdoors is very different to the unknown."

I lay back, locking my fingers behind my head and staring up at the sky. "Look on the bright side. At least *you're* used to sleeping on the floor." After the tournament, we'd stuck to one room, Jack again insisting on sleeping on the floor. It was a wonder he'd gotten any decent sleep. Although, judging by the dark shadows under his eyes, it hadn't been as satisfying as he'd made out. If he carried on like this, I might have to do something completely uncharacteristic like offer to take the floor in the next tavern we spent the night in while he had the bed.

Jack picked up a stick and poked at the fire in a way that said the volatile streak that was always so close to the surface with him was in danger of escaping once more. "You're not funny. And… I don't know why we couldn't have had two rooms."

"You could have paid for your own room."

"What? With my *twenty* gold coins."

"Exactly."

A furrow appeared on his brow as if that thought had never occurred to him. "I need my money."

"I need *my* money."

"For what?"

I turned my head to the side so I could see him better. "I have a long way to go."

He came to stand in front of me, staring down at me with his hands on his hips. The flickering firelight lent his features an ethereal quality that made him look even more handsome than he was already. "Where are you going?"

"To Knightshade."

Jack screwed his face up as if trying to recall whether he'd ever heard of the place. "What's in Knightshade?"

"Bad men, and a very high tower."

"Sounds delightful. Why on earth would you want to visit a place like that?"

I sat up, clasping my knees under my chin as I faced him. I was surprised it had taken Jack this long to start asking questions. He really should have asked them before agreeing to travel with me, but then, I was learning that Jack had an impulsive streak a mile wide. It was one of the things that made him so intriguing. "To rescue a prince, of course."

"A prince...?" His eyebrows met in the middle as he gave my words time to digest.

I nodded. "Prince Montgomery from the kingdom of Quatasta. He was abducted one rainy night during a festival and spirited away from under the king and queen's noses. As the oldest son and heir, they were quite rightly shocked and devastated. A ransom has been requested for his safe return, but it isn't a ransom that anyone, even royalty, is capable of paying without unrestricted access to a gem mine, and a thousand men to mine it." I pulled a map out of my pocket and spread it across the ground, the firelight bright enough to show the details. I gestured for Jack to sit down, and despite a slight eye roll, he did as I'd asked, positioning himself on the opposite side of the map.

Jack's gaze dropped to the map as I placed a finger on it. I took the opportunity to study his features without the weight of his shrewd gaze on me. He had very long eyelashes and a mouth that, when it wasn't twisted in derision or open to lash someone metaphorically with his tongue, was made for kissing, the lower lip plump and full. And I was optimistic enough to believe that once I worked out a way of getting through that prickly exterior, I might get to experience it one day. That and a hell of a lot more.

"Well?" Jack's voice was laced with impatience, bringing me back to earth with a bump.

I reluctantly tugged my gaze away from his face and focused on the map instead. "That's Arrowgarde, the capital of Quatasta. That's where the young prince was abducted from. Where would you take a prince from there?"

"I don't know. I've never abducted a prince. It always seemed like too much trouble. And what would I do with one? Stick him in the middle of a field and use him as a scarecrow?" I stared at him until he finally leaned forward to study the map, his fingers tracing over its surface until they paused at a spot covered by trees. "There's a forest there. That seems like a good place to hide out if you don't want to be discovered."

"It would be. If it wasn't full of giant basilisks. Only an idiot ever sets foot in that forest. Therefore, not a viable option."

Jack's gaze sought out mine. "Basilisks?"

He was endearingly clueless sometimes. "Giant reptiles." He shook his head and I sighed. "Didn't you learn anything about the world on your farm?"

"I didn't think I needed to know about a forest hundreds of miles away where I never planned to visit."

He had a point. "Basilisks are deadly. They kill in two ways—with their stare, and if that's not enough of a deterrent—they leave poisonous secretions. Hence the no one going in there."

Jack's finger moved the other way on the map. "Here, then. In Cragwall."

I peered at where he was pointing to. "That village has been abandoned for a long time."

He raised an eyebrow. "So... a perfect place to stash a prince, then."

"It's abandoned because it floods at least twice a year, with water often reaching a height of five meters." There were only two directions left for Jack's finger to travel on the map. I pre-empted the first by moving my finger there instead. "This is Lastwick. Lastwick is a center for trade and therefore extremely busy. You'd have to be crazy to try to hide someone there and think they would remain undetected. "Which... only leaves..." I slid my finger across the map. "The Solace Tower in Knightshade."

Jack stared at the map for a long moment. "They could have taken him farther away."

I shook my head. "Why would they when there's a perfectly good tower only too easy to defend? Besides... the tower is where they've been keeping him. That's where his parents have been sending regular payments of the ransom. But at the current rate, it will take them one hundred and eighteen years to pay it off. By which time, the prince will be long dead."

Jack's expression turned stormy. "Why didn't you just say that in the first place?" He waved a hand at the map. "Why did we have to go through all this rigmarole?" I gave him a sweet smile and he pulled a face at me. "So why don't they just rescue him?"

"Many have tried, and many have failed. Some of whom were never seen again. The basilisks are probably to blame for that one. Or they were staying in Cragwall when the waters came." I gave a dramatic sigh. "Therefore, it's time for me to step in so the poor prince doesn't have to spend his whole life locked up in a cold, drafty tower and can instead recommence his life of luxury, and one day be king. His father suffered a fairly nasty spell of sickness only a few months ago."

Jack blinked. "You?"

I nodded. "Me!"

He tilted his head slightly to one side, studying me as if I'd just grown an extra nose. "What's in it for you? I find it hard to believe you're doing this out of the goodness of your heart."

"And why is that?"

Jack fixed me with a stare. "You're a man who robs people and refuses to give them their money back, even when you're caught red-handed. The two things don't go together. I'm assuming that if they've been giving all the coin they have to ensure the prince's continued survival, a cash reward will be difficult for them. So..." He dragged the word out. "I'll say it again. What's in it for you?"

I folded the map up and put it back in my pocket. "They've offered the prince's hand in matrimony to whoever can liberate him from his stone prison." I didn't know what reaction I'd expected, but it certainly wasn't for Jack to burst into laughter. Not a small laugh either, but a great big belly laugh, that if I hadn't witnessed first-hand, I would have doubted he was capable of. And it went on for a while, Jack forced to wipe moisture away from his eyes when he finally managed to bring himself back under control. "What's so funny?"

Jack sat up straighter, his eyes still shining with mirth. "I can't decide what's funnier, the idea of *you* marrying a prince—"

"What's wrong with me?"

He waved a hand down the length of my body as if that was meant to explain everything. "You're hardly prince-marrying material, are you? But apart from that, the idea of you marrying anyone is hilarious. *You* are definitely not the marrying kind."

"No? So, what am I?"

Jack considered the question for a moment. "You're the sowing your wild oats kind. I can't imagine you settling down with one man. Or one woman."

I lay back down and continued my scrutiny of the sky. "I could, if it was the right man." I didn't include women. Women were lovely and while I couldn't say my tastes had never wandered that way during a dry spell, men were most definitely my preference.

Jack's snort was loaded with disbelief. "Yeah, right. What do you even know about this prince? What if he's ugly?"

"He's a prince. Princes are always handsome. They come from a long line of handsome people. My future fiancé will turn heads wherever he goes. He will be tall and dashing. He'll be good with a weapon and kind to animals. He'll be brave and honest. He'll be cultured and educated. He'll..." I paused and turned my head away so Jack couldn't see the smile hovering on my lips. "He'll know what a basilisk is without having to be told."

Jack made a tsking sound in his throat before climbing to his feet to tend to the fire. A few minutes of silence hung between us before Jack finally broke it. "What are we supposed to eat?"

"The fresh air is my food."

"Very poetic, but not very nutritional." He gave the fire another hard poke before lifting his stare to the line of trees a hundred or so meters away. "Do you think there are animals in the woods?"

"I'll protect you."

"Sweet!" He said the word like it was anything but. "But I was thinking more of using my bow to catch something that we can roast over the fire."

I rolled onto my side and propped myself up on one elbow. "That sounds good."

There was a decidedly wicked glimmer in his eye as his glance came my way. "But you have your fresh air."

"I could probably manage food as well."

"I tell you what..." The sparkle in his eye grew more pronounced, something close to a smile pulling at the corners of his mouth. "I'll sell you dinner for one hundred and eighty gold coins."

"You have to catch something first."

He picked up his bow and slung it over his shoulder before turning to face the trees. "If I don't catch anything, it's only because it's getting dark. I'm an excellent shot."

"Of course you are."

"I am."

"I was agreeing with you."

"You were..." He shook his head. "It doesn't matter."

I sat up as he strode off in the direction of the trees without another word. "Be careful." No response. "Remember goats are food, not sexual partners."

I got the finger for that jibe. I laughed and then lay back to contemplate the sky once more. I doubted he'd catch anything. Like he'd said, it was starting to get dark, and there would be even less light away from the fire in the midst of the trees. In fact, I probably should have stopped him from going on what would no doubt be nothing but a waste of time and energy. But then, Jack was strong-willed. I doubted I could have dissuaded him even if I'd tried. So it was better not to waste *my* time and energy. With that in mind, I closed my eyes. No doubt Jack would take great pleasure in waking me when he got back.

As rude awakenings went, being lifted ten feet into the air by an enraged orc had to rank among the rudest. "Ul-gan!" My attempt at saying his name came out as more of a strangled squawk due to the thick fingers wrapped around my neck. It was those fingers that were to blame for my elevated status, my legs kicking feebly in the air in a fruitless attempt to find purchase. I'd known he was tall, but along with that height apparently came great strength too.

One thick green finger jabbed me in the chest. Was he related to Jack? They both had the same approach to solving a problem: poke the other person until they'd had enough and agreed to anything you wanted. Which begged the question, what did he want? He'd obviously followed us all the way from Cloudwater, neither Jack nor I noticing a seven-foot orc skulking in the undergrowth. I'd be having words with Jack about his observational skills later. Assuming I survived. "Whaaaat d'youuu waaant?" The words were difficult to squeeze out through the iron grip on my neck. "Youuuu have veeeery strooong finnnngersss."

I was lowered slowly, which was good. At least until the downward progress stopped way before my feet reached the ground, Ulgan's face looming close to mine. "What do I want?"

God, he was ugly. What if he wanted me sexually? I liked to think of myself as pretty cosmopolitan. I'd definitely bedded a few elves in my time, and there'd been that one drunken incident with a banshee that I preferred not to think about. But I'd never gone for bulging eyes, green skin, and protruding teeth, and I was pretty sure that as far as orcs went, Ulgan wasn't one of the more attractive ones. Next time I bumped into a lady orc, I'd have to ask. Perhaps he was. Perhaps orc attractiveness operated on a different scale. Could I do it? I angled my head downwards the best I could to see his lower body. Okay, that was one big bulge in his loincloth. Too big. Way too big. He'd split me in half.

Ulgan let out a sound that was half hiss and half growl. I really hoped that wasn't how orcs demonstrated their arousal. "I want my money. The money you cheated me out of. I don't know how you did it, but I know you did. And then I'm going to break a finger for every ten gold coins you stole from me."

I did a quick calculation. "Only... got... ten... finnnnngers. That'ssss one hundred... gold coins."

Deep ridges appeared on the orc's brow as he contemplated my words, his yellow eyes narrowing. "Then I'll break your toes as well. What does that add up to?"

"Twoooo hundred. That... works."

"Perfect."

He gave me a little shake, my entire body dancing like I was a puppet on a string. It made it even harder to speak. "Whatttt... animal... are... yoooou... sssscared offff?"

"What!?" His voice was almost a roar. "Speak properly."

"Sssstop ssssshak...ing meeee... and I will." I was suddenly still, the fingers around my neck slackening slightly. "I said... what animal... are you scared of?"

The fingers tightened again as Ulgan's chest puffed out. "I AM ULGAN. I AM NOT SCARED OF ANYTHING. HOW DARE YOU INSULT ME BY ACCUSING ME OF SUCH A THING?"

I'd started with an enraged orc, and I'd now got one suffering from whatever came after enraged. Apoplectic maybe. Okay, I'd just have to go for something big and hope for the best. A woolly mammoth, perhaps. Extinct animals always seemed to give a person more pause, like they were struggling to believe the evidence of their own eyes. Or a dragon. Gold sparks were already starting to trickle from my fingertips. I just needed to decide on a shape to form them into. Dragon or woolly mammoth?

I was still pondering the choice when a voice rang out through the darkness. "I suggest you unhand him immediately. If not, I'll have no choice but to shoot this arrow into some fleshy part of your body."

Ulgan swung around, my legs kicking out due to the rapid momentum. Jack was standing there, his bow drawn back and the arrow trained on Ulgan. I stilled the magic and raised a hand in a wave. "Jaaaack! Hiiiiii Jaaaaaaaack."

Jack didn't lift his head or offer a greeting, all his focus on his aim. He looked cool as a cucumber, like he threatened giant orcs every day before breakfast. He tilted his chin slightly, one eye slightly squinted to sight down the arrow. "I'm thinking that I aim for your eye. How do you fancy wearing an eyepatch for the rest of your life? It would ruin your..." A slight furrow appeared on his brow. "... looks." He was probably thinking the same thing I was, that actually it was more likely to improve them. "Or..." Jack paused dramatically, his gaze lowering to the loincloth and his eyes widening. "What about your cock? Do you need that? Can you manage without it?"

I didn't know about Ulgan's cock, but mine had given a definite twitch at hearing the word spill from Jack's lips. I could definitely enjoy that in a different context, like where he was talking about mine instead of an orc's.

Ulgan let out a loud bellow. "YOU DARE THREATEN ME, TINY HUMAN."

Jack pulled the string of the bow back a fraction. "I dare. Now... I asked you to unhand him and you still haven't done that, so I'm thinking an eye *and* your cock. Maybe both eyes. I'm guessing if you were blind, your card-playing days would be over. Hopefully, you have another source of income. If not, I suggest you let him go."

Ulgan let go. It was just unfortunate that it was from a great height, the wind knocked out of me as I hit the ground. He loomed over me, saliva dripping from his protruding teeth. "Don't think you've heard the last of this. I will return. And I will have my revenge on you."

I wanted to say something dry and witty, something that would leave a lasting impression, and maybe even make Jack laugh. All I managed was a cough, my lungs still working on taking in oxygen. Footsteps thundered away, Ulgan no longer making an effort to be stealthy as he returned to wherever it was he'd come from.

Jack lowered his bow, and I peeled myself off the ground and flung myself at him, using the element of surprise to draw him in tight and wrap my arms around him in an embrace that didn't make it easy for him to extricate himself. And he definitely did try before giving in to the inevitable. "You saved me from the mean, nasty orc." I buried my face in his neck and squeezed even tighter, my hands drifting down his back.

"Do *not* put those hands any lower."

I turned my head away to grin so that he couldn't feel it against his skin. He couldn't blame a man for trying. "You're my hero!"

"Yeah, whatever." He endured the embrace for a few more seconds as I clung to him like a limpet that had found the rock it intended to stay on for the rest of eternity. Jack cleared his throat. "Please let me go."

"Why?"

"Because... I asked. Because... I'm not feeling comfortable. Because—"

"But it's nice. I just suffered a great trauma. A hug always helps after a traumatic experience."

"I think... two people have to be involved in a hug. A hug is usually given or shared. You've..."

I prompted him when nothing else was forthcoming. "I've?"

"Taken it."

"Huh!" I treated myself to one last lungful of Jack before pulling back, Jack wiggling out of my arms as soon as he was able.

He retreated to the opposite side of the fire, his gaze on the flames. "Why did he think you'd cheated him?"

I lowered myself to sit on the ground and shrugged. "No idea." I raised a finger to my temple and whirled it around. "He's clearly loco. And a sore loser."

Jack still didn't lift his head. "Hmmm..."

"But you rushed to my rescue, so it's all good." I lifted my fingers to my neck and gave it a quick probe. "Although, you should probably check my neck out. He had a grip like you wouldn't believe. It was like being squeezed between five rocks."

"I should, should I?"

"I don't see anyone else around."

"I don't have any medical knowledge."

"What do you do on the farm when the animals are injured?"

Jack came back around the fire to stand looking down at me, his expression inscrutable. He leaned forward to peer at my neck. "I put them out of their misery."

I scuttled back. "Well, as I said, I'm absolutely fine. There's nothing to see here."

"Your voice is quite hoarse."

"You say hoarse. I say husky. Husky is sexy."

Jack was grinning as he returned to where he'd left the bow. He picked something up off the ground and held it aloft, two furry things dangling from his fist. "I caught some rabbits."

"You did?" Realizing the amount of surprise in my voice probably wasn't polite, I corrected myself. "You did. You're quite the font of hidden talents, aren't you?"

"I'm good with a bow." Jack seated himself cross-legged, the two rabbits laid across his lap. "Do you know how to skin a rabbit?"

"Me? Do *I* know how to skin a rabbit?" Jack lifted his gaze to mine, and I wilted beneath it. "No."

Jack sighed. "Why am I not surprised? I guess I'm doing everything, then. Catching the food, preparing the food, *and* cooking the food."

I wasn't used to feeling useless, but at that moment I came the closest I ever had to it. "You're going to share it, though, aren't you? I mean"—I gestured at the rabbits—"you caught two."

There was a long pause before Jack answered, as if he'd had to examine his own response a little too carefully before it had made it to his lips. "Yes, I'm going to share. If not, you'd moan, and you'd watch me eat with a sorrowful expression that would be enough to put me off my food. Therefore, my sharing is for my benefit, not yours."

Jack pulled out a sharp knife and set about skinning the rabbit. I watched him for a few minutes, impressed by how easy he made it look. "You could teach me."

Surprise was written all over his face as he raised his head. "Yeah?"

I nodded. Jack turned out to be a good teacher. He even managed to remain patient when I discovered that it was nowhere near as easy as he'd made it look, his rabbit looking like the finest cut of meat, whereas mine looked like it had been run over by a cart a time or two. They both tasted good, though, my stomach full by the time we'd eaten our fill with enough meat left over for breakfast.

There wasn't much to do after that except bed down for the night, Jack choosing a spot on the opposite side of the fire from mine. I lay there for a moment and then I got up, his eyes tracking me in the darkness. "What are you doing?"

I lay down behind him, leaving a good meter of space between us. "I think we should be closer."

"I think we were fine where we were. You're farther away from the fire now. You're going to get cold."

"I'll be fine." I shuffled a little bit closer.

"I can hear you moving."

"I'm just... getting comfortable."

"Why has your voice gotten louder then?"

"Probably something to do with your ears. Did you yawn?"

Jack made a huffing sound. "Don't push it, Sebastian. Don't go thinking that just because I didn't want you to be killed by a great big hulking orc means anything. I would have done the same for anyone. It's what people do. They help each other."

"I know that." I shuffled closer again, cutting the distance between our bodies down to about half a meter. "And call me Bass."

"Sebastian."

"Farm boy."

"A farm boy who saved your ass and provided dinner."

I gave up on getting any closer and rolled onto my back. "My neck hurts. I've got orc fingerprints embedded in it. I don't know if I'll be able to sleep."

"Well, just make sure you don't keep me awake."

"Wouldn't your mother be upset at your lack of caring?"

"My mother... would take one look at you, and..."

"And what?"

Jack sighed. "I don't know. I'm tired. Can I just sleep, Sebastian? Please."

"Of course, you can sleep."

"That would require you to stop talking."

I stopped talking.

Chapter Six

JACK

I awoke to the words "big orc" being whispered into my ear. I launched myself to a seated position, Sebastian's head dropping from my shoulder and his arm untangling from where he'd had it wrapped around my waist, as a result. "Where?" A careful scrutiny of the campsite revealed no orc to be seen.

Turning my focus back to Sebastian revealed that he wasn't even awake, his eyes still screwed tightly shut. He was sleep-talking again. I stared at him for a moment, his mouth moving for a moment in a restless motion before more words came out. "Big balls."

I frowned. Was he...? There was silence and then, "I can't fit that in my mouth." I almost swallowed my tongue. He was. I hit him on the chest, hard, Sebastian's eyes immediately jerking open. He rubbed at his chest with a wounded expression, tendrils of blond hair hanging down to cover his face. "What was that for?"

"Where do you want me to start?"

Sebastian brushed his hair back, the complete confusion on his face not appearing at all manufactured.

I sighed. "Well, let's start with the fact that I woke up with you almost on top of me."

His eyebrows shot up. "I was? Huh! I'm sorry I missed that."

I ignored him. "Or... you could take it as payment for the lurid sex dream you were having about orcs, the details of which you felt the need to whisper in my ear." It was a slight exaggeration, most of it having come after the point I'd already pushed him away. But he didn't need to know that.

Sebastian's brow scrunched up. "What was I saying?"

"How big everything was. How you couldn't possibly fit a certain organ in your mouth."

Sebastian blinked. "I said that. I actually said organ."

I smiled, enjoying the lie as it slipped from my mouth. "You did. You described it in great detail. I know you get around, Sebastian, but I didn't know you had a thing for orcs. I should have left you two alone yesterday. I didn't realize that what I was witnessing was actually foreplay."

Sebastian clambered to his feet, brushing bits of twig and leaves from those impossibly tight trousers of his. "I don't have a thing for orcs, trust me."

"If you say so."

"I don't."

"I believe you."

"I don't!"

I hid my smile as I started doling out the leftover rabbit. It felt good to get one over on him. How annoying for Sebastian that he couldn't control what came out of his mouth when he was asleep. I could claim he'd said anything, and he wouldn't be able to deny it. I was definitely going to squirrel that nugget of information away until it proved useful.

I stared in disbelief at the village Sebastian had just walked straight past. "We've been walking all day. Why can't we stop here? What makes Redview so much better than this place?"

Sebastian didn't slow, and I was forced to jog to catch up with him to hear his response. "Hot springs."

"Which means?"

He frowned. "Exactly what I said. Redview has hot springs. Oldshire doesn't. Don't tell me you wouldn't go for a hot bath in water that doesn't get cold? It bubbles as well."

It did sound good, but I wasn't going to give Sebastian the satisfaction of admitting that. "How much farther is it?"

"Couple of hours."

I groaned. "We should have stopped anyway, to ask about my sister."

Sebastian stopped so suddenly I almost walked into his back. When he turned, there was a look of genuine remorse on his face. At least I assumed it was genuine. "We'll go back."

I turned to look at Oldshire. It was tiny, even smaller than Riverbrook. Did it look like a place my sister would stop? I didn't know. I was beginning to think I didn't know her at all. I shook my head. "It doesn't matter. Skipping one place isn't going to make much of a difference. If she was here, I don't think it's a place she would have stayed. She would have moved on, probably to somewhere with hot springs."

Sebastian smiled. "Exactly."

Redview turned out to be a village hewn almost completely out of rock, even the houses largely consisting of a hodge-podge of different types of rocks. Sebastian seemed to know exactly where he was going, passing most of the houses to walk to the far side of the village where a white stone house loomed over the other buildings. Sebastian paused for a moment with his hand on the door. "Welcome to one of the best inns in the kingdom."

"Is it?" I might have taken some time to peer through one of the windows to ascertain just how true that statement was if it wasn't for the fact that Sebastian was already stepping inside.

A tall, wiry youth immediately rushed from behind a counter to seize Sebastian by the shoulders and pull him into a long hug. "Oh my God! When did you get here? Is it true what I heard? How long are you staying? Are you hungry? Does my uncle know you're here? Did you really beat Ulgan? Are you tired? Where are you heading to? How much did you win? Who's this? How long has it been since you were last here? Was Ulgan as scary as they say? Do you need to sit down?"

The questions were never-ending and delivered without a single pause for Sebastian to actually answer any of them. Perhaps he wasn't meant to. Sebastian had a huge grin on his face when he finally eased himself out of the embrace. "Slow down, Ansel."

He turned to me. "This is Ansel. Ansel, this is Jack."

There was no time to avoid it, and I found myself caught up in a similar hug to the one Sebastian had endured, Ansel hanging on way past the time when it had already grown excruciatingly awkward. It was a little reminiscent of the one Sebastian had given me the previous night, but then, at least I knew him. Sort of. And I'd put his overexuberance down to having escaped an irate orc. Whereas I had no such excuse to use for Ansel.

"Ansel." Sebastian sounded amused. "Jack's not a big hugger. Let him go. I think he might need to breathe again." The grip didn't slacken in the slightest. "Ansel!"

He finally eased back. "I just wanted to be friendly."

I coughed. "And you were. Very friendly."

Sebastian shot me a warning glance, which I took to mean I shouldn't hurt this rather strange boy's feelings. I didn't need it. My sharp tongue was reserved for Sebastian and Sebastian alone. Ansel hadn't robbed me with a monkey. Not yet, anyway. Although, the day was still young.

Ansel rushed over to a large open ledger. He drew his finger down the entries and frowned. "We've only got one room left. I could—"

Sebastian cut in. "One is fine. Jack likes to have me close. He says it makes him feel safer."

My snort was loud and drawn-out. "Jack has never said any such thing. Jack would feel far safer if Sebastian was in another kingdom. Jack is very much just putting up with Sebastian for reasons unbeknownst to himself that he keeps questioning daily."

Sebastian smiled sweetly and fluttered his eyelashes. "Why is Jack talking about himself in the third person?"

I glared at him. "Jack is…" I stopped myself. "*I am just so utterly flabbergasted by the lies that trip off your tongue so easily.*"

Ansel was grinning in a way that said our altercation was amusing. Well, I was glad someone was amused. And it certainly wasn't me. Safe, when I was close to Sebastian? As if. He was the one I needed to keep an eye on, or before I knew it, he was wrapped around me like a snake, muttering orc-related filth in my ear.

Ansel reached beneath the counter and pulled out two large fluffy towels, which he offered to Sebastian. "Room is the one at the top. I'm assuming you'll want these first?"

Sebastian gave him a grin as he took them. "Definitely. I'm so ready for a hot bath."

A look of alarm suddenly crossed Ansel's face. "What happened to your neck?"

I almost felt guilty that I'd refused to comment on the livid bruises that stood out on Sebastian's neck. Almost. But not guilty enough not to get in there first. "He tried breath play with an orc."

Ansel's eyebrows shot up. "Really? Wow! I didn't know you were into orcs. Good on you, Bass." He winked. "You should try everything once, right?" His expression sobered. "Be careful, though. That shit's dangerous. Especially when your partner is so much bigger and stronger than you are. And make sure you use lots of lubrication." A dark flush crept into Ansel's cheeks. "You know, because they're very well endowed, or so I hear."

The sideways glance my way from Sebastian should have been enough of a warning that I wasn't going to like the next words out of his mouth. "Jack struggles to understand the attraction of anything with two legs. He likes goats. The bigger and hairier the better."

I was treated to another raise of Ansel's eyebrows as his gaze trailed slowly down my body, as if he was expecting to see tufts of goat hair sticking out of my clothes from my last encounter. "Oh! I see. Well… to each their own. We don't have any goats here, sorry. But I'm sure Bass can conjure one up for you. Or would that be weird? It would be weird, right?"

We left Ansel pondering his own question, Sebastian leading me out of a back door and down a long, rocky path. Eventually we came to a cave, the interior lit with lanterns and surprisingly expansive. At its center was a large pool emanating steam.

Sebastian held out an arm. "See. Hot springs. How do you like that, farm boy?"

I liked it a lot. I could already imagine how good that water was going to feel against my skin. The fact that it was empty except for the two of us was an added bonus. "How come there are no other guests here?"

Sebastian was already unbuttoning his shirt. "Limited hours."

I turned to look behind me, gold sparks dancing in the corner of my eye as I faced front again. "What was that?"

Sebastian paused with his fingers on a button. "What was what?"

"I keep seeing…" Too worried about sounding like a lunatic, I didn't finish my sentence. "Nothing. Never mind. What do you mean by limited hours?"

He peeled his shirt off and let it drop before starting on his boots. "Guest hours are between nine and five only. And then a late-hour session at ten. The pool's only for family use outside those hours."

I frowned. "But aren't we guests?"

Sebastian waved a dismissive hand. "I'm special."

I rolled my eyes. "And if you keep telling me that, I might believe it one day."

"Duly noted. I'll aim for three times a day."

Sebastian's fingers went to the fastening of his trousers. He made short work of it before starting to pull them down. I swallowed and looked away. Except… he had his back to me. He was the one unashamedly undressing in front of me, so why the hell shouldn't I look if it was right there. It didn't mean

I liked him. It just meant I could appreciate a nicely toned ass. And his was definitely that—firm and muscular and...

Sebastian's throaty laugh cut into my thoughts. "Jack, you little devil. I'm not a piece of meat, you know."

He still had his back to me. Therefore, there was no way he could know I was looking at him. I let out a sound of disgust. "I'm not remotely interested in your naked body, so you can keep your wishful thinking to yourself."

"Liar!"

There was a great deal of conviction in Sebastian's voice. Confused, I looked up to find a hawk perched on a rocky outcrop looking down at us. It hadn't been there when we arrived, and it being here now didn't make sense. Where had it come from? I tilted my head to the side, and it did the same. I was dimly aware of Sebastian wading into the water as I continued to stare at the bird in an attempt to work out what it was doing here.

Gold sparks.

Suddenly, it made perfect sense. Those same gold sparks had been there on the very first day that I'd met Sebastian, when he'd waved a hand and the monkey had disappeared to turn his blatant lie that there was no monkey into a warped version of the truth. And come to think of it, those gold sparks had also been there last night when I'd arrived back at the camp to find Sebastian dangling from the orc's meaty fist. "Were you going to summon an animal last night?"

Sebastian eased himself down in the water and laid his head back against the side of the pool with a groan of satisfaction. "Possibly."

"So I didn't really save you?"

He considered the question for a moment. "Well, yeah, you did. You didn't know that I could have gotten myself out of that situation. You rushed in there with no thought of your own personal safety, like some sort of guardian angel with a bow."

"Why hadn't you summoned anything? You were just sort of hanging there." Something suddenly occurred to me, my face screwing up with a disgust I couldn't manage to hold back. "Oh my God! Were you enjoying it? Were you secretly getting off on it? I was joking when I said I was interrupting, but was that true?"

Sebastian blinked a few times. "No! Can you get this ridiculous idea out of your head that I am into orcs? I'm not... orcist, but they don't do anything for me."

I raised an eyebrow. "So why are you having sex dreams about them?"

"I'm not."

I inched the eyebrow a little higher. "You were dreaming about sucking his cock."

A slight smile appeared on Sebastian's lips. "I do love hearing that word on your lips. Can you say something else lewd?"

"Like what?"

The smile grew wider. "How about, if you're a very good boy, Bass, I'll let you suck my cock."

"That's never going to happen. My *cock* will never get anywhere near your lips. Not even if some sort of nasty accident should befall me and said organ became detached from my body. I'd still find some way to keep it away from you."

Sebastian grimaced. "You had to go and spoil it, didn't you, by talking about detached organs?" Sebastian's gaze lifted to trail down my body in a lazy scrutiny. "Speaking of which, are you going to undress and come in, or are you just going to stand there?" He made a little splashing motion with his arms. "The water is absolutely divine. You do not want to miss out."

Ignoring him, I lifted my eyes to the hawk again, something tickling in the back of my brain. "Why the hawk?"

"Force of habit."

"Which means?"

"I can close my eyes and still be able to keep a lookout. It pays to be prepared. For all we know Ulgan is still following us. I'd rather not find myself dunked under the water by giant, green fingers while taking a bath."

"So... you can see through the hawk's eyes?"

Sebastian nodded.

It was a clever—and I imagined very useful—trick to be able to pull. My cheeks burned at the confirmation that Sebastian had indeed been able to see me checking him out. Luckily, the knowledge of his magical powers had opened up far more important lines of enquiry. "But that would mean that your monkey, or should I say *you*, targeted me on purpose."

Sebastian shrugged. "I would suggest not leaving your money pouch on the table where anyone can see it."

"I didn't know that I had to guard against marauding monkeys."

"Well, now you do." He paused for a beat. "You're welcome."

I ignored him, my mind already on something else. Where else had I seen the gold sparks? Something told me it was important. And then it came to me. I'd seen them when Sebastian had been taking part in the tournament. "I'm an idiot!"

Sebastian shifted lazily in the water. "Now, don't be too hard on yourself, Jack. You've spent all your life on a farm. You could probably leave money scattered around there and no one would touch it, but out here in the real world, you can't be that trusting. You need—"

"Not about that." I glared at him. "I was stupid not to put two and two together and work out that pigeons don't just happen to fly into crowded taverns and sit directly above gaming tables. And that the likelihood of one being ejected and then flying back in is extremely low. That's why you started losing. You'd lost your eyes." I ran a hand through my hair, disgust settling in every atom of my body. "You did cheat! I should have let Ulgan have you. Next time, I will. Go on, try and deny it." Sebastian stayed silent. "See, you can't, can you?"

"It really depends on your definition of cheating."

I placed my hands on my hips. "Could you or could you not, see all his cards via the medium of pigeon?"

Sebastian cleared his throat. "Not all of them. Sometimes he held them at a strange angle and the pigeon struggled. He's a pigeon, not a contortionist."

"Just admit it. Just say you're a huge cheat. At least that would be honest. God knows there's been very little of that since I met you."

"Say what? Sorry?"

My fury grew exponentially, my voice getting higher. "Are you listening to me?"

"I'll admit that I'm a little bit distracted, you know, given the... er"—Sebastian lifted a hand from the water to wave it in my direction—"nakedness."

Nakedness! Had he gone insane? I dropped my gaze, realization sinking in that I'd been so caught up in ferreting out the truth that I hadn't registered ripping off my clothes at the same time, my brain wanting one thing while my tired limbs craved the heat of the water. And now here I was, hands on hips, providing Sebastian with an unobstructed view of everything I had.

I waded into the water, leaving as much space as I could between myself and Sebastian before sitting down, the water in that part of the baths reaching up to the middle of my chest. I'd like to have believed that my cheeks were burning from the heat of the water, but I knew it had absolutely nothing to do with that, and everything to do with having paraded naked in front of Sebastian. "You cheated. You're a big cheat. And a thief. And a... libertine. One who has sex dreams about orcs. I don't know how I got mixed up with you."

"I'm not into orcs."

"But you're fine with the rest?"

Sebastian sat up straighter, the water level dropping to his waist. "How do you think Ulgan won for five years straight?"

"Luck."

Sebastian's snort reverberated around the enclosed space. "Yeah, right! He was cheating. I happen to think that cheating doesn't count if you're cheating a cheat."

"How was he cheating?"

"I don't know."

"So you've got absolutely no proof?"

He shrugged. "Doesn't mean I don't know it to be true. There are numerous ways he could have done it."

I eyed him warily, surprised by the extent to which I wanted to believe him. "Like what?"

"He could have visited a witch or a warlock. They have all sorts of tricks up their sleeve. Luck spells. The power to see through things. I don't know. I'm not an expert."

I made a considering noise. "Wouldn't those things be terribly expensive?"

Sebastian gave a long, slow nod. "Probably something that only a man who'd won a tournament five years in a row could afford."

He had a point. "It doesn't make it right. And you didn't have to get me involved in it."

"I never asked you to chase my monkey."

"No, you would have been happy for me to be penniless and forced to sleep rough, where I would probably have been eaten by a bear."

"There aren't any bears in this kingdom."

"A lion, then. I don't know. Something that eats humans. My point is that you hadn't considered what would happen to me once you left me without any money."

"I didn't know you."

"Hmm..."

A loud voice suddenly rang out across the cavern. "Bass, you useless reprobate. I thought Ansel had been on the magic mushrooms again when he said you were back. But here you are, in the flesh."

I turned just in time to witness a swarthy dark-haired man not even hesitate at the entrance to the pool. Instead, he waded in fully clothed, Sebastian rising in a torrent of water and the two of them embracing, the stranger apparently not caring one jot that Sebastian was naked. What did that make them? Lovers? Something more?

I averted my eyes from Sebastian's taut, rounded ass, the hawk still there to catch me in the act should I be tempted to dwell on it. I'd have to be even more on my guard around Sebastian. He literally had eyes in the back of his head. At least when there was a summon around.

The two men finally broke apart, Sebastian sliding back into the water as the other man stood thigh deep, his white shirt damp from where Sebastian had been plastered against him. His gaze slid my way, and he made no attempt to hide his curiosity. I slid deeper into the water beneath the force of his scrutiny, the water lapping at my chin. He gave me a crooked smile. "Who's this?"

Sebastian waved a hand in my direction. "This is… Jack." What was with the pause before he'd said my name? Had he been about to introduce me as farm boy? If so, it was a wise decision not to have gone ahead. There'd been something strange in his voice, though, when he'd said my name, some sort of edge to it, like he'd been going to say more but had stopped himself. "Jack, this is my good friend, Leofric."

One of Leofric's dark eyebrows shot up. "Jack?"

Sebastian nodded. "Jack."

What was with everyone repeating my name? It was enough to make a person feel decidedly uncomfortable, like there was a whole conversation going on beneath the surface that I hadn't been made privy to. And where did I recognize the name Leofric from? Right. That was it. Sebastian had muttered something about a Leofric in his sleep that first night when I'd been forced to share a room with him. I mumbled a greeting before closing my eyes and letting their conversation wash over me.

CHAPTER SEVEN

JACK

I'd found myself sharing a table with Leofric as we'd eaten dinner. He and Sebastian had sat with their shoulders pressed together as we'd devoured a thick, plentiful stew with meat and vegetables, and then washed it down with large tankards of ale.

The inn had filled up in the interim, most of the guests keen to hang out and enjoy the hospitable atmosphere. And I had to admit that it was hospitable. Even without the access to the hot springs, this was one of the nicest places I'd ever set foot in. The décor wasn't too shabby either, the inn a mixture of dark wood and polished stone.

Once he'd finished eating, Sebastian had wandered off and was currently deep in conversation with a tall male elf. His departure had left me alone with Leofric, who seemed only too happy to sit with me. I opened my mouth to tell him that he could get on with whatever it was he'd normally be doing, that I didn't require a babysitter, but he got in there first. "He likes you."

I played dumb. "Who?"

His lips curled up into a knowing smile. "Bass. I've known him for a long time, ever since we were kids. I know everything about him, and he knows everything about me."

That made them sound like they were two peas in a pod. I had to admit that physically, they were pretty similar, both muscular and blue-eyed with long hair. Only where Sebastian was fair, Leofric was dark. Without the difference in coloring, you would have been forgiven for thinking they were brothers. "Do you rob people with monkeys as well?"

Leofric threw his head back and laughed. "Alas, I have to admit that I'm all out of monkeys. Bass told me how you two met. It sounds like him. He does have a habit of making a dreadful first impression." He leaned forward slightly. "Ask me how I met Bass."

I took a drink of my ale while I contemplated lying and telling him I had zero interest. I sighed and gave in to the inevitable. "How did you meet?"

"Little Bass"—Leofric lowered his hand to about a foot off the floor to illustrate his point—"conjured up a snake in my bed as a prank. Not a grass snake. No, nothing so innocuous for Bass. He's never done things by halves. He conjured up a viper, a bright green one. I didn't know anything about it until it slid under my nightshirt. I cried for hours and then refused to sleep in my bed without someone checking it first for months. Bass's mother forced him to apologize to me, but the damage had already been done. I still check a bed before getting into it to this day, the bastard."

He'd said "bastard" with a great deal of fondness, like Sebastian was actually no such thing. "And you still became friends after that?"

Leofric grinned. "Bass has a way of grinding you down. He's a force of nature. You can no more say no to Bass than you can hold water in your hand."

I crossed my arms over my chest. "Oh, I can say no to him just fine."

Leofric took a sip of his ale, his gaze meeting mine over the rim of the tankard. "Yet, here you are." Curiosity sparked in his eye. "Do you realize you watch him? Even while we've been talking, you keep one eye on him."

I gave the loudest and most convincing scoff I could. "I don't. What a ridiculous thing to say."

Leofric rested his head on his hand and regarded me without speaking, his silence far more effective than any words could have been. "If I do"—I illustrated the point with an outstretched finger—"it's simply to make sure he's not robbing anyone, or seducing any virgins, or cheating anyone out of their livelihood. *Someone* needs to keep an eye on him."

Leofric hid a smile behind his hand. "And are you the man for the job?"

I narrowed my eyes at him. "What's that supposed to mean?"

"You and Sebastian. He could do with a steady hand to guide him."

I stared at him incredulously, barely able to believe what he was suggesting. "Me and Sebastian! There is no me and Sebastian. There will never be any me and Sebastian. Not while I'm still breathing. I dare say that if I died, there's nothing I could do to stop him requisitioning my corpse and propping me up in a corner. But that would be the only way there would ever be a me and Sebastian. Why would you go and say a ridiculous thing like that?"

"I told you, he likes you."

"He likes everybody."

Leofric nodded. "He does, but he *likes* you."

I concentrated on polishing the rest of my ale off, Leofric immediately waving Ansel—who had turned out to be his nephew, Leofric's sister being the owner of the inn—over to give me a refill. My gaze skittered over to Sebastian of its own accord, all his attention still on the elf. "He likes me so much that he's over there."

I wanted to take the words back as soon as they'd left my mouth. I couldn't have sounded more like a spurned lover if I'd tried.

Leofric's grin told me he thought so too. "He's just being friendly."

"I'm surprised he hasn't taken his shirt off yet." Mind, I was aiming that comment at the wrong man—Leofric's was undone almost to the navel. I didn't have the same burning need to look at him, though. I could appreciate the view without being tempted to wallow in it.

Sebastian chose that moment to turn, his gaze meeting mine. He lifted his hand and curled his fingers to gesture me forward. "Jack, come here."

The glare I shot him was wasted due to the fact that he'd already turned back to the elf, as if it hadn't even crossed his mind that I wasn't at his beck and call. What did he think I was? Did he think he could whistle, and I'd bound across there like a dog desperate to find out what his master wanted?

I stayed resolutely in place, ignoring the chuckle that came from Leofric. A minute passed before Sebastian turned again, his face the picture of confusion when he discovered I wasn't there. "Jack?"

I got up, my comment to Leofric coming from between gritted teeth. "Just so we're clear, the only reason I'm going over there is to give him a piece of my mind, to let that big lummox know that he doesn't get to order me around, that if he tries it again, he's in danger of losing an important part of his anatomy."

Leofric gave another chuckle. "Of course."

I was dimly aware of Leofric following as I made my way over to Sebastian. He probably didn't want to miss the show. I doubted there were that many people willing to take Sebastian down a peg or two, but I certainly was.

As soon as I was close enough, Sebastian's fingers curled around my arm, my intention to cut him down to size forestalled by the words out of his mouth. "Ayas saw a red-headed woman a few days back."

I gaped at him before flicking my eyes to the elf, hope flaring in my chest. If someone had seen Annabelle, then I still had a chance of finding her. Guilt for judging Sebastian so harshly came hand in hand with the sense of hope. I'd thought he was flirting, when what he'd actually been doing was asking questions about my sister. Questions I should have been asking instead of sitting and sulking in a corner. "Is that true?"

Ayas nodded. He gestured at his head. "She had a hood on. It was pulled up to cover her hair, but she lowered it, just for a moment. The sun was out, and her hair lit up like a flame. That's why I noticed her. Hair like that is very rare. Very beautiful as well. She was obviously going to great pains to hide it."

Excitement bubbled in my chest. "How tall was she? Where was this? Could you tell what color her eyes were? Where was she going? What was she doing?" I'd turned into Ansel, the torrent of questions bubbling out of me like water.

Sebastian moved to wrap an arm around my shoulders, and for once I didn't mind. It was somewhat reassuring, like we were in this together. "Slow down, Jack. Ayas will tell you everything. I called you over as soon as he told me he'd seen her." He paused, his brow furrowing. "You must not have heard me the first time."

Leofric cleared his throat. "Who's the red-haired woman?"

"My sister."

I looked to Ayas. "Tell me what you know, please."

Ayas nodded, his expression earnest. "She was in Brittleharbor."

"Brittleharbor?"

Sebastian supplied the answer. "It's on the coast."

"What's in Brittleharbor?"

"Not a lot, apart from ships." Sebastian frowned. "Would your sister have any reason to be seeking out a ship?"

I shook my head. "Not that I can think of. Perhaps she was just passing through."

Ayas rubbed his chin thoughtfully. "Perhaps. I didn't get that impression, though. I saw her again the next day. She was talking to a ship's captain. She had the hood up, but I recognized her cloak from the day before. And her eyes were green." He held out a hand in front of him, the level well below his chin. "She was about this height. Maybe a bit taller."

I couldn't help the grin that broke out across my face. "It's her." Still smiling, I turned to Sebastian, my usual antagonism lost beneath a huge wave of relief. "I have to go there." I disentangled myself from him, dimly aware that the loss of warmth from his body felt like a much bigger deal than it should have done. "Where's your map? Which direction do I need to go in? I need to leave immediately."

My shoulders were gripped, Sebastian slowly turning me to face him, his blue eyes intent on my face. "It's dark, Jack. You can't go now. I know this is the first lead on your sister that you've had, but you can't go off half-cocked. It's safer to wait until the morning. You're not going to help your sister if you get yourself killed. We'll set off at first light. I promise."

"We?"

Sebastian's lips curved up into a smile. "Of course. We're in this together."

My heart gave a funny little skip. "Isn't it out of your way?"

He shrugged. "What's a little detour between friends?"

I stared at him, our gazes locked, something I didn't want to think too much about passing between us. I was relieved when Leofric spoke, his announcement breaking the charged moment. "I'll come too."

Sebastian turned to him and raised an eyebrow. "Stocking up on seafood?"

Leofric's grin was lazy, his eyes sparkling with amusement. "Something like that."

I couldn't decide whether Leofric's company would be a blessing or a curse. I was yet to work out the specific nature of his and Sebastian's relationship, and I wasn't sure I wanted to.

There might only have been one room available, but the room at the top of the inn was clearly one of their most prestigious, everything in it either dark wood or white silk, except for the lit red candles. Both the bed and the windows were huge.

Sebastian seemed to follow my thought processes, providing the answer without me having to ask. "This is the bridal suite."

"The what?"

Sebastian started taking his boots off. Of course, his clothes were coming off. He'd been in the room for longer than a second. "The room for people who were married recently." His shirt followed the boots.

"So why are we in it?"

He grinned. "You heard Ansel. It was the only room left."

There'd been a moment tonight where I'd almost had this room to myself, Leofric telling Sebastian he should bunk with him. And then the next thing I'd known, Sebastian had said something to Ayas, and the elf had cozied up to

Leofric, Leofric seeming only too happy with the attention. "Why aren't you staying with Leofric?"

"Because…" Sebastian started on the fastenings to his trousers. "He's having some private time with Ayas. I would have been in the way."

"It happened very fast. What did you say to Ayas?"

A look of innocence came my way, blond lashes fluttering down to hide the blue gaze. "What do you mean?"

"You said something, and then the next moment he was all over Leofric."

Naked, Sebastian pulled the covers back and got in the bed. He pulled the white silk sheet over his lap and then lay on his back with his fingers interlocked behind his head. "I did a bit of matchmaking, that's all. No big deal."

I walked over to stare out of the window. "I thought you and Leofric were…"

I winced at my own words, quickly trying for a bit of damage control. "Not that I give a damn. I was just surprised when he went off with Ayas instead of you."

"We were once, but that was a long time ago."

"So, you're just friends?"

"Yep. Why?"

I shrugged. "No reason." I turned to face him. "Actually, there is a reason." He raised an eyebrow and I continued, a plausible excuse for my query only just having come to me. "If I'm going to be traveling with both of you for the next couple of days, and it's true what Ayas said about there being little accommodation between here and Brittleharbor, I'd rather not have to listen to the pair of you screwing while I'm trying to sleep. That's all."

"We won't be screwing."

"Good." I pulled my boots off. "For the reasons I said, because who wants to play third wheel?"

"Leofric, apparently."

"What?"

Sebastian blinked. "Nothing. I was just thinking aloud."

"Well, don't."

"Don't think, or don't do it aloud?"

"Both."

"Got you. No more thinking. I will just act on base impulse in the future."

I narrowed my eyes at him. "That doesn't sound wise. There must be a middle ground."

Sebastian rolled onto his side and propped himself up on one elbow. "Has anyone ever told you that you're very bossy?"

"No." I stared at the bed and then the floor, and then the bed again.

"Probably because they were too scared to."

"I'm not scary." Bed. Floor. Bed. Floor. I didn't want to sleep on the floor, but the bed had a naked Sebastian in it.

"Not scary!" Sebastian let out a snort. "You scared a seven-foot orc away with only a bow and arrow. I mean, you did threaten to take his eyes and his cock, so words were involved as well."

I stalked over to the bed and pulled the sheet back with a flourish which dared him to comment on it as I climbed in.

"You're not going to take your clothes off?"

"No."

"Fair enough."

I rolled onto my side so that I had my back to him. "If I was that scary, you'd abandon this bed for the floor."

"I'm a very brave man."

"You're an idiot."

"I'm a very brave idiot."

I hid my smile in the pillow. "Go to sleep. And keep to your side of the bed. And do not start whispering filthy things about orcs in my ear."

There was a rustling of sheets as Sebastian lay down. "Very bossy."

"Shhhh."

"Night, Jack."

There was a beat of three seconds where I tried not to say it, but somebody else seemed to have taken over my tongue. "Night, Sebastian."

"Bass."

That, I managed to ignore.

CHAPTER EIGHT

SEBASTIAN

Leofric waved a hand at Jack's back, my companion setting a punishing walking pace while Leofric and I tagged behind. "What did you do? I thought I'd detected a certain amount of softening toward you after you found out about his sister, but you seem like you're back to square one today?"

I contemplated the question, deciding Leofric knew me far too well to lie. "He took umbrage with me not keeping to my side of the bed. Like I can be held responsible for what I do while I'm asleep. He called me a... What was it? Ah, that's right—an opportunistic octopus. Those two words don't even make sense together."

Leofric chuckled. "You've certainly got your hands full with him."

"I did." I smiled at the memory of a warm and pliant Jack in my arms. It had almost made waking so early worth it. "That's what he took exception to. Oh, and he claims I talk in my sleep as well."

"You do talk in your sleep."

I gave him a sideways glance. "You've never mentioned it."

Leofric shrugged. "I figured you knew. You have full-scale conversations sometimes. It's just something you do."

"Huh!" A change of topic was definitely in order. "How was your night with Ayas? I thought you might have changed your mind about coming with us."

Leofric's smile was tinged with fond remembrance. "It was good. A very unexpected bonus to your inability to let Jack out of your sight even for one night."

"You don't know how determined he is, or how stubborn. He would have left for Brittleharbor in the middle of the night."

"So you were left with no choice but to pin him down with your body?"

I ignored the jibe. "You weren't tempted to stay?"

Leofric shook his head. "He had business to attend to. He said he would call in to Redview on his way back. I'll have returned from Brittleharbor by then."

After a long day of walking, I was glad to make camp, Leofric and I working together to build a fire while Jack disappeared with a determined look on his face.

Leofric inclined his head in the direction Jack had gone a good hour earlier. "Where's he gone?"

"To catch something for dinner, I assume."

His eyebrows shot up. "Really? I thought the bow was just for decoration."

I shook my head. "He caught two rabbits earlier in the week. They were very tasty. There's a lot to be said for fresh meat."

"Huh." Leofric tore a blade of grass off a nearby clump and twirled it between his fingers. "Good-looking *and* useful to have around. No wonder you're panting after him like a dog on heat."

I shot him a glare. "I am not panting after him. I have a normal, healthy interest in him which currently isn't being reciprocated, but I'm patient, I can wait."

"Jack is..." Leofric suddenly stopped talking.

I leaned forward, eager to know what he'd been about to say. I'd noticed the two of them talking the previous night. Had Jack let slip something that would give me hope my attentions weren't going to be thrown back in my face forever? "Jack is, what?"

Leofric lifted a hand to point. "Jack is... back."

He was, breezing into camp like he'd only been gone for a few minutes. He held out a large leaf and I stared at the green mush contained within its curled-up sides. I leaned forward to sniff it, immediately recoiling from the pungent scent. "What the hell is that? Whatever it is, I'm not eating it."

I received a familiar look of disdain. "You're not meant to eat it, you absolute nincompoop. It's Crawling Polkweed..." Both the sigh and the eyeroll that followed demonstrated Jack's irritation at me for not having a clue what he was talking about. "Crawling Polkweed, when mixed with Angel Grass, both of which I managed to find, are good for healing." He waved a hand at my neck. "It looks sore, that's all."

It was sore, the orc's fingermarks now lurid purple and green marks on my skin. I was just surprised Jack had noticed, especially since he'd barely looked my way all day. It was sweet of him to have gone out of his way to find the ingredients. Of course, if I told him that, he'd no doubt fling the whole lot in the river and deny any such thing. So instead, I found myself staring up at him, at a loss for what to say.

I was dimly aware of Leofric rising to his feet in my peripheral vision. He cleared his throat. "I'm going to take a walk. A long one."

I nodded to show I'd heard, but I didn't take my eyes off Jack. "That's very... considerate of you."

He shrugged and offered me the leaf again. "Do you want it or not?"

I tipped my head to one side, baring the side of my neck where the most damage had been wrought. "You should do it. You know, make sure it's been administered correctly."

"You just smear it on. It's not that difficult."

When I made no move to take it from him, Jack let out a gusty sigh. But he did step closer, so close that I could feel his body heat. He dipped his fingers into the green gunk and began to dab it gently on my neck. "I should have made this for you a couple of days ago. It would have prevented some of the swelling and bruising. Sorry."

I almost swallowed my tongue. "What was that word you just said? Did you just apologize to me? Or does this stuff cause instantaneous auditory hallucinations."

Jack's fingers stilled. "I can be a bit..."

"A bit what?"

His fingers started to move again, the action of him applying the salve soothing. "You know."

"Judgmental?"

He shook his head.

"Obnoxious?"

He frowned. "Are you deliberately getting this wrong so you can call me names? Moody. I was going to say moody."

"Ah, moody. Of course. Not obnoxious or judgmental. You would never be either of those things."

"I'm trying to be nice here, Sebastian."

I stifled a smile at the sharp note in his voice. Only Jack could claim he was trying to be nice while simultaneously getting irritated. "You are being nice."

He stood back to admire his handiwork. "How does that feel?"

"Cold." I had to admit, though, that the dull ache in my neck was already beginning to subside slightly.

Jack scooped out another handful. "Other side."

I obediently tilted my head the opposite way, Jack moving my hair out of the way, an action I was grateful for. "I'm going to smell like pond scum."

"Lucky that you and Leofric are just friends, then, and you're not trying to make yourself attractive for him. And that there's no one else for miles."

I gave him a narrow-eyed glare which he studiously ignored. I tried a different tack. "While we're doling out the apologies, I apologize for this morning."

Jack let out a little huff. "What are you apologizing for exactly?"

"For... wrapping myself around you like a..."

"Octopus?"

"I can't help it if I gravitate toward warmth while I'm asleep."

"Are you apologizing, or are you once more telling me that it's not your fault? Because I feel like we already had one of those conversations."

"I'm apologizing."

"Go on then, because there seems to be a certain word missing."

"Sorry for using you like my own personal teddy bear."

Jack's hand dropped from my neck. "Apology accepted." He paused for a beat. "I'm not going to have sex with you, Sebastian."

And there it was in perfect clarity, the matter-of-fact way it had been laid out causing my stomach to lurch and something sharp to splinter in my chest. "Why not?"

Jack let out a little laugh that was half amusement and half disbelief. "Because it would be a terrible, terrible mistake, and I'd regret it the next morning. I'm not like you."

"And what am I like?"

"You're more worldly than I am."

"And that's a bad thing?"

He gave a little shake of his head. "No, it's just... different. *We're* too different. I wanted to be straight with you. You're going out of your way to travel to Brittleharbor with me, and I would hate it if the only reason you were doing that is because you think you might win me over in the end. It's not going to happen."

"You're attracted to me. I've seen how you look at me."

Jack spent far more time placing the leaf on the ground and wiping his hands on the grass than the task warranted. "You're an attractive man. You know that."

"But?"

He looked up to meet my gaze. "I can enjoy looking at something without having to touch it."

"Can we be friends?" The silence while I waited for him to answer felt like eons passing.

His reply when it came was hesitant. "I don't know. Can we?"

"I don't see why not."

Jack strolled over to the log that Leofric had vacated. "I'm really glad we had this discussion and got everything sorted out."

Had we? It didn't feel like it, a gnawing feeling in my gut I wasn't accustomed to making it hard to say anything. Anyway, it was probably better not to push.

"Will you and Leofric part company with me tomorrow?"

"Why would we do that?"

"Because... I just told you that I'm not going to have sex with you, and because I'm well aware that there's a prince who needs rescuing, a prince that I'm delaying you from getting to. It makes no sense for you to come with me."

It made perfect sense to me, even after Jack's announcement, but I wasn't about to try and explain that to him. "No, we're still coming."

"Yeah?" There was no way I could miss the relief in his voice.

"You're a long way from home. What kind of friend would I be if I just abandoned you? Besides, I might never have met your sister, but I feel like I have. I'd like to find her safe and well just as much as you."

"That's..." Jack didn't seem to know how to finish the sentence and I didn't push him on it. Silence fell for a few minutes until Jack broke it. "How do you come to have magic?"

I eyed him warily. "Is this where you accuse me of having stolen it?"

"Did you?"

"No."

"So you were born with it?"

I nodded.

Jack contemplated that for a few moments. "That's really unusual."

"Why?"

"In Cerensai, magic is rare unless you're royalty."

"I'm not from Cerensai."

He sat up straighter, a curious look on his face. "Where are you from?"

"Same place as Leofric. Over the sea." An arch of Jack's eyebrow had me elaborating. "Padora. Have you heard of it?"

"I've heard of it."

"But you've never been?"

He gave a soft laugh. "I can count the times I left Riverbrook before this on the fingers of one hand. Is that pathetic, that I'm twenty-six and had never strayed far from my own village before?"

"Were you happy there?"

"Mostly."

I shrugged. "Then it's not pathetic. Most people who roam are looking for something. If you have everything you need, then there's no need to go looking for anything else. You're only here now because you're searching for your sister."

Jack thought about my words for a moment. "What are you looking for?"

"A lost prince."

There was a slight twist to his mouth. "Who you're going to marry and live happily ever after with."

I lifted my chin, the cynicism bothering me. "Why do you say that like the idea is ridiculous? Do you not have a romantic bone in your body? Do you have someone waiting for you in Riverbrook? Is that it? Does farm boy have another farm boy there?"

Jack shook his head. "No. I guess my dreams are more rooted in realism. I just want someone nice. He doesn't need to be a prince. He just..." Jack's gaze turned distant as if he'd become lost in his head.

"He just, what?"

He gave a guilty start. "I guess, he just needs to put me first. To see something in me that no one else can and to be a good man through and through." He laughed. "Do you know what, mine is no more rooted in realism than yours is." He lifted an imaginary tankard. "To your prince and to my Mr. Considerate. May both men cross our paths before we're too old to appreciate them."

I raised an imaginary tankard back, not liking the sense of melancholy that had stolen over Jack. I flicked a finger, the gold sparks transforming into a butterfly the color of Jack's eyes. I sent it across the divide between us, the butterfly settling on his nose until he raised a hand with an indignant splutter and knocked it away. I redirected the butterfly to the back of his hand, Jack lifting it close so he could scrutinize it. "Is this you?"

"It is."

He tilted his hand slightly, the butterfly fluttering its wings. "And you can see through its eyes?"

"I can." And at the moment, the close-up view of smiling lips and emerald-green eyes was a rather beautiful one. I didn't mind Jack when he was scowling, but when he smiled, it was like witnessing the sun coming out from behind the clouds.

Jack tilted his head to one side. "Can you make anything? Or are there, I don't know, size limitations or something?"

"I can make anything as long as I can picture what it looks like. Small is easier than big, though."

"Easier?" Jack sounded genuinely interested.

"Summoning an animal uses magical reserves. The bigger the animal and the longer I need to keep it around, the quicker those magical reserves are used up. Once they are, there's a period of time where I'm not able to summon anything else."

"How long?"

"It depends on a number of factors."

Jack's brow furrowed. "Like what?"

I was discovering new things about Jack all the time. He clearly didn't like not knowing how things worked. "How well I've slept. How much I've eaten. My mood. Everything, really."

Jack studied the butterfly. "Can you feel it in you, the magic?"

I nodded.

"What does it feel like?"

I'd been asked that question before and it never got any easier to answer. The magic had always been there, even before I knew how to use it, so how could I possibly compare it to someone who didn't have magic when I didn't know how that felt.

Jack picked up on my silence. "How can you tell when your magical reserves are low?"

I thought hard. "The magic is like a constant buzz beneath my skin, a warmth. When there's less magic, it's colder and quieter." Jack's lips twitched, and I frowned at him. "What?"

"Nothing."

"I can change that butterfly into a bear in a matter of seconds."

He schooled his face. "Internal warmth. I was just thinking that might explain your penchant for taking your shirt off. It would be nice to have an explanation that's not just extreme vanity."

I stared at him. "I'm not vain."

Jack laughed so hard he almost fell of the log, and I was forced to send the butterfly into the air. It didn't like the extreme vibrations. It might have been a summon and under my control, but it was still capable of independent feeling, the two of us linked so closely I could feel its apprehension. Jack was clutching his stomach by the time his laughter subsided. "Ah, that's really funny."

"I'm not."

"Tell that to your hair."

I frowned. "What does that mean?"

He mimed tossing his head back, lifting his hand to brush back imaginary hair in a dramatic gesture as he did so.

"I don't do that."

"You do it *all* the time."

Did I? If I did, I didn't do it deliberately. I sent the butterfly on a lazy circuit of Jack's head, Jack craning his neck to follow the movement. "It's very pretty."

"It's the color of your eyes." I cursed myself for the slip up. I'd just gotten him to agree to be friends. I didn't need him to change his mind within the first five minutes. I quickly changed the subject. "Anyway, in answer to your earlier question before you succumbed to a bout of unexplained and completely unnecessary hilarity, I do run hot."

Jack nodded, but his eyes were still on the butterfly. "Can you make it change color or would you have to make a whole new butterfly?"

"What color do you want it to be?"

"Blue." He hesitated. "The color of your eyes."

Something unfurled in my stomach, and I was forced to ignore it. I flexed my fingers, the butterfly losing its green color and turning blue. "How's that?"

"Jack shook his head. "Not the right color. Too pale. Your eyes are darker."

"I can't see my eyes."

Jack waved a finger at the butterfly and raised an eyebrow. "Yes, you can."

I sighed, but I maneuvered the butterfly away from Jack and toward me, manipulating the color to match the view I had of my own eyes.

Jack smiled. "Perfect."

For a few moments, I let the butterfly dance in the space between us, both of us watching it, Jack even lying down so that his head rested against the log. It didn't take long before his eyelids started to droop. When his breathing evened out, I made the butterfly disappear and I watched him instead, his face younger and far less guarded in sleep. It was a peaceful moment with just the two of us and the crackling of the fire.

CHAPTER NINE

JACK

Something was wrong. I couldn't quite pinpoint what it was, but it was enough to force me out from the layers of sleep that had only recently taken hold. And then it came again. Breathing. Far too close. Something solid but insistent pushing at my crotch. "Stop it, Sebastian."

"Not me."

With my eyes still squeezed tightly shut, I frowned. It was obvious he was speaking the truth, his voice far too distant for him to be responsible for the rather intrusive touch. But then if it wasn't him, who was it? Leofric?

I opened my eyes. The yellow, slitted eyes of a wolf stared back at me. The wolf broke eye contact first, its muzzle dropping to nose at my crotch once more. Anger curled around my nerve endings. So much for Sebastian and I having reached an agreement about our 'relationship.' I should have suspected that he wouldn't give in so easily.

I'd even found the whole butterfly thing charming, my feelings toward him softening greatly. But this... This wasn't a butterfly. This was a great big hairy wolf with its nose stuck in my crotch like it was hunting for treasure. Did Sebastian really think I'd find this funny?

I grabbed its snout and forced its head away. The wolf wasn't about to be deterred that easily and it was back in seconds. This time, I hit it, delivering a blow to the side of its neck.

"Erm... I wouldn't..."

I ignored Sebastian, more interested in the snarl that revealed the wolf's razor-sharp teeth, and the low growl that had started in the back of its throat. "This is not funny, Sebastian. Take it away. The butterfly was pretty. This isn't." The wolf growled louder as if it didn't like being compared to a butterfly and found wanting. I hit it again, the creature giving a surprised yelp before recommencing its growling.

Sebastian's voice was full of lazy amusement as it floated my way. "I feel like this might be an opportune time to tell you that the wolf has absolutely nothing to do with me, so you might want to stop agitating it by hitting it."

I froze. "Don't be stupid. Of course, it's got something to do with you. You sent it over here to dig its nose into my crotch because that's exactly the kind of thing you'd do."

"Maybe. If I'd thought of it, but I didn't."

"But if it's not you, that would mean..." I swallowed with difficulty, my mouth drying up halfway through the sentence.

"Yep. Stay still."

Well, it wasn't like there was anywhere for me to go, was it? Not with the log at my back and the wolf right in front of me. Eyes still fixed on the wolf, I reached out to the side for my bow. If I could manage to notch an arrow, it might be enough to frighten the beast away. Fingers scrabbling blindly in the dirt, I came up with nothing, my heart sinking as I recalled having left my bow on the other side of the camp.

"It's on its own. Lone wolves away from the safety of their pack aren't usually dangerous unless you aggravate them."

If I'd been brave enough to look away from that mouthful of teeth, I might have offered Sebastian a withering glare. As it was, I had to settle for demonstrating all my scathing criticism in nothing but words instead. "I pushed it and I hit it twice. I think we're way past the stage of me not aggravating it."

"I tried to tell you."

"Do you think you could choose a different time to say I told you so? Like, maybe a time when I don't have a slavering wolf who looks like it wants to eat my face nearly on top of me."

"Sorry." Sebastian's apology sounded way too cheerful.

The wolf came a step closer. Still snarling. Still growling. "Don't apologize. Do something."

"I'm working on it. Wolves don't have many predators. There are humans of course, but you're a human and it doesn't look remotely scared of you."

"There must be something."

"I think..."

I let out a long breath, frustration and fear coalescing into one tangled mass of emotion. "If I could rewind time, I'd definitely let Ulgan have you.

In each and every way. And I'd stand there and watch. Maybe I'd applaud the particularly gruesome bits. And if he needed help digging a grave, I'd help him with that too. When the authorities came calling, I'd deny all knowledge of you. And I'd quite happily give Ulgan an alibi as well."

"That's not very nice."

I could almost picture the hurt expression on Sebastian's face. I pulled some long-forgotten snippet of information out of the recesses of my brain as the wolf took another step. "Tigers. Tigers eat wolves."

"A tiger I can do." Familiar gold sparks filled the air. And then a huge orange and black striped beast was coming right for me, its roar drowning out the sound of the wolf. The wolf gave a high-pitched yelp and then turned tail and ran. From somewhere, I found the strength to scramble over the log, the tiger far more terrifying than the wolf had been. It was definitely bigger. Way too big. It also had rather peculiar ears. I didn't get an opportunity to study them and work out what was strange about them before it disappeared in a cloud of gold sparks.

With my heart beating so fast it made me feel dizzy, I carefully eased myself to standing, my legs none too steady. For the first time since waking, I lifted my gaze to Sebastian. He was standing casually against the fire with one hand propped on his hip. He looked like absolutely nothing of note had happened. I dragged as much oxygen in as I could and then released it again, forcing myself to breathe evenly. "I think I hate you."

He turned, flicking a lock of blond hair back behind his shoulder, his lips pursing. "I didn't do anything."

I shook my head wearily, my heart still beating furiously. "You thought it was funny."

Sebastian bit his lip in an effort not to give in to his amusement. "You were hitting a wolf. I couldn't decide whether you were just insanely brave or... well, just insane."

I cast an eye around the camp. "Where's Leofric? Did he not come back?"

"He came back while you were asleep, and then he went to take a dip in the river."

As if on cue, Leofric strolled into view, his hair damp, and his shirt draped over his arm to leave his chest bare. He looked at Sebastian and then at me, one eyebrow raised. "Did I miss something?"

Neither of us answered.

Brittleharbor was a mass of narrow, winding streets, the houses tiny and scattered haphazardly to give the town a somewhat chaotic appearance. It was quiet as well, with barely anyone on the streets. I had Sebastian and Leofric on either side of me as I rounded a corner, the sight that met me bringing me to a premature halt and seizing hold of the breath in my chest. All I could do was stare at the expanse of blue that dominated the horizon.

Sebastian and Leofric carried on for a few paces before realizing I'd lagged behind. They turned in unison, Sebastian grinning at the expression on my face. "I'm guessing you've never seen it before. What do you think, farm boy?"

"It's so... big."

"I know. But what do you think of the sea?"

Leofric snorted, but I was still too awestruck by the view to give Sebastian's double entendre the scorn it deserved. "Do people really set sail on that? How do they know there's anything at the end of it? It looks like there's just endless nothingness."

Sebastian returned to my side and took my arm, the action forcing me into forward momentum once more. I let him lead me the rest of the way down the street, Leofric falling into step beside us once we reached him. From there, we traversed a long flight of stone steps that led down to the harbor, boats and ships stretching in a long line as far as I could see in both directions. All of the people missing from the town appeared to be here, the harbor a buzz of activity. Shaking my head, I stopped again, this time for an altogether different reason. "This is going to be like looking for a needle in a haystack."

Sebastian slid an arm around my shoulders, his lips close to my ear. "Have faith. Ayas saw your sister here. This is the best lead we've had. We could turn a corner and she could be stood right there."

"He's right, Jack," Leofric said.

"But there's so many ships. It's going to take forever to talk to everyone. And what if no one's seen anything? Or Annabelle has sworn them all to secrecy?"

Sebastian's brow furrowed. "Is your sister a witch?"

Slipping free from his grasp, I mirrored his frown. "No."

"A femme fatale?"

I threw him a look of disgust. "Not everyone is as free with their body as you are."

Sebastian pressed a hand to his chest and fluttered his lashes. "Thank you."

"That was not a compliment, and you know it."

Out of the corner of my eye I saw Leofric turn his head away, the action an obvious attempt to stifle a laugh. I was glad someone found Sebastian amusing. I was beginning to think that Leofric had deserved that snake in his bed. Maybe he'd even like another one. I just needed to find one first.

Sebastian waved a hand at the row of ships. "I'm just struggling to work out how your sister could have sworn so many men to secrecy without the aid of magical powers or feminine wiles."

I glared at him. I didn't have the patience for logical thinking, not when I was operating on nothing but blind emotion. I wanted to find my sister so badly that it hurt. I wanted her home where she belonged, not rampaging around the kingdom doing lord knows what. She was no more worldly than I was. I'd thought her escapades would have taken her no farther than a few villages away, but here we were miles from Riverbrook with no guarantee that she was even here.

Leofric cleared his throat. "I suggest we split up. We'll cover more ground separately. And that way you two won't kill each other either. Amusing as it is to listen to the two of you exchange barbs, and trust me it is, we've got more important things to do today if we want to question everyone we can before nightfall."

Guilt settled in my gut. Neither man needed to be here. Yet, they'd both chosen to help me. It would serve me well to remember that. I took a deep breath and resolved to be more patient, to not let Sebastian get to me so easily. I already knew he enjoyed winding me up, but I didn't have to take the bait every single time. He flashed me a smile and I attempted to force my lips upwards, the action feeling decidedly forced, and I assumed not that convincing. Sebastian didn't seem to care, his smile growing wider. "We're going to find someone who knows something about your sister. I can feel it."

I hoped he was right. Once we'd figured out our plan of attack and agreed to signal the others if we discovered anything, I squared my shoulders and set off toward the first ship. It was huge, but then most of them were. Its deck was a flurry of motion, men busy loading huge crates from the dock onto the ship. I stood for a moment, completely lost as to where I was supposed to start. Everyone was so engrossed in what they were doing, I doubted they'd be willing to give me the time of day.

"Not there, you pair of blithering idiots. At the back. If you tried listening for once, you'd know that."

The voice had come from a tall, dark-haired man with a short beard standing over to one side. Given the beady eye he had on everybody and the insults he kept shouting to anyone who stepped out of line, he seemed to be in charge. He didn't look like a captain, but then, I didn't really know what a captain was supposed to look like. I approached him cautiously, the man seeming oblivious to my presence even as I stood right next to him.

"For God's sake, put it down gently. I'd say I'd take any breakages out of your wages, but I'd have all your money for the rest of your life. You know where that crate is going, right? It's going to the palace at Arrowgarde. What d'ya think is in it? Straw?" One of the men carrying the crate muttered something under his breath. "What was that, Hawkins? Do you think my ears are for decoration? You want off this ship, just say the word. I can go down to the tavern and find someone to replace you in seconds. Some drunk that can barely stand should be a fair swap." His gaze snapped the other way. "Fucking hell! Put your back into it, Kavanaugh. My mother could lift that better than you."

"Your mother's built like a brick shit house," was Kavanaugh's response to that, the rest of the men chuckling until the dark-haired man's icy stare reached them. At which point the mirth died out as quickly as it had started.

He let out a sigh. "What do you want?" I didn't realize he was talking to me, until dark eyes turned my way, his gaze scouring me from head to toe in a clear attempt to size me up. "If you're after a job, I don't take anyone without previous sailing experience. Try The Floating Duck..." He lifted a heavily tattooed arm, the muscles bunching as he pointed in the direction Leofric had gone. "Carruthers will take anyone, no matter how useless they are." His hand shot out, steely fingers wrapping around my biceps. "You're strong, though, so once you get sick of worrying you might sink at any given moment, and you realize what a shitshow he runs, come back, and I'll give you a trial. If you're any good, I'll rescue you before he kills you with that rusty tub of his he insists on calling a ship."

"I'm not a sailor."

"No?" I was subjected to a longer and slower scrutiny, a lot of it seeming to focus on my crotch, as if his aim was to see through the fabric of my trousers to what lay beneath. I resisted the urge to cover myself with my hands, but it was a close-run thing. "Are you here to offer your services to my men?"

I frowned. "My services?"

The corners of the man's mouth twitched up. "Because if so, I might keep you for myself. They'll complain"—he cast a narrow-eyed look at his men—"but what the fuck don't they complain about? What are your rates?"

"My rates?" I seemed to be stuck in a loop of repeating what he said.

He leaned closer, something glittering in his dark eyes. "How much do you charge for a fuck or a suck?"

I stared at him. "Nothing. I—"

"Nothing!" He let loose a whoop of elation. "Now, we're talking." He grabbed hold of my arm and started to steer me toward the ship. "Let's go to my cabin. I've got time for a quickie before we sail."

How had this conversation gotten out of hand so quickly? Was everybody outside Riverbrook completely insane? Although, I supposed I should have been glad he'd offered to pay me. Whereas Sebastian, smug git that he was, had expected me to pay him. I struggled out of his grasp. "I'm not a whore."

"No?" Dark eyes blinked at me in confusion. "So why are you offering to have sex with me in the middle of the day? You're going to get yourself quite the reputation that way."

I was quickly revising my opinion about Sebastian being the most insufferable man alive. It seemed there were people in the world who were even more annoying than he was, and I'd just met one of them. I took a deep breath, my words pushed out through gritted teeth. "I didn't offer to have sex with you. I have no interest in having sex with you. I will never have sex with you. Is that clear enough?"

The man crossed his arms over his chest and tipped his head to one side. "So you're not a sailor... you're not a whore... What are you?"

"A farmer, if you must know."

"Huh!" He inclined his head toward the sea. "Not much to farm around here."

"I'm looking for my sister. I wanted to know if you'd seen her. She has long red hair, but it seems she's been covering it with a hood. Someone saw her here in Brittleharbor a couple of days ago. She's shorter than me, but we look similar apart from the hair."

"Why didn't you just say that in the first place?"

I resolved not to lose my temper. "Have you seen her?"

My face was subjected to almost as detailed a scrutiny as my crotch had been. Finally, he shook his head. "I haven't seen a red-headed woman. In fact, I haven't seen any women. Sorry." His head suddenly shot up, his gaze alighting on something over my shoulder, a ruddy flush blossoming on his cheeks. "What the fuck do you think you're doing? You leave it balanced like that and it's going to fall. It falls and everything inside it breaks. Fuck! Sometimes I wonder if you all pay for your ale in brain cells. It's the only reason I can come up with why they seem to be fewer and fewer as time passes."

Assuming the conversation was over, I took the opportunity to take my leave. Thankfully, the next few inquiries were far more straightforward, with no one assuming I was a sailor, and no one accusing me of being a whore either. The story remained the same, though. No one had seen Annabelle.

I was in the middle of being told the same thing again by a captain, who despite appearing to be in his sixties looked like he'd win any arm-wrestling match with ease, when a shout came from along the dock. I turned in that direction to find Leofric waving his arms in a clear bid for attention. "Jack! Come here."

CHAPTER TEN

JACK

I broke into a run, the surge of hope in my chest lending me extra speed. Sebastian reached Leofric at the same time as I did, both of us skidding to a halt in front of Leofric and the man he'd been talking to, who sported an impressive array of facial tattoos. Leofric lifted a hand in his direction. "This is Mannix. Mannix, this is Jack, and that's Sebastian."

Not prepared to wait the extra seconds for polite introductions to reach a satisfactory conclusion, I cut in rudely. "Yeah, yeah, Mannix, got it. Pleased to meet you and all that. What did you see?"

Mannix looked toward Leofric and he gave an encouraging nod. "I saw a red-headed woman. Very pretty she was too. She had green eyes like yours. She said her name was Belle."

Excitement bubbled through my veins. "She calls herself Belle sometimes. What did she say to you? What did you talk about?"

Mannix cleared his throat and stood up straighter, as if he'd just realized that what he was about to say was of the utmost importance and he wanted to give the moment the reverence it deserved. "She wanted to travel on my ship."

I looked past Mannix to where his ship lay, this one much smaller than the one where I'd been accused of being a whore. "Is she here? I need to speak to her. Can you get her?"

Mannix seemed to shrivel in on himself, his shoulders drooping. "Ah, about that. I said no to her. I didn't have a cabin for her. Not without her having to share with one of the men, and I didn't think that was a good idea."

"When was this?"

Mannix stroked his chin thoughtfully. "Two days ago."

Frustration pressed down on me like a ten-ton weight. If Mannix had said yes to her, she'd be here. I would have been able to talk to her and bring an end to whatever madcap scheme had brought her here, and then take her home where she belonged.

Sebastian moved closer to me, his shoulder a surprisingly warm and reassuring weight as it pressed against mine. I was relieved when he seemed to sense my inability to speak and took over. "Where is she now? Do you know? Did you see which direction she went? It's really important that we find her."

Mannix's face twisted into an expression I didn't like the look of at all. "You won't find her round here."

I found my tongue again. "Why not?"

"I might have said no, but Carruthers didn't. He's the captain of—"

"The Floating Duck." I finished the sentence for him, both Leofric and Sebastian looking at me with surprise. "I've heard all about Carruthers, and how he'll accept anyone on board his apparent deathtrap of a ship."

A faint smile appeared on Mannix's face. "Well, I wouldn't go that far. It's certainly had more than its fair share of repairs, that's for sure, but those who say that it's held together by nothing but glue and prayers are exaggerating. I'm sure your sister will be fine."

I stood up straighter, my spine ramrod straight. "Oh, she will be, because I'm going to go over there now and drag her off the ship, even if I have to put her over my shoulder. I'm afraid her little adventure is over with."

"Good luck with that."

I stared at Mannix. "What do you mean by that?"

"They set sail yesterday."

It felt like someone had stolen all the air from my lungs. "To go where?"

Mannix shrugged. "I can't tell you. Some ships only sail a set route. If it was one of those, I'd be able to give you some idea. But, The Floating Duck, now she goes everywhere. She might go south. She might go north. Carruthers likes to say that the sea is his hunting ground." He paused for a moment to scratch his head. "Although, none of us have worked out what it is that he's hunting." He let out a little chuckle. "Probably spare parts to patch up the latest damage. If there's a rock in a cove, he always seems to hit it."

I did my best not to panic. "When will The Floating Duck be back?"

Mannix pulled an exaggerated thinking face, his brow scrunching up. "Months probably. Could even be a year. It's doubtful that your sister will be on it, though. I'd assume she's trying to get somewhere. There doesn't seem much point in returning to where she started. Unless she's got a hankering to be a sailor. Has she?"

My chest tight, I shook my head. "Not that I know of. But I'm beginning to think I don't know her at all." I backed away from the group, dimly aware of the conversation continuing. I'd heard enough. I didn't need to take part in any of the further pleasantries going on. All I needed was to sit down.

Heading over to a nearby bench, I sat and buried my head in my hands. What was Annabelle playing at? I could almost buy her leaving home for a few weeks because she wanted an adventure, but getting on a ship of her own accord, actually choosing to be at the mercy of that huge expanse of water, especially in a ship that had a reputation for being none too seaworthy. She must have lost her mind.

A warm weight settled across my back, fingers curling around my shoulder to pull me closer, my head coming to rest on his shoulder. Sebastian. I could tell from his scent. Sebastian was warm spices and sunshine. The thought caused something to jerk in my chest even as I gave in to it. When had I noticed what Sebastian smelled like? Probably during one of the times he'd wrapped himself around me like a monkey clinging to a tree. Sebastian was always touching me. Which was all the more reason to push him away and sit up. I didn't, though. What would a few more seconds hurt? I was miles from home, and I'd just reached a dead end in my reason for leaving in the first place. Surely, I deserved to wallow for a little while.

The silence was peaceful, with nothing but the sound of breathing and the gentle lap of waves. I could have stayed like that forever. I would have stayed there longer if it wasn't for Sebastian finally speaking.

"She'll be alright, you know."

I pulled away and sat up, opening my eyes to find Leofric standing in front of us with a strange expression on his face. It felt almost intrusive, him being there, which was a ridiculous thing to think. He looked away as I met his gaze, almost like he felt the same. I turned to face Sebastian. "You don't know that."

"Your sister's old enough to make her own decisions. She made a decision... Well, a series of decisions which brought her here, and then she made another decision to get on the ship. I can't pretend to understand her motives, but... she wasn't coerced. No one brought her here."

I knew what he was saying, but that didn't make it any easier to listen to. "I have to let her go... is that what you're saying?"

He gave a nod.

"So... I just..." I shook my head. "I go home, is that it? I tell my mother that Annabelle has sailed off somewhere and we may never see her again."

Sebastian held my gaze. "It's the truth." His gaze lowered to his lap. "And you don't have to go home."

"Where else would I go?"

His lips quirked up into a half-smile. "You could come with me. You could help me rescue a prince."

In all the anxiety-fueled emotion of the last couple of days, I'd almost forgotten about the prince trapped in the tower and Sebastian rushing to his aid. Although, I supposed I needed to drop the rushing part given the detour Sebastian had taken for my benefit.

"What prince?" Leofric looked puzzled.

Sebastian lifted his head to address him. "Prince Montgomery of Arrowgarde, who was cruelly snatched from his birthplace and forced into an existence a man of his status shouldn't have to endure."

Leofric's brow scrunched up. "Right. I heard about that. What are you getting out of it?"

A laugh escaped from me as Sebastian narrowed his eyes at his friend. It seemed Leofric really did know Sebastian. "He's going to marry him," I offered helpfully.

Leofric's confusion grew more pronounced. "That doesn't make any sense. Why would you need to marry a prince? You're—"

Sebastian suddenly sat forward on the bench and clapped his hands together. "I don't think we need to go into the details. By the time I get there, someone else may have rescued him anyway." He turned back to face me, his smile crooked. "So what do you say, Jack? One more adventure?"

I had the strangest urge to say yes. It was an urge I really didn't understand.

But then, when were you ever invited to take part in a daring rescue? If nothing else, it would be a great story to share once I returned to Riverbrook. A far better story than that of chasing my sister halfway around the kingdom only to be too late to stop her sailing off into the sunset.

"Jack?" Sebastian's voice was soft and cajoling. It promised excitement and intrigue. It promised a journey that would never be forgotten. And it promised something else as well, something that had heat spreading through my chest and lower parts of my anatomy awakening too. It had only been two days since I'd categorically stated that I would never have sex with Sebastian, and I was already wavering on that decision. What would it be like? I suspected he'd be a generous lover. He certainly wouldn't lack experience. Why shouldn't I have a bit of fun before I returned to Riverbrook? Would it be so terrible to give in to the mutual attraction? "I…"

"Sebastian Beau! It is you. I thought I was seeing things when I looked across the harbor and saw you standing there. But here you are. Aren't you a sight for sore eyes?"

I looked up as Sebastian was tugged to his feet by the same man who'd mistaken me for a whore. He stared at Sebastian for a few seconds before taking him in his arms and pressing his lips to his. Leofric seemed just as surprised as I was.

The kiss went on for a long time. A very long time, Leofric and I cast as awkward observers. And it certainly was awkward. Where were you supposed to look when someone was basically being devoured in front of you? In the end, I settled for glaring daggers into the back of Sebastian's head. Had I really been considering having sex with him? It seemed I'd have to join a queue.

And still the kiss was going on. I had the absurd urge to grab the backs of their heads and prize them apart like you might a toy from a dog's mouth. Instead, I endured it. In the end, it was Leofric who spoke up. "Bass, are you going to introduce us?"

Sebastian slowly peeled himself away from the other man, a slightly dazed look on his face. "This is Cassemir. We go way back. Cassemir, this is Leofric." He turned my way. "And this is Jack."

Cassemir grinned when our eyes met. "I've already had the pleasure. Although, we didn't get as far as exchanging names. He did, however, tell me that he would never have sex with me."

He held out his hand and I studiously ignored it, settling for glowering at him instead.

Sebastian laughed. "Don't take it personally. Jack tells everyone that. Don't you, Jack?"

I threw him a dirty look. "Only the people who seem to think that sex should be a financial transaction. Your *friend* here thought I was a whore."

Sebastian blinked. "Really? He's definitely not a whore. What made you think that?"

Cassemir shook his head. "It's been a long day and I've had a lot of fools to suffer." He smiled, but it bordered on lascivious. "It was probably wishful thinking. Anyway…" He focused back on Sebastian. "What are you doing here? Where are you headed?"

"Knightshade."

Cassemir's grin grew wider. "Well, you're in luck. We're headed to Maplewater, and I happen to have a spare cabin. We could drop you off at Dawnport and save you a few days' journey, if you feel so inclined?"

Sebastian didn't even take time to think about it. "Definitely. Count us in."

"Us?" My voice sounded flat.

Sebastian frowned. "You were going to say yes. I could see it in your eyes."

I could hardly deny it, not when it was true. "That was before."

"Before what?"

Before you kissed another man right in front of me and I realized it bothered me. Except, there was a far bigger problem than that one. "Before you were getting on a ship. I don't... That is, I can't. I've never..."

Sebastian stepped closer. "The sea isn't that scary." He held out a hand. "Let me show you."

I stared at his hand, but I didn't take it. It might not be that scary to him, but to me it was an insurmountable obstacle. I was perfectly happy on dry land. The sea had already swallowed my sister whole. It didn't need to take me as well. I took a step back and shook my head, Sebastian's hand dropping to his side and his shoulders drooping.

Cassemir wrapped an arm around his shoulders. "We've got to leave within the hour, Bass, so say your goodbyes. You know my ship, right?"

Sebastian nodded and Cassemir turned, raising a hand in farewell. "Nice meeting you all."

I stayed silent. Leofric drew Sebastian into a hug, the two of them exchanging a few words before Leofric wandered away to leave me alone with Sebastian. The moment felt strangely charged, my heart speeding up and my palms clammy. I raised my chin and met his gaze, refusing to let him see that I was anything but nonchalant about our parting. Which I was. I'd known him, what? Six days? Seven? It was a ridiculously short time for him to mean anything to me. And that was before you took into account that he was on his way to marry a prince. Well, the prince was welcome to him.

Sebastian smiled, but there was a tinge of sadness to it. "Is there anything I can say that will change your mind?"

"No."

"Okay." His gaze dropped to his feet. "So... I guess this is goodbye."

"I guess it is." My throat felt tight, an emotion that I told myself was all about my search for my sister coming to such an abrupt and unsatisfactory end and absolutely nothing to do with the man in front of me.

A slight smile played on Sebastian's lips. "Maybe I'll visit Riverbrook one day."

I laughed at the absurdity of the idea. "Going to bring your prince?"

The smile grew wider. "No. He can stay home."

"And warm the bed?"

"Exactly."

And there it was, the reminder I needed that Sebastian wasn't someone to pine over. He had a string of conquests as long as my arm, and I didn't need to add myself to that number. "You better get to your ship."

Sebastian reached for my hand, and I realized his intention too late to stop him from pressing his lips to the back of it like I was some fair maiden. They lingered there for a moment, my skin tingling and my cheeks heating. "It's been a pleasure, Jack Shaw. You might be a farm boy, but you're a farm boy like no other."

My throat thickened again, the words sounding so sincere that something I didn't want to examine too closely opened up in my chest. "I bet you say that kind of thing to everyone."

He let my hand drop and took a step back. "I really don't."

"Go." I needed him to do what I said before I did something stupid like shed a tear.

He took a few more backward steps. "I'll be seeing you."

I met his stare. "Not if I see you first."

He grinned and then spun around, his steps taking him away from me and toward Cassemir's ship. I watched his departing back for a few moments before taking my seat on the bench again, where I concentrated on breathing in and out and thinking about anything except the tumult of emotions that raged inside me. The bench gave slightly as Leofric seated himself next to me. I didn't look at him. He probably thought I was a gullible idiot to have fallen for Sebastian's charms despite my numerous protestations to the contrary.

"I was hoping you'd go with him."

I let out a choked laugh. "Why?"

"Because..." Leofric paused for so long that I thought he'd changed his mind about offering any sort of explanation. I turned my head to find him with a ponderous expression on his face. "Numerous reasons."

"Name one."

"Bass has a habit of launching himself into things without thinking too much about the consequences."

An image of thick green orc fingers wrapped around Sebastian's neck as he dangled helplessly in mid-air came to mind and I smiled. "I can see how that would be a problem. But what's that got to do with me?"

"He could do with someone to watch his back. Someone who's not afraid to say no to him, and who will point out when his schemes are particularly hare-brained and likely to end in disaster."

I raised an eyebrow. "Sounds like you should go with him."

Leofric grimaced. "I would if I could, but I'm needed back in Redview. My sister has got too much on her plate as it is. It was a luxury to take these few days, and I only got away with them because I'm going to be returning laden with salted herring which will make us a healthy profit in the next week."

I studied the ground for a few seconds. "You said numerous reasons. What else?"

The corners of Leofric's mouth tugged up. "He's different around you."

"Different?"

"Softer. More open."

I let out a snort. "That's softer. I'd hate to see him when I'm not around, then. What does he do, murder people instead of just robbing them?"

Leofric laughed. "It's difficult to explain. But you two together, you just work."

I rolled my eyes. "I don't know what you've been watching. We argue constantly. I don't think we've ever agreed on anything. If I said the sky was blue, he'd no doubt claim it was another color entirely."

"You say arguing, I say flirting."

I stared at him incredulously. "You need to get your eyes and ears tested if you think that's flirting."

"If you say so."

"I do!"

"So, you have no feelings for him at all?"

"Oh, I have feelings, but most of them are negative." Leofric studied my face for a moment, his expression saying he didn't believe a word of it. I broke eye contact first. "Besides, it doesn't matter, does it? He's on his way to rescue a prince and then marry him." I couldn't quite keep the note of bitterness out of my voice.

Leofric gave a slow shake of his head. "He's not going to marry a prince, trust me."

There was an awful lot of conviction in his voice. "Why do you say that?"

Leofric's eyes sparkled with amusement. "Because..." He paused and then seemed to change his mind about what he'd been going to say. "Can you picture Bass lazing around in a palace all day?"

I shrugged. "I don't know him well enough to have any idea how he'd choose to spend his day."

"He'd hate it. It's not a life he'd ever want to lead. He'd be bored after the first week, and he knows that."

"So why would he say he's going to marry him?"

Leofric smiled fondly. "Who knows? I love Bass to death, but even I don't know how his brain works most of the time." He cast a sideways glance my way. "Maybe you were meant to be jealous."

The sound I let out in response to that statement was halfway between a snort and a scoff. "As if." I lifted my head to stare at the ship. All but five of the crates were now loaded. I assumed that once they were all on board, they would set sail. "He just kissed another man in front of me."

"Is that what you saw?" There was a note of curiosity in Leofric's voice.

I frowned. "That's what happened."

"No... That was your interpretation of what happened."

I threw Leofric a disdainful look. "And I assume you're going to enlighten me on what *you* think happened?"

"Bass was kissed in front of you. I didn't see a lot of mutual passion going on. Bass was just too polite to push him away."

I replayed the moment in my mind, grudgingly admitting that Leofric might have a point. Sebastian *had* been very still, his arms remaining at his sides the entire time. "Is there anyone in this kingdom he hasn't slept with?"

Leofric laughed. "Probably. If you look hard enough. Listen, Bass is a red-blooded male, and he's a long way from being a virgin, but that doesn't mean he can't commit to someone. He just needs to find the right person. And he's certainly loyal. He's the one person that if I ever found myself in trouble, I know I could call upon and he'd come running. There's not a lot of people you could say that about. He's got a good heart." He leaned forward, his eyes intent on my face. "You know that Ayas wanted *him* the other night, don't you? That I was the consolation prize. But he turned him down because he wanted to be with you."

Something caught in my chest, and I couldn't look at him. "You don't know that."

"Yeah, I do. Why else would he have turned him down?"

Three crates left to load. I sat up straighter. "The sea... it scares me. If he wasn't going on a ship, then maybe..."

Leofric nodded understandingly. "Being scared isn't a bad thing. Letting fear rule your heart to the point where it stops you from getting what you want is, though. Facing our fears is what makes us grow as a person."

"Like having a fling with someone who is never going to be a viable long-term prospect?"

Leofric's lips twitched. "Like living in the moment and letting the future sort itself out."

I closed my eyes and thought about what he'd said. My world had been so small before I'd left Riverbrook. There'd been numerous flings with strangers passing through, some of them even lasting a couple of weeks before they'd moved on, so it wasn't that I was opposed to them, that I held some higher moral code. It was just that this felt different. Bigger, somehow. Was it because I sensed a man like Sebastian would be capable of breaking my heart if I let him? But then, that was the key, wasn't it? I just had to be careful not to give too much of myself, not to get carried away. Sex and love were two distinctly different things. As long as I remembered that, everything would be okay.

"Jack?" Not Leofric's voice. Sebastian's. I jerked my head up to find him standing in front of me, his hand outstretched. "I thought you might need this." He unfurled his fingers to reveal ten gold coins resting on his palm.

Ignoring the way my pulse sped up, I arched a brow. "You're giving me money. You? What's the catch? What do I have to do for it?" I paused, putting just the tiniest bit of huskiness in my voice as I peered through my eyelashes at him. "I'm not sucking your cock." Now, that was flirting. Leofric needed to take note of the difference.

Sebastian's breath hitched slightly, and I smiled with smug self-satisfaction. "No catch. You've just a got long way to travel and I want to make sure you get home safely. You can pay me back when I come to visit."

"With interest?"

He shook his head, one corner of his mouth lifting. "Same amount."

I stood to put us on the same level. "Of course, I could argue that I really shouldn't be paying you back, that that's just my fair share of your winnings."

"You could. You do love a good argument."

"I like people to be fair."

Sebastian threw a glance over his shoulder. There were no crates left on the dock. "I have to go. The ship's ready, and Cassemir's keen to set sail as soon as possible."

I took a deep breath, and as I carefully picked the gold coins off Sebastian's palm and placed them in my money pouch, I made a decision. One I hoped I wasn't going to live to regret. "Thank you. Although, you needn't have bothered."

Sebastian's brow scrunched up. "No? Why not?"

"Because..." I glanced at Leofric, and he gave an encouraging nod. I gave him a hard look in return, one I hoped that conveyed that he would be to blame if this went horribly wrong. "I'm coming with you."

Sebastian appeared to have been struck dumb, the only sign of life a slow blink. I turned to Leofric. "Safe journey home, Leofric. Thanks for the talk."

He winked. "Any time."

I started to walk toward the ship, the prospect of spending more time with Cassemir almost as distasteful as the thought of being at the sea's mercy. I could see him on the deck waiting for Sebastian. Speaking of Sebastian, where was he? I turned back to the bench to find he hadn't moved. "Are you coming?"

Rousing himself from whatever reverie he'd been caught up in, he fell into step beside me. "What changed your mind?"

I sighed. "I've got nothing better to do. The fields are still going to be there when I get back. My brother will have taken good care of everything."

"There's only one cabin."

"I'll cope."

"It's tiny. The bed's really small, and there's no floor space." He needed to make up his mind whether he wanted me to come or not. He'd spent all that time trying to convince me and now that I'd given in, he was trying to dissuade me. "You realize, the money was meant to be for if you didn't come?"

I bit my lip to stop myself from smiling. "I realize that."

"So, are you going to give it back to me?"

"No."

"That's what I figured."

I came to a stop in front of the gangplank, my heart racing and my legs suddenly weak. The sea beneath it seemed full of a dark threat. How deep was it? Surely, a lot deeper than any of the rivers I'd bathed in. I sighed. I could stand here and picture a number of things that could go wrong, or I could do as Leofric had suggested and face my fears. I squared my shoulders and marched over the gangplank, the slight rocking of the ship's deck as I set foot on it doing nothing to make me feel better.

Cassemir raised an eyebrow as I approached. I met his gaze with my head held high. "I changed my mind."

He nodded. "I can see that. Welcome to The Jellicoe." He gave a little bow that seemed somewhat mocking. "My ship and I are at your service."

CHAPTER ELEVEN

SEBASTIAN

I peeled back the sheet, Jack's dark head still making me smile even if I couldn't see his face, buried as it was in the pillow. "You can't stay in here forever."

"Yes, I can. Tell me when we get to Dawnport."

"I emptied your sick bucket." Jack mumbled something that could have been thank you but was just as likely to have been fuck off. We'd barely been an hour into the journey when he'd started throwing up. His seasickness came and went, with early mornings seeming to affect him more strongly. And no matter how many times I told him that fresh air on deck would do him far more good than being cooped up in the cabin, he ignored me and refused to move. He'd been so ill that he didn't even complain when I spooned him at night. Not that there was an alternative when the bed was so narrow. I hadn't been lying about that, the cabin designed for one rather than two.

"Jack?" He didn't stir. I reached out a hand and stroked his hair. "You need to get up."

"Go away. Go and play with Cassemir."

"Cassemir's busy. He's got men to shout at."

He rolled onto his back, the paleness of his face only serving to make his eyes appear even greener. "What's with that? Why don't they leave?"

I shrugged. "I don't know. I guess they're used to it. Cassemir's not too bad apart from the shouting. I'm sure there are worse captains."

Jack heaved himself up a little to lean his head against the wall. It was the most life I'd seen out of him since we'd set sail. Maybe he was starting to feel better. His gaze drifted over my bare torso. "I see you've lost your shirt again."

"It's hot in here." It was. In fact, hot was an understatement, the weather growing steadily warmer the farther we sailed south. The cabins being in the belly of the ship meant that no air reached them, fresh or otherwise.

"What's the story between you and Cassemir?"

I eyed Jack warily. "Story?"

He rolled his eyes at the attempt to pretend I didn't know what he was talking about. "How did you meet?"

"In a tavern. We were both drunk."

"And you fell into bed together?"

"You say that like it's a bad thing."

Jack shrugged. "He seemed *very* pleased to see you again."

I knew he was referring to the kiss. The kiss that I'd endured while trying to work out how you were supposed to extricate yourself from such an embrace, which wasn't a state of affairs I was used to. But I'd been very aware that Jack was watching, that he'd be putting his own little spin on it. I probably should have been glad that his incessant vomiting had saved me from being quizzed on it earlier. In retrospect, the last couple of days had been rather peaceful. There'd been no insults. No arguing. No glares. It had all been rather... Well, boring. It had been boring. "He spends most of his time at sea. He's pleased to see anyone who's not one of his men."

Jack looked thoughtful. "You should... reconnect."

"Should I?" I studied him.

"Of course." Green eyes stared back without blinking. "And then I can have this cabin to myself, and I won't have to spend my nights feeling like I'm being attacked by an over-amorous squid."

"Oh, I'm a squid now, am I? I was an octopus before."

"Squid. Octopus. Same thing. Both have lots of tentacles."

I leaned closer. "But we've come so far. Remember when you used to insist on sleeping on the floor. Now you happily share a—"

"Happily?"

"Now you share a bed, and I'm still breathing when I wake up in the morning."

"If that's your definition of progress, you must not expect much from life."

"On the contrary, I expect a lot." I held his gaze. "And I don't give up until I get it."

Jack started to slide down the bed again, his intention clearly to return to the fetal state I'd found him in. I grabbed his arm. "Oh no, you don't. You're coming outside. You need to see that the sea is not the monster you've built it up to be in your head. What happened to the brave man who stood up to a murderous orc single-handedly with little to no thought to how he might get hurt? Where's he gone?"

Jack's eyes narrowed on my face. "I vomited him up, and he was disposed of in a sick bucket. He's probably halfway to Shimid by now."

Despite my best intentions, I couldn't stop my lips from twitching. I dropped my voice to a cajoling tone. "Come outside. I promise I won't let anything bad happen to you."

"No."

I sighed. "You're not leaving me a lot of choice here, Jack. I can't leave you festering in here. Not when I know it's making you worse. A good friend sometimes has to take measures the other person might not like, but they wouldn't be a good friend if they didn't do it anyway." Getting up, I placed my knee on the bed, the action bringing me closer to Jack.

He attempted to shuffle back but there was nowhere for him to go. "No!"

"No, what?"

"No to whatever you're thinking of doing."

"It's for your own good."

"I don't care."

I made a lunge for him, Jack's two days of lying in the bed like a stranded jellyfish leaving him with little defense against my onslaught. He swore up a storm as I dragged him from the bed and heaved him over my shoulder. "Jack Shaw, does your mother know you talk like that? You're going to be really at home amongst the sailors once we get on deck. They have a certain turn of phrase as well."

"I'm not fucking going on any cock-sucking deck. Put me the fuck down. And don't bring my fucking mother into this. She'd fully support me sticking up for myself if some complete bastard tried to abduct me."

I ignored the fists flailing at my back as I hefted him higher. I'd never hear the end of it if I dropped him. "I really don't think a deck could suck a cock. You know, on account of it very much lacking a mouth or any ability to have sexual feelings." It was tricky, but I managed to get him through the door without either of us suffering a decapitation. It took a while but eventually he went slack, apparently resigned to his fate.

"I hate you."

"I know, so you keep telling me."

"I really do this time."

"You can tell me that all you want once we're on the deck. The words will sound so much sweeter with a fresh breeze on my skin."

"I will. Don't think I won't."

I navigated my way up the stairs, all heads turning our way as I appeared on deck, a mixture of laughter and cheers meeting our arrival.

"They better not be laughing at me."

Jack sounded so belligerent that I couldn't help but smile. "I'm sure someone just told a particularly hilarious joke. They wouldn't dare laugh at you when you've got such sharp arrows."

"Where is my bow?"

"Back in the cabin." I made my way over to the far side of the ship before relieving myself of my heavy load by dumping him on the wooden deck. I was fully prepared to sit on Jack if he attempted to make a run for it in a bid to return to the cabin. As it was, apart from heaving himself to a sitting position, he didn't move, his eyes squeezed tightly shut and his body language screaming discomfort. "Open your eyes."

"Get stuffed. I'll open my eyes when I'm ready."

"It's really not that bad."

Jack opened one eye and then just as quickly closed it again. "I can see sea."

I laughed. "Funny that, when we're in the middle of it." I sobered quickly. "What is it that scares you so much?"

Jack pulled in a shaky breath. "Being surrounded by water. There being no escape from it."

"You can see land."

"Yeah?" There was a hopeful note in his voice. "You're just saying that to try and get me to open my eyes."

I shook my head before realizing he couldn't see it. "We're following the coast. There won't be any point in this journey where we won't be able to see land unless it gets really foggy. Does that help?"

One eyelid cracked slightly open. "Maybe."

"Take a look, Jack."

A noise in his throat betrayed how unenthused he was about the idea, but he did open his eyes. He climbed to his feet warily, his gaze fixed on the horizon. "Where's the land? Did you lie? You better not have lied. If you lied, I'll..."

I took his arm and steered him around in the opposite direction. "There." It was distant, but it was unmistakable.

Jack took the few steps needed to reach the railing, bracing his arms against the side. Taking the risk of him pushing me overboard, I went to stand next to him. "See. It's not that bad."

"The land does make me feel better. Like we could change course and be off this thing in a matter of hours."

"Well, good luck convincing Cassemir to do that, but I know what you mean."

Jack's gaze lowered to the water. "Is it less rough today?"

I nodded. "Which probably accounts for the fact that you're not throwing up. All in all, it's a good day."

Jack turned his head to stare at me, his gaze frosty. "Easy for you to say. You haven't been abducted from a cabin."

"I think you secretly enjoyed it." I delivered the words and then waited for the inevitable explosion to hit, Jack not disappointing in the slightest.

"Enjoyed it? Why would I enjoy being manhandled by a brute like you? If I wanted to come on deck, I would have come on deck. I don't enjoy my choices being taken away from me. Not even slightly. You discounted all my opinions on the matter, and you threw me over your shoulder like I was some sort of maiden. You were extremely lucky that I didn't have my bow or I would have…"

I twitched my fingers and conjured up a small bird, its plumage a bright yellow color. I sent it fluttering around Jack for a moment before making it land on his shoulder.

"… and you can't charm me with a bird, either, no matter how cute it might be. And don't make it chirp, that's not going to fix anything."

I moved the bird closer to Jack's face, the small head brushing his cheek as it continued to chirp. Jack let out a long sigh, his torrent of words coming to an abrupt end. The thing about Jack was that he might burn hot when he was annoyed, but he ran out of steam just as quickly as it had flared up in the first place.

I pointed to the door that led back into the bowels of the ship. "You can go back in if you want."

He held up his hand and I sent the bird from his shoulder to his outstretched finger. "In a bit." He studied the bird. "Is this a real bird? I've never seen one like this."

"It's native to Padora. It's called a Goldenia. The males have a yellow breast and the females a yellow stripe on their head."

"Where is Padora?"

I squinted at the sun in an attempt to get my bearings, turning until I knew I was facing east. "In that direction. We're too close to Cerensai to be able to see the coastline. If we sailed for a couple of days that way, we'd be able to see it."

"What's it like?"

I shrugged. "It's a beautiful place."

"Why did you leave then?"

"Too many expectations." Jack turned to face me, his eyes full of curiosity. He already looked better, the fresh air and sun bringing some much-needed color to his cheeks. I should have ignored his protestations and forced him to leave the cabin days ago. I'd file that away as important information to bear in mind for the future.

He frowned. "What sort of expectations?"

Much as I preferred him talking to me rather than growling obscenities, I'd already said too much. "Just… things. Nothing important."

"So you left?"

I stared out across the sea. "So I left."

"How long ago?"

"Years."

My vague answers didn't seem to be deterring Jack in the slightest. If he could tell they were questions I didn't want to answer, he was intent on ignoring it. "How many years?"

"Six."

"And where's home now?"

It was a good question, and one I'd been asking myself for years. I coughed to hide the lump in my throat. I flew the Goldenia in a circle, the bird providing the perfect excuse to focus on something else for a moment while I gathered myself. At the end of the loop, I recalled the magical energy, the bird disappearing to leave nothing but a trail of gold sparks which quickly dissipated into the air. "Home is… everywhere."

Jack's brow furrowed. "That answer makes no sense. Why don't you go back to Padora?"

I shook my head. "I don't want to. Life's different there. I can't explain." I could, but it wasn't a conversation I wanted to have. Not with Jack, of all people. I'd never met anyone who didn't treat me differently once they knew. And I didn't want him treating me differently. I'd take him as he was, all fury and bristling indignation to hide the soft heart that I already knew lay beneath, and that he took great pains to hide.

"Will you ever go back?"

He'd drawn so close that we were barely inches apart, the warmth of his skin sinking into my bones. My fingers twitched, but not with magic this time, with the urge to bury them in his hair and tip his head to the side, to create the perfect angle to fit our lips together. "I don't know." It was an honest answer.

"Do you have family there?"

I nodded. "A mother. A father. Brothers and sisters."

"Don't they miss you?"

"Probably."

"Do they know where you are?"

"Probably."

Jack tipped his head to the side, confusion dawning in his eyes. Now that was the perfect angle to kiss him. "How can you not be sure if they know where you are? They either know or they don't."

"It's complicated." I moved closer and Jack didn't move back. "Jack…"

His tongue darted out to moisten his lips in what I took as the perfect invitation. "Sebastian." I didn't even care anymore that he refused to shorten my name. In fact, I liked it. It made him different. The whole world could call me Bass, and he could call me Sebastian, especially in that tone of voice so uniquely him, where I was never sure whether he wanted to stab me or kiss me. Or stab me and then kiss me. I moved another inch forward, Jack meeting me halfway, my head tipping one way and his the other. His teeth sank into his bottom lip, and I imagined soothing it with my tongue. It was one of many things I wanted to do with my tongue.

Closer. Almost there, the moment suspended in time, hanging there deliciously. Balanced on that precipice between the anticipation of not knowing what it would feel like, and the satisfaction of knowing nobody could take the memory of what it had been like away from me.

"Bass!" The voice was almost as much of a cold shower as the hand that landed on my shoulder a few seconds later, Jack already turning away to lean back on the railing and stare over the sea. If I'd had a weapon to hand, it was quite possible I would have stabbed Cassemir in the heart, free voyage or no free voyage. Could he not tell what had been about to happen? Or maybe that was it, he had been able to tell, and he'd been determined to stop it before it happened. He'd certainly made it more than clear over the last couple of days that his cabin door was always open. And normally, I would have taken him up on it. We'd certainly had fun together in the past; what Cassemir didn't know about using his mouth on certain parts of the body was not worth knowing.

Scraping the shreds of my patience back together, I turned to face him with my best attempt at a smile on my face. "Cassemir."

Cassemir inclined his head toward Jack, who seemed intent on pretending Cassemir wasn't there, and I had to say was doing a pretty good job at it. "I see you got him out of the cabin. I was beginning to think that him being there was a story you'd made up to cover up the fact that you'd thrown him overboard."

Jack's slight eyeroll gave away the fact that he was listening. "He was somewhat reluctant to come out."

Cassemir grinned. "So I saw. So *everyone* saw. My men are still chuckling over it. It made their day."

Jack's fingers tightened around the railing, his knuckles going white. I steered Cassemir away out of Jack's earshot. "Don't. I've just got him to calm down."

Cassemir's eyes narrowed as he looked back over at Jack. "He does seem somewhat volatile. He must be very good in the sack for you to put up with that." He arched a brow, the look on his face saying he knew perfectly well that we weren't sleeping together.

"We're friends."

A slow smile spread across his face. "In which case, he won't have any issues with you coming to my cabin. You've played nursemaid for long enough. I've got a bottle of whiskey that I've had tucked away for a special occasion in there. I've just been waiting for the right company to share it with. What do you say? We can catch up. I'm sure you've got some fascinating stories to tell since I last saw you. I heard about your big win in the tournament. You can start with that. You can tell me all about how you got one over on Ulgan. I hear he's gunning for you by the way, something to do with a puny human threatening to put an arrow through his cock." He inclined his head in Jack's direction. "Your new *friend*, I assume?"

I nodded, something like grudging respect settling on Cassemir's face. "He can come to my cabin too if you like. A few shots of whiskey and I bet he'd be a different person. I don't mind sharing."

I gave myself a moment to imagine it, the scenario Cassemir was painting difficult to visualize. "I doubt it. I expect Jack's a belligerent drunk. In case you haven't noticed, he doesn't like you very much. He has issues with people who mistake him for a whore."

"He'll come round."

I shook my head. "You don't know Jack. He can bear a grudge like no one else I've ever met."

Cassemir smiled. "Just me and you, then." He reached out to lay a hand on my arm, his gaze hot and hungry as it roved over my bare chest. "It'll be just like old times." I should have been tempted. Cassemir was good-looking and fun in bed. But I wasn't tempted. Not in the slightest.

Cassemir leaned forward with a seductive smile on his lips. "He won't care, if that's what you're worried about."

I gave a wry laugh. "He told me to play with you."

"Well, there you go then. What more proof do you need? Let's go. What are we waiting for?"

I shook my head and stepped back, Cassemir's fingers falling from my arm. "I need to make sure he doesn't fall overboard. I was the one who dragged him up here so it would be my fault." As excuses went, it was a weak one. Jack was an adult. He was quite capable of looking after himself.

Cassemir seemed to think so too if the twist of his mouth was anything to go by. "You used to be fun, Bass. What happened?"

I forced a smile. "Old age, probably."

"Well, good luck." It was said in a way that made it clear he wished me anything but that, and that he wasn't taking the rejection too well. He threw a steely glare in Jack's direction. "You're going to need it." He swung on his heel and strode off.

I made my way back over to Jack and took up a position on his right-hand side, my arms braced against the railing in a perfect mirror of his own posture. There was silence for a few moments before Jack spoke. "You turned him down?"

"I..." I trailed off, not sure what I was supposed to say.

Jack turned his head my way, his gaze fixing on my face. "What's wrong? Are you ill?"

I smiled. "Something like that."

He raised his eyebrows and then returned to his scrutiny of the sea. "You don't think his offer of a cabin was contingent on the expectation of you putting out?"

"I'm not a whore." His lips twitched, but he didn't say anything. "We can sleep on the deck if that's the case."

"*You* can sleep on the deck."

"Well, unless *you're* going to sleep with Cassemir, he's not going to look any more kindly on you than he does me. Especially, given the fact that you just pretended he didn't exist."

"I did no such thing."

I made my snort particularly loud so that it could be heard over the wind. "I must have missed your friendly greeting."

We lapsed into silence, and I studied Jack's face in profile, his expression earnest. "What are you thinking about?"

He took a deep breath in before letting it out. "Home."

"Do you miss it?"

He considered the question for a moment. "I miss the people. I miss my parents and my brothers and sisters. That's why I don't understand you being so offhand about your family."

I smiled. "Our situations are very different."

"Are they?"

Jack turned his head and I found myself the recipient of the full force of his gaze. I looked away and changed the subject. "What about your farm? Are you worried about that?"

Jack shook his head. "It'll be fine. My family will take care of it. It's what we do, help each other out."

I nodded and we lapsed into silence once more as I contemplated the fact that I was happier spending time with Jack without talking than I would have been in Cassemir's cabin. What a strange turn of events that was. Maybe I was ill.

CHAPTER TWELVE

JACK

It may have been overkill to fall to my knees and kiss the ground to celebrate being back on dry land, but I didn't care, not even with Sebastian watching with an amusement he didn't even try to hide. Still on my knees, I held up a finger. "Don't say a word."

Sebastian flicked his hair back, the cool breeze sending blond tresses into his face. "I didn't say a thing." The corners of his mouth curled up. "I've never been jealous of the ground before."

I shot him an evil glare as I rose to my feet. I didn't need a reminder of that crazy moment on the ship, where relief at finding that life above deck wasn't as horrid as I'd feared had almost led to me throwing caution to the wind and kissing Sebastian. I might not have been a fan of Cassemir, but I owed him for disrupting that charged moment. I had no idea what that one kiss might have led to, but given that we'd spent two more nights glued together in the narrow bed of the cabin, I was relieved not to have found out. Something twanged in my chest, and I had to remind myself that I *was* relieved. "What now?"

Sebastian stared off into the distance for a moment, his eyes narrowing as if he was concentrating hard. "We travel to Embercliff and spend the night there. From there we go on to Steelmeadow. From Steelmeadow, we travel to the tower and rescue the prince. It should take three days at most. Once we have Prince Montgomery in our safe keeping, we travel to Lastwick. It should be too busy there for anyone to make a move if we've been followed. And from there, it's a matter of a few hours to Arrowgarde, where we hand Prince Montgomery to his grateful and emotional parents and the people rejoice at our bravery."

"And you marry a prince?" I studied Sebastian as I said it, Leofric's surety that Sebastian would do no such thing still ringing in my ears. Would he laugh at the notion and give away his true feelings on the subject?

Sebastian nodded, his expression as earnest as I'd ever seen it. "And I marry a prince."

I rolled my eyes. "Poor Prince Montgomery. Locked up in a tower for months and then when he's finally liberated, he has to marry you. Hardly seems fair, does it?"

Sebastian puffed out his chest. "I'll have you know that I'm quite the catch. No doubt the king and queen will be beside themselves with relief at their son having brought home such a good match."

"I hope they're good actors, then." Despite not having a clue what the prince looked like, I gave myself a moment to picture it. No doubt they would make a striking couple. "Will you be faithful to him?"

Sebastian's response didn't hold even the slightest hesitation. "Of course. The man I choose to marry will be very special indeed. There's no question of me not being faithful."

I couldn't hold back on my snort. "Lucky him." I ignored the faint ache in my chest as I scanned our surroundings, the sprawling houses of Dawnport lying to the left while a long dirt road led off to the right. It would have been nice to spend the day in Dawnport celebrating the fact that the ground no longer moved under my feet, and to sleep in a bed where two could fit comfortably without the constant banging of knees and elbows during the night. But apparently, that wasn't the plan.

I set off down the dirt road, Sebastian following. We walked for most of the morning, conversation limited to safe topics like how long our supply of water would last and the likelihood of meeting anyone coming the opposite way. We hadn't so far, the road remaining empty.

The sun was blazing in the sky by the time we reached a fork in the road, sweat soaking the back of my shirt. Sebastian had long since taken his off, of course. It wasn't like he needed an excuse. When he came to a halt with a thoughtful look on his face, I waited for him to share what was on his mind. When nothing was forthcoming, I was forced to prompt him. "What?"

He lifted a hand to gesture to the road that went left. "Do you see those trees?"

"What, the big, green leafy things? Yes, strangely enough I haven't lost the power of sight during the last few hours and can indeed see them."

"If we go that way, it cuts hours off our journey. We'd reach Embercliff well before nightfall." He lifted his hand to point at the fork that went right. "Whereas, if we go this way, we might still reach Embercliff, but it's more likely we'll need to camp out and won't get there 'til tomorrow."

Great! While I didn't mind the sleeping under the stars part, the hardness of the ground was another thing entirely. I invariably woke up the next morning so stiff and sore that I felt like I'd aged considerably in the space of a few hours. Whereas Sebastian always managed to appear as fresh as a daisy, his long hair not seeming to suffer from the harsher conditions of being outdoors. Add to that the fact that I was hot, and somewhat irked by the way my gaze kept straying to the play of Sebastian's muscles beneath his skin as he walked. Therefore, to me, the choice was obvious. "I vote for the short way." Sebastian didn't even try to hide his grimace at my decision. I blew out a frustrated breath. "What aren't you telling me?" I eyed the forest curiously. "What's in there? Animals?" I hefted my bow higher. "I'll protect you."

Sebastian gave a slow shake of his head. "Not animals. Bandits... maybe. They've been known to lie in wait for unwary travelers. But..." His brow creased.

I sighed. "But, what?"

"If we move fast enough, we should be able to avoid them."

"Great. So let's do that, then, let's cut hours off our journey and move fast." I started walking toward the trees but stopped after a few steps when I registered that Sebastian wasn't following. "What are you waiting for?"

"We should take the safe route."

I stared at him. "You're on your way to rescue a prince from an impenetrable tower. You cheated a seven-foot orc out of his money. I wasn't aware you knew the meaning of the word."

Gold sparks danced between Sebastian's fingers, and I narrowed my eyes. "What are you...?"

He didn't need to offer an answer, a glossy black horse appearing between us only a few seconds later. Sebastian wasted no time in vaulting onto the horse's back. The leap would have been somewhat impressive, given the way Sebastian's muscular thighs and backside flexed, if I was prepared to allow myself to be impressed by him, which I most definitely wasn't. He held out a hand, and I stared at it. "So, you're telling me that all this time we've been walking, you could have made things a lot easier. And you wonder why I call you insufferable."

The horse gave a little prance, Sebastian moving with the motion easily despite the lack of saddle. "Diminishing magical energy, remember? So I'd appreciate it if you got your peachy little ass on here as quickly as possible, given that you're the one so determined to take a shortcut. There's no way we can walk through the forest. We'd be sitting ducks for bandits."

I hadn't heard any of what he'd said after peachy little ass, the rush of warmth through my body enough to make me feel momentarily dizzy. "Peachy little ass? You shouldn't be looking at my ass."

A slow grin spread across Sebastian's face as he flexed the fingers of his outstretched hand in invitation. "I can't help myself. You may as well tell me to stop eating. Both actions are as natural as breathing."

I took his hand, Sebastian pulling as I leapt, the two of us working together until I was eventually seated in front of Sebastian. His arms came round me as he buried his fingers in the horse's mane. I'd grown used to having him so close. Even so, the wall of heat and muscle wrapped around me, and the muscular thighs pressed to mine, caused my cock to give an interested twitch. We couldn't have been any closer if he was penetrating me. And I really needed to stop having those sorts of thoughts.

He spurred the horse into motion, and I settled in, glad for an opportunity to take the weight off my feet for a while.

Sebastian leaned in, his breath warm on my face as he spoke directly into my ear. "You've gone very quiet, Jack."

"Just thinking."

"About?"

"I was wondering if your lines actually work on people. You know, the whole I could no more not look at your ass than I could give up breathing."

A low chuckle vibrated near my ear. "I said eating, not breathing."

"Do they work?"

"I don't normally need lines."

Despite it being wasted because he couldn't see it, I rolled my eyes. "Let me guess... you just stand there, take your shirt off, let your hair blow about in the breeze, and admirers flock to you."

"I would say that's fairly accurate, yes."

"Have you ever considered being humbler?"

There was a slight pause while Sebastian thought about it. "No. I can't say I have."

"I didn't think so." I went quiet as we entered the forest and the trees swallowed us up. It was darker and denser than I'd expected it to be. I shivered, the abrupt change in temperature chilling the drying sweat on my skin.

"Having second thoughts?"

"No." It was a lie. I was having second and third thoughts. Sebastian was the risk-taker, not me. Therefore, I probably should have taken more notice of his caution. If he'd had doubts about this being the right course of action, then perhaps I'd been a little hasty in pushing him, just because I wasn't keen to sleep rough. "Perhaps, we should have..." An owl hooted in the distance, Sebastian going rigid at my back. Forgetting what I'd been about to say, I laughed. "Don't tell me you're scared of owls."

"How many owls do you know who come out during the day?"

It was a valid point. There were plenty of owls who hunted close to the farm in Riverbrook, but I only ever heard them once the sun had gone down. "What does that mean? Is this a different species of owl?"

Sebastian dug his feet into the horse's flank, the horse immediately responding and breaking into a trot. "It means, it's probably not an owl at all."

I pondered his words for a moment. Was it my imagination or did the horse seem nervous? "If it's not an owl, what is it?"

"Communication."

"Between who?" But I already knew the answer to that, didn't I? It wasn't like Sebastian hadn't warned me about bandits. I'd just chosen to ignore it. "What do they usually want?"

Sebastian's pause was long enough to know I wouldn't like his answer. "Money. They'd sell their own grandma if they could get a good price for her."

I released a slow breath. "And here we are, carrying a considerable sum. We may as well have given them a written invitation." Another hoot came from the undergrowth, this one closer and from a different direction. "How much farther?"

"Another couple of miles."

That wasn't far on horseback. I breathed a little easier. We'd make it and then we'd laugh about this later, about how a few owl noises had been far scarier than an enraged orc. I'd of course blame Sebastian and deny my part in having been the one to put us in this situation.

A rustle came from my right. I jerked my head around to examine the undergrowth. Nothing there. Nothing I could see anyway. Just grass and bushes. I laughed at how jumpy I'd become, the laughter dying in my throat as I turned back to the front in time to witness the dark shadows detaching themselves from the trees, the figures spilling out of the undergrowth to block the path in front of us. Three were on horseback and one was on foot.

I turned to look behind us, thinking we could turn around and go back the way we'd come, but there were men there as well, the sound I'd heard no doubt the result of one of them moving into position. We were well and truly surrounded.

The horse came to a sudden stop, Sebastian struggling to hold it still as it tossed its head. It continued to paw at the ground as our welcoming party formed themselves into a line across the path. They were all dressed in black, with a multitude of weapons on display: bows, knives, and swords.

One of the men swung off his horse to drop to the ground with cat-like grace, the man on foot taking the reins of his horse as he came to stand directly in front of us, the other men falling into formation at his back. He was good-looking in a scruffy sort of way. "Bass! Well, well, well. I wondered when our paths would cross again."

What? "You know him?" Given the man knew his name, it was a rhetorical question, so I didn't wait for an answer. "Let me guess, you've slept with him?"

If Sebastian had heard my question, he didn't show any signs of it, his attention focused on the man barring our path. "It's been a while. Jack, this is Mad Dog Keaton."

Mad Dog Keaton! What a charming name. I had enough sense not to share my thoughts, though. If someone was called Mad Dog, you treated them with caution. Even I knew that. They didn't get a name like that without having earned it in some way.

Mad Dog lifted a hand to scratch idly at the stubble on his chin, his eyes narrowing on Sebastian. "How long has it been? Ah, that's right. Three years since you snuck out in the middle of the night and took my money with you."

I didn't even try and temper my sigh. "So you did sleep with him. And then you robbed him. Good work there, Sebastian. We've not only run into bandits, but we've managed to find one that's pissed at you. I can't imagine how this could have anything but a happy ending."

Sebastian's arms tightened around me. "It's not as bad as it sounds."

"Why don't you get off the horse, Bass, and we can talk."

Sebastian's weight shifted behind me in a move that I suspected meant he was weighing up our odds if we were to make for a break for it. Given the number of bows aimed our way with arrows already notched, I assumed he came to the same conclusion that I had, that it had zero chance of success. He gave me a gentle nudge and I took the cue to slide off the horse, Sebastian landing next to me, and the horse ceasing to exist shortly after we reached the ground.

Was Sebastian calculating what other animal he could conjure up? Did he have enough magical reserves left? It was hard to see how one animal could take down numerous armed men in one attack before they could retaliate, though. Could his summons be hurt and killed? I had no idea. The horse had felt as solid as any horse I'd ever ridden. Therefore, it seemed likely they were just as prone to injury—or death—as any other animal.

I roused from my thoughts to find Mad Dog regarding me with open curiosity. I met his stare, doing my best not to show that I was intimidated. Mad Dog dipped his chin in my direction, his gaze straying to Sebastian. "Who's this?"

"Jack. My name's Jack."

Mad Dog raked his gaze along the length of my body. "And what's your link to Bass?"

"Traveling companion."

Mad Dog's lips twitched with barely concealed amusement. "Right. Course you are."

"I am!" I jabbed Sebastian in the ribs with my elbow. "Tell him."

Sebastian doubled up in pain, the jab perhaps having been a little too brutal. It would probably be wise to remember that it was two against seven. Therefore, it would be better if I didn't incapacitate the only man who was on my side.

Sebastian eventually unfurled himself, one hand rubbing at the area where my elbow had dug in. "He is. Although, he does somewhat take the word companionable out of companion. He's more of a... traveling one-man conscience that I never asked for."

Mad Dog's eyes kept flicking between the two of us, the furrows on his brow giving the impression that he wasn't quite sure what conclusion he was meant to come to about the two of us. He stepped conspiratorially close, his voice a stage whisper. "You should watch him, Jack. He'll rob you. Mark my words."

I laughed. "Already been down that road, but thank you." It was somewhat of an incongruous warning to get from a bandit, and I couldn't stop myself from pointing that out. "But isn't that what you do?"

Mad Dog blinked. "Yeah, but I don't pretend to be anything else, do I?" He waved a hand down his body. "Dressed like a bandit." He withdrew a rather evil-looking sword from a scabbard and hefted it in the air, the blade glinting. "Armed like a bandit." He waved a hand at the trees lining the road. "And we were hiding in the trees like bandits."

He seemed rather proud of the fact that they weren't pretending to be anything but what they were. I gave a nod. "True."

A strange silence followed before Mad Dog clicked his fingers. "I haven't introduced you to the men, have I?" He clapped a hand on the shoulder of the man next to him. "This is Ralph Eyepatch." I gave a nod to the man wearing a black eyepatch over his right eye. "On the horse, you've got Chadwick Scarface." The man turned his head, the livid scar on his face stretching all the way from his jaw to his temple. Mad Dog pointed behind us and I was forced to turn. "Toothless Damon." The man grinned to reveal just the one tooth in his mouth. "Colborn Blue Eyes." The man didn't smile, his bright blue eyes narrowing. "In the middle you've got Pierce the Brute." Pierce would have given Ulgan a run in the height stakes, his shoulders just as broad and the expression on his face none too friendly. Mad Dog pointed to his left. "And last but not least, you've got, Jeffery Threefingers. You're probably wondering why he's called that."

I stared at him, but Mad Dog seemed genuinely earnest. "I'm guessing he's only got three fingers."

Mad Dog's eyebrows shot up. "Yes! How did you work that out?" Jeffery Threefingers gave a three-fingered wave as Mad Dog turned around to his men. "We've got a clever one here, boys."

I turned to Sebastian, hoping my look adequately conveyed what I wanted it to, which was, "Seriously, you slept with this man. THIS MAN. What were you thinking?"

Sebastian gave a little shrug, but there was a definite tinge of sheepishness to it. So far, this had all been relatively civilized. Was this how bandits usually operated? I hadn't thought so, at least not the ones I'd conjured up in my imagination. I cleared my throat. "Well, it's been nice meeting all of you, but we should probably be on our way. We're looking to make Embercliff before the sun goes down."

Mad Dog stared at me and then threw his head back and laughed. They all joined in one by one until it was like being surrounded by a pack of hyenas. Mad Dog clutched at his chest in a way that said it hurt. "That's a good one. You're very funny, Jack." He turned to Sebastian. "He's very funny."

Sebastian didn't say anything, and I steeled myself for whatever was about to come next. Mad Dog tilted his head to one side, his smile crooked. "You see. It doesn't work like that. You're in our territory, so you have to pay a toll."

"A toll? How much would that be?"

His eyes narrowed, the air of friendliness he'd worn so far disappearing. "How much have you got?"

He might not be that bright, but there was a definite air of menace to him. "Not much."

Sebastian stepped back, the left-hand side of his body hidden behind mine. To an innocent onlooker, it might have given the impression that he was trying to hide, but I got it immediately. It meant they couldn't see his hand. If they couldn't see his hand, they couldn't see the gold sparks that were about to emanate from his fingertips, therefore giving him the element of surprise. His lips lowered to my ear. "Get ready to run."

Mad Dog scowled. "Hey! No whispering. Makes me think you're up to something, and I already don't trust you, Bass."

Sebastian made a hurt noise of protest. "Well, that's just mean, Keaton. Why would you say such a thing?"

"You robbed me."

Now, there was a sentence I could have said myself. And if there hadn't been six other armed men present, I might have felt some sort of kinship with Mad Dog. But given the presence of his gang, he'd clearly robbed a lot more people than Sebastian had, so quite honestly, it was hypocritical of him to take the moral high ground. Whereas I'd never robbed anyone. I'd never even thought about it. I figured that gave me far more of a right to use it as a stick to beat Sebastian with than it did Mad Dog.

A warm tingle crept up my back. I'd never been close enough to realize that Sebastian's magic was something that could be felt. It was an interesting sensation, one that rapidly spread to my groin. And then he was pushing me out of the way. "Run."

I ran. I didn't wait to see what animal Sebastian had gone for. Something big and scary, I hoped. With bandits in front and behind, the only place I could run was into the trees, the crashing noise behind me signaling that I was being followed. I glanced back to see Pierce the Brute in hot pursuit. He was big. That meant slow, right? That meant I could outpace him.

I'd lose him, and then I'd meet up with Sebastian again. I'd mock him for his terrible taste in men and the fact that he seemed to rob everyone he met. I was looking forward to using the new ammunition I'd gained.

The thick root seemed to come out of nowhere, my foot finding it with unerring precision. There was a moment where I thought I was going to be able to stay on my feet, but it proved to be nothing more than misplaced optimism as I pitched forward to meet the ground with a sickening crunch.

I was on my feet within seconds, but hands were already on my shoulders, Pierce living up to his name and flipping me over as easily as if I weighed no more than a feather. I opened my mouth to say something, but there was already a fist coming for my head.

The world went black as quickly as if someone had hidden the sun.

CHAPTER THIRTEEN

JACK

The first thing I became aware of was the steady drip of water, the sound making very little sense. The ground was particularly hard. And extremely cold too. I didn't even have the comforting warmth of Sebastian wrapped around me. Where was Sebastian? And why was it so cold? There was a funny smell too, my lungs filling with a mixture of urine and damp every time I inhaled. Why the hell had we camped here? And why couldn't I recall where here was? The last thing I remembered was...

I opened my eyes. Not that it made much difference given how little light there was. Was it the middle of the night? An attempt to sit up was met by a wave of dizziness. Persevering, I managed to lever myself up bit by slow bit to a seated position, my back against a wall.

"You were out for the count when they brought you in. You've been out for hours. I thought he'd hit you so hard you might never wake up."

I automatically turned my head toward the croaky voice, finding a tall, skinny man crouched nearby, his long, straggly hair and beard making it difficult to pinpoint his age. "Who hit me?" But I was already remembering the dash through the forest followed by the impact of Pierce the Brute's fist as it drove into my skull.

I lifted a hand to probe my forehead, the lump the size of an egg and sore to the touch. From what the man had said, that had been hours ago. Ignoring the incessant pounding in my head that accompanied each beat of my heart, I clambered to my feet. I was in a cell, one wall entirely made up of metal bars. It was a fairly small space, that I apparently shared with one other occupant.

There wasn't much else in the cell apart from the man, a ratty blanket, and a bucket which I assumed served as a latrine, its contents probably accounting for the smell. "Who are you?"

The man pulled the blanket over his lap. "Name's Efrain. You?"

"Jack. How long have you been here?" I went over to the bars while I waited for his answer, pressing my nose to them in order to be able to see better. The cell was at one edge of a fairly large space, the poor light due to its distance from any of the lit torches mounted on the walls. The walls were rock, which led me to believe we were in some sort of cave. Wooden furniture, which looked like it had been liberated from a number of different sources, none of it matching, was dotted around. A table here, chairs there. There was a fire pit at its center, which seemed to act as a focal point for the bandits. Most of them were sat around drinking while a few played cards. One of them threw knives at a target. I couldn't see a door, the far side of the room just seeming to disappear into shadows. Definitely a cave, then.

My hand went to my trouser pocket, the familiar bulge of my money pouch predictably missing. I'd been robbed. Again. Only this time, there'd been three times the amount of money in it.

"A man loses track of time."

It had taken Efrain so long to answer the question that I'd almost forgotten I'd asked it. "Days? Weeks? Years?"

"Oh, definitely years."

I turned back to face him. "Why? What did you do?"

Efrain picked at the corner of the blanket. "Tried to stop Keaton from making a big mistake."

The note of fondness in his voice was unmistakable, and completely absurd given the circumstances. "And who's Keaton to you?"

"My son." Efrain said it like the answer should have been all too obvious.

I blinked a few times, the action doing nothing for the pounding in my head. "And he keeps you locked up in here?"

Efrain shrugged. "He took a wrong turn. He was always such a good boy as a child. He'll come to his senses one day."

I turned back to the bars just as the man we'd been discussing appeared from the shadows on the far side of the large space. I slammed my hand on the bars. "Hey!"

Mad Dog lifted his head, a toothy grin breaking out on his face as his gaze met mine. A few of the other men also looked my way, but after a brief glance went back to what they'd been doing as if I was of no great concern. Mad Dog strode toward me, coming to a stop at the other side of the bars. He was close enough to grab, but I doubted that would do me much good in the long term. "Hey, you're awake. Welcome back to the world of the living. I thought Pierce had gotten a bit carried away. Man doesn't know his own strength."

A grunt came from a table in the corner where Pierce appeared to be sharpening a knife. I tore my gaze away from him and back to Mad Dog, my fingers curling around the bars. "You have to let me out."

Mad Dog's brow furrowed. "Do I? Why?"

"Because..." I was struggling for a reason, my thought processes decidedly fuzzy, probably as a result of the blow to my head. "Because you can't just keep people locked up." Given he'd kept his own father locked up for years, I doubted it was the most convincing reason I could have come up with.

"I'm not going to keep you locked up."

A wave of relief washed over me. "Of course, you won't. I knew you were a reasonable man." I waved a hand at the lock on Mad Dog's side of the door. "So... unlock the cell, and I'll be on my way. No hard feelings."

Mad Dog tilted his head to one side and studied me with a slight frown. "How would keeping you locked up make me any money? That makes no sense. I'm not going to keep you here like some sort of pet. I'm going to sell you."

A boulder settled in my stomach. "Sell me! To who?" Fearing my inquiry sounded a little too reasonable, I added, "And you can't just sell people. People aren't a commodity."

Mad Dog's lips curled up into a smile. "These bars say you are, that you're my conomodity." He frowned. "Codomity. Codonomity." He shook his head. "What's with the big, fancy words? We don't need those. I'm going to sell you to Chalia Perrieth."

I swallowed. "Who the hell is Chalia Perrieth? And why would she have any interest in buying me?"

It was Efrain that answered, his voice floating from the back of the cell. "Chalia is a bad bitch elf. She'd knife you as soon as look at you. She sells slaves. That's what you'll end up being. Shipped off to another kingdom and bought by the highest bidder. If you're lucky, you'll end up as a pleasure slave. If you're not so lucky, well, I hear the quarries in Krizar are a particularly bad place to end up. They always need fresh slaves because the ones they have don't tend to last that long. You seem like a nice young man. I'll keep my fingers crossed that you don't end up there."

"Thanks."

Mad Dog leaned to the side so he could see past me and raised his hand in a cheery wave. "Hi, Dad."

"Hi, Son. You shouldn't sell people, you know. Your mother wouldn't have approved."

Mad Dog gave a tut a teenager would have been proud of. "Yeah, Dad, whatever. Mum was an assassin, remember."

"But she didn't sell people."

"No, she killed them instead. Should I kill Jack? Would that make you feel better?" Mad Dog raised his eyebrow in expectation of an answer, but whatever it was that his dad muttered in response wasn't loud enough to be heard.

"I'd rather you didn't kill me."

Mad Dog offered me a sunny smile. "Well, there you go. I knew you'd come around to the idea of me selling you eventually. I appreciate your cooperation." He jerked his chin to the back of the cell. "And don't listen to the old man, Chalia's not that bad as long as you stay on the right side of her." He tapped his nose. "Piece of advice for you because I'm a generous man... just nod and smile when she asks you something. She likes that."

"Nod and smile... right." I leaned forward as far as I could in an effort to see more of the room outside the cell. "Is this the only cell you have?"

Mad Dog nodded. "Why?"

I picked my words carefully. "What happened to...?"

"Bass?"

"Yeah."

Mad Dog's face took on the look of someone who'd sucked on a very large and very sour lemon. "Slippery fucker got away." His mouth settled into a firm line. "He always was annoying, but you tend to forget that because of how pretty he is." His stare turned distant. "You know, with that hair, and those eyes, and those muscles." He gave himself a shake. "Anyway... he's probably in Embercliff by now. That's where you guys were heading, right?" He didn't seem to expect an answer, so I didn't provide one. Mad Dog thought hard for a moment. "You're not expecting him to come and rescue you, are you?"

Was I? It was unlikely, wasn't it? Sebastian had a prince to rescue. I wasn't a prince. I was a nobody. Just someone he'd amused himself with for a while, a bit of company until something better came along. He was probably already in Embercliff, regaling them with tales of his recent adventure. My name probably wouldn't even come up unless he was going to blame me for having been in the forest in the first place. He probably thought I'd gotten my just desserts. I sighed. "No, I don't expect him to come and rescue me."

Mad Dog looked pleased with my answer. "Good. So you won't be disappointed then, when he doesn't show up. I hate disappointed captives. They're so miserable to look at. They really put a downer on your day."

"When are you going to... er...?"

"Sell you?"

I nodded.

Mad Dog stood up on his toes, his grin strangely childlike. "Well, that's where I've got really good news for you."

"You have?"

He gave an enthusiastic nod. "The timing couldn't have been more perfect. Normally, you'd be stuck here for a month, but Chalia is due in the area the day after tomorrow. Isn't that great?"

"Fantastic." I couldn't have sounded any less enthused about it, but if Mad Dog picked up on it, he didn't bother to comment. "Do I get any food?"

Mad Dog reached through the bars to give my arm a pat. "Course you do. Gotta keep you looking good for Chalia. The better you look, the more I'll get for you. Isn't that right, Dad."

"You shouldn't sell people."

Mad Dog rolled his eyes. "He's like a broken record, bless him."

A shout came from the other side of the room, Mad Dog turning on his heel and striding away to see what they wanted. I went back to the spot where I'd woken up. No blanket for me, apparently. No wonder I'd been cold when I'd regained consciousness.

Efrain cleared his throat. "It might not be that bad, you know."

"What might not be?"

"Life as a slave."

I closed my eyes. "Oh, I'm sure it'll be great fun. Why would I have issues with someone transporting me to another kingdom, dictating how I spend my day, deciding how much I get to eat, and basically working me into the ground until I die? It's what every boy dreams of."

Efrain went quiet. He was evidently a little better than his son at picking up on sarcasm.

Dinner arrived in the form of a thick soup with great clumps of an unidentifiable meat floating in it. No vegetables. Efrain polished his off in record time, forgoing the use of utensils to drink straight from the bowl. He celebrated the completion of his meal with an almighty belch. I took my time with mine, trying not to think too hard about what the meat might be, and focusing on the fact that I needed the protein.

After dinner, I was given a blanket, but it was no match for the dampness of the cell, our position too far from the fire to get any benefit from the flames.

The shivers that ran through me at regular intervals combined with the lingering nausea from the bump on my head didn't leave me in the best of moods. Efrain liked to sing as well and seemed to have an extensive catalogue of songs from which to choose, at least five of them sounding exactly the same but with different words, which made me think he was making them up.

He didn't stop singing until Ralph Eyepatch threw an apple at his head, the aim needed to get it between the bars rather impressive. Efrain grinned and held it up like a prize, the next few minutes quiet except for the sound of crunching. He offered me a share of it, but I declined. I figured if I wanted one that badly I could sing a few of my own songs, a little ditty based around the lyrics of Mad Dog Keaton being a dick sprung immediately to mind.

I glanced over at Efrain. "Aren't you cold?"

He shook his head. "You get used to it after a while."

Something brushed against my foot, and I looked down to see the biggest rat I'd ever seen, and I'd seen some pretty big ones on the farm. "Aw Shit! There's rats in here as well." I aimed a kick at it, and it jumped backwards. It didn't run for cover like I expected, though, its whiskered face twitching as it stared at me.

I picked up the spoon from my soup bowl and threw it, the rat dodging out of the way just in time. This time, it did run away, disappearing through the bars. A slight kerfuffle broke out as Jeffery Threefingers and Chadwick Scarface spotted it and attempted to catch it, the two of them not succeeding in anything more than banging their heads together as the rat darted between their legs. If nothing else, it had produced an amusing interlude, the two bandits still rubbing their heads and looking confused.

As for the rat, it was nowhere to be seen. Knowing there were rats wandering about in the bandit hideout wasn't going to make me sleep any better. Mind, it was hardly surprising. The bandits weren't exactly house-proud, at least not judging by the bones littering the floor from previous meals.

Preparing myself for a sleepless night, I tucked my blanket around me as best I could and lay down on the floor. I wasn't wrong, waking more times than I cared to count during the night, the symphony of snores from the sleeping bandits doing nothing to improve my disposition. At one point during the night, I'd even gotten up to see if there was any way of reaching the lock on the door, imagining the look on their faces if I managed to escape while they were sleeping. But with no key, it proved fruitless, and I had no choice but to return to huddling under my blanket.

It was the creak of the cell door opening that had me opening my eyes in what I assumed was the morning. It was hard to tell when it was always dark. I leapt to my feet just in time to witness a man being shoved inside before the cell door was closed and locked again, Pierce the Brute lumbering away with a grunt. He was definitely a charmer, that one. I stared into familiar blue eyes, desperately trying to quell the fluttering in my chest and the temptation for my lips to curve upwards.

Sebastian had no such qualms, a wide smile dominating his features as he looked me over. "Jack! I missed you."

"Sebastian." I aimed for cool and might have pulled it off if it wasn't for my voice going up at the end.

His brow suddenly furrowed. He stepped forward, reaching out with surprisingly gentle fingers to trace the contours of the bump on my head. "Who did this? Was it Keaton? If it was Keaton, I'm going to be having strong words with him. Robbery and imprisonment are one thing, but injuring someone is taking it too far."

I let out a snort. "So, you do have a moral compass. I guess it just starts at a different place than most other people's. And it wasn't Keaton, it was Pierce. You know, the man with fists the size of most people's heads. I can attest to their effectiveness."

I don't know what I'd expected Sebastian to do, but it certainly wasn't to lower his head and press a gentle kiss to the swollen area. His fingers curled around my shoulders to push me back a step, his blue eyes blazing with a fierce heat as his gaze held mine. "He'll pay for that."

"Will he?" I found myself unable to look away, the fury and sincerity shining from him somewhat hypnotic. I cleared my throat in an effort to ground myself. "What are you doing here anyway?"

Sebastian smiled once more. "What do you think I'm doing here? I've come to rescue you."

I let my gaze drift over Sebastian before pointedly looking at the cell door. The closed cell door. The closed, *locked* cell door. "I hate to be the one to break it to you, but rescue involves removing the person from captivity. This is more of a... joining than a rescue."

Sebastian made a tutting sound. "Give me a break. Plans take time to implement, you know."

My heart rate quickened. "There's a plan?"

He gave an eyeroll. "Of course there's a plan." He held up a hand with one finger in the air. "Step one, find out where you were. That took a while. And..." He looked suddenly affronted. "While we're on the subject, I did not appreciate you trying to kick my rat or throwing a spoon at its head."

"That was you?"

"Of course it was me. Did you think one random rat just happened to wander in here?"

That's exactly what I'd thought, but Sebastian was right. It did lack a certain amount of logic. Sebastian stared at me intently until I was forced to say something. "I'm not thinking straight. I have a head injury."

His features immediately softened, and I found myself pulled against his chest, my nose buried in the curve of his neck. I drank in his warmth, one night in the cell having left me feeling like my bones were infused with the damp that hung in the air. "You need a bath."

Sebastian's hands tightened on my back, his fingers stroking down my spine in a way I wasn't at all opposed to. "So do you. You smell like a wet dog."

"Thank you. What was the rest of the plan?"

"Infiltrate the bandit hideout and pretend I was giving myself up."

"And then?"

"Release some sort of wild beast to cause havoc. Although, I'm aware that didn't work out too well in the forest."

I burrowed deeper into Sebastian's arms. "Yeah, what happened there?"

"My magical energy sort of fizzled out. You know, after the horse. A horse carrying two people on its back consumes a lot of energy. The lion I conjured got a couple of attacks in and then... poof... it was gone."

"A lion?" I couldn't help but be impressed. "I've never seen a lion."

Sebastian's hand lifted to stroke the back of my head. "I'll conjure another one for you. A bigger one."

I forced myself to lift my head so I could look him in the eye. "Before you got locked in here would probably have been a good time."

Sebastian grimaced. "Ah, yeah, about that. That's where the plan may have gone a little awry."

"A little awry?"

He held up his wrist and I stared at the metal gauntlet that now adorned it. "Huh! New jewelry. It's very nice, but I fail to see what that's got to do with anything, apart from making me pissed because you obviously took a detour to rob someone while I was locked up in here."

He turned his wrist, the keyhole on the other side of the gauntlet coming into view. "It blocks magic. I can't use any while I'm wearing it, which... kind of ruins the plan."

I blew out a long breath. "Well, that's... fantastic." I let the knowledge sink in for a moment. "Who has the key?"

"Keaton."

"'Keaton.'" I said it in a sing-songy voice, not even trying to hide my derision. "It's sweet that you're on first name terms. It's a shame that didn't stop him from having you locked up, and"—I waved a hand at his wrist—"you know, magically binding you so that you can't even summon a fly."

"I don't think a fly would be very useful."

I narrowed my eyes at him. "Oh, I don't know, you could fly it up your ex's nose."

"He's not my ex."

I fixed my gaze on him. "So what is he, exactly? What happened between the two of you?"

"You really want to know?"

I crossed my arms over my chest. "If I didn't, I wouldn't be asking."

Sebastian scratched his head. "It's a very short story."

I cast my eyes heavenward. "Yet, you haven't started telling it."

He let out a sigh. "We met in a tavern. I'd had quite a bit to drink. He was very... persistent."

I raised an eyebrow. "A very familiar story as well, but we'll ignore that for now and concentrate on the relevant parts. He was persistent... and you just couldn't say no?"

His lips twitched. "In my defense, this was well before his days of being a bandit."

"So, you did the dirty deed and then you robbed him?"

Sebastian grimaced. "You make it sound way worse than it was."

I shook my head. "What did you steal from him?"

"Just some coins. I can't remember how much." He shrugged. "It certainly wasn't enough for him to bear such a grudge."

I stared at him. "I would assume it was more the principle of the thing. You know, the fact you had sex with him and then instead of saying goodbye like a normal person would, you ran off with his money. People are funny like that."

"People are way too sensitive." Sebastian's brow creased. "Besides, he's just taken way more off me than I took from him. I worked hard for that money."

I laughed. "You played a few games of cards and cheated an orc."

He stared solemnly back. "Exactly. It was hard work. It required cunning and skill."

I paced a few steps. Not that there was far to go within the confines of the cell. I wanted to be angry that Sebastian hadn't foreseen Keaton having a way to block his magic. But then how could I be? Sebastian could have continued on his way, but he hadn't. He'd come to rescue me.

Sebastian's eyes narrowed. "Why are you looking at me like that?"

"Like what?"

"Like... fondly. Like you don't hate my guts. Stop it. It's weird. It makes me think being hit on the head left permanent damage. I want the old Jack back."

I smiled. "I'm just grateful you came to rescue me." I left a deliberate pause. "Even if you have done an awful job of it, and the upshot of your rescue is I'm no better off than I was before you arrived, and you could argue that I'm worse off because this cell wasn't that big to start with, and now there's another body in it. Now, Keaton can sell both of us tomorrow."

"Tomorrow?"

I nodded. "Apparently, some important player in the slave trade world just happens to be passing. I'm guessing he'll sell you too."

"That doesn't leave us much time to come up with a new plan."

"Like what?"

"You need to seduce him."

Sebastian almost jumped out of his skin as the voice came from the back of the cell, Efrain seemingly having woken up at some point during the conversation and unwrapped himself from the blanket where not one inch of skin had been showing. Sebastian stared at him, wide-eyed. "Who the fuck is that?"

"That's Efrain. Efrain, Sebastian. Sebastian, Efrain."

Efrain nodded but Sebastian was still too busy staring at him. "Why didn't you tell me we weren't alone?"

"You have eyes." That wasn't completely fair, given the poor light in the cell and how well Efrain had been camouflaged.

"Who is he?"

I sighed. "You can talk to *him*, you know."

"Who are you?"

In the end, I answered anyway. "Efrain is Keaton's father."

Sebastian's eyebrows shot up. "And he keeps you locked in here?"

Efrain nodded. "But he's a good boy, really." He waved a dismissive hand. "Anyway, do you want to get out of here or not?"

Sebastian and I exchanged a look and then both nodded.

Efrain sat forward, gesturing us both closer. We both went, the pair of us crouching down in front of him to better hear what he had to say. Efrain pointed at the gauntlet on Sebastian's wrist. "You need to get close enough to him to get the key. It'll be in his pocket. He always carries important things around with him." He puffed out his chest proudly. "I taught him that as a boy, that the safest place to keep something is on your person. Plus, you need to get out of this cell. So the answer is obvious, isn't it? You seduce him. You get him out of his clothes, and you get hold of the key. He's very easily seduced, my boy. A pretty face has always been his downfall."

Sebastian was staring at him like he thought Efrain was quite mad. "I'm not seducing him."

Efrain's brow wrinkled. "Why not? What's wrong with my son?"

Sebastian gave a short, sharp laugh. "Do you mean besides the fact he leads a pack of bandits, sells men to slave traders, robs anyone he meets, and he kidnapped a friend of mine?" He turned to me with an almost apologetic look on his face. "I'm not seducing him. I know you don't think I've got a lot of morals, and in the past, you might have been right, but a man can change. I can change. I just needed someone to change for, a light in the dark, a yin to my yang, a…" He stopped suddenly. "Jack, are you listening to a word I'm saying?"

I started. I hadn't been. I'd switched off at the point he'd said he wasn't going to seduce him, because I had to admit that Efrain's plan made a lot of sense. I'd seen the way Mad Dog Keaton looked at Sebastian. Not to mention the way he talked about him, like Sebastian was every man's wet dream. He was definitely still interested in him. If Sebastian played his cards right, he could have Mad Dog eating out of his hand. I rose slowly to my feet. "Efrain is right. You need to seduce him. It's the only way. And he's not exactly the sharpest tool in the box, so as long as you're convincing, he won't suspect a thing."

Efrain coughed, and I spared him a fleeting glance. "Sorry, but it's the truth."

"Apology accepted."

Sebastian stood too, the expression on his face a strange one. "You want me to seduce him?"

I ignored the sharp pang in my chest at the thought. "I want to get out of here. I definitely don't want to be sold to some bad bitch elf and then sold to someone else. So… unless you've got a better plan?"

Sebastian shook his head. "How… er… far am I meant to take this seduction thing?"

I pondered the question. "As far as you need to. Show no mercy." I eyed him critically, making absolutely no effort to hide my grimace. "I have to say you've looked better. You're somewhat disheveled." Unusually for Sebastian, he was. I stepped forward. "Okay... we can make a few improvements." I started with his hair, picking a leaf out of it before finger combing it to bring it back to some semblance of order. It wasn't perfect, but it would do. Next, I used my sleeve to remove as much dirt and dust as I could from Sebastian's face. I took a step back to admire my handiwork. It was better, but it still wasn't enough. I made an attack on the buttons of his shirt. "We need to get this off."

Sebastian dropped his chin to watch as I undid his buttons. "You know, it's funny, when I've thought about you undressing me, I never considered it being for another man."

"Shhh." I pulled the shirt off his shoulders. "We all have to take one for the team sometimes. Besides..." I smiled as I said the words that I knew couldn't fail to get through to him. "You want your money back, don't you?"

"Very much so."

"Well, there you go then. This is the way to get it."

I frowned, still not completely happy with the tableau. "Do a few push-ups. You need to pump your muscles up a bit."

Sebastian obediently dropped to the floor and did as I'd asked. I watched him for purely scientific reasons—just to make sure he was putting enough effort in—as his muscles tightened and bulged.

Once Sebastian was back on his feet, Efrain piped up again. "You need to undo a button on his trousers. Keaton's never been one for subtlety."

I dropped my hands to the fastening on Sebastian's trousers, but he batted them away. "I can do it." He sounded almost annoyed.

I studied him. "What's eating you?"

Sebastian met my gaze. "Absolutely nothing. Everything's fine and dandy. Never been better." He held his hands out to the side. "Do I pass muster?"

I let my gaze travel slowly over him, my throat drying up at the sight. He was goddamn beautiful, but I was hardly going to tell him that. "You'll do." I cleared my throat as I rearranged a lock of hair to hang provocatively over his chest, fighting down the urge to tell him that I didn't want him to do this. We needed that key, and this was the only way to get it.

Sucking in a lungful of stale air, I pushed him toward the bars before I could change my mind. Sebastian didn't look too happy about it himself as he glanced over his shoulder. "I've never had to seduce anyone I didn't like before."

"You'll be fine. It's just acting." I pointed to Mad Dog, the bandit deep in conversation with Toothless Damon on the other side of the room. "Call him over. Make sure you touch yourself a lot while you're talking to him. And say nice things. It'll be easy."

CHAPTER FOURTEEN

SEBASTIAN

To say I wasn't happy about Jack pushing me to seduce another man would have been an understatement. But what choice did I have but to go along with it, and pray I didn't mess it up when his freedom hung in the balance. Mine too. Therefore, all I could do was try not to take being told to take the seduction as far as I needed to as a personal affront. Success wasn't exactly a foregone conclusion, given that I didn't normally need to employ such tactics. Which probably went a long way to explaining why I hadn't gotten anywhere with Jack.

I let out a long sigh. "I'm not feeling too good about this."

Jack's eyes flashed. "Suck it up, Buttercup." He appeared at my side with a familiar spoon in his hand, one I'd last seen winging its way through the air toward my rat. Without further ado, he proceeded to bang it against the bars, the clanging sound echoing throughout the room. "Hey, Keaton. Mad Dog? Over here. Sebastian needs a word with you."

A frown was pasted on Keaton's face as he turned our way. He hesitated for a moment, as if considering ignoring us altogether before finally crossing the room in our direction, his steps slow. Jack covered his mouth with his hand, turning his head my way to speak in an exaggerated stage whisper. "I've had an idea."

I kept my eyes glued to Keaton, trying to gauge his mood. "Another one?"

Jack let out a little huff. "If you recall, *this* idea was Efrain's actually, but it just occurred to me that we should make it a little more interesting, put a little more icing on the cake."

I didn't like the sound of that. "What do you mean?"

Jack lowered his voice, Keaton now only a few steps away. "We make him think that he's stealing you away from me. It'll feed his ego and make being with you an even more attractive proposition. And hopefully, make it seem less like it's some sort of plan. Just... follow my lead."

He stepped back into the shadows at the back of the cell as Keaton arrived at the bars with a look of suspicion on his face. "What? I can't think of anything we've got left to say to each other, Bass."

Not a promising start. Now what? There seemed to be an awful lot of things to remember. *Touch myself. Be nice to him. Follow Jack's lead.* I felt like I was in a play that no one had given me the script for. I could have done with some time to prepare, a few minutes at least. Jack's belief that I was some sort of smooth-tongued lothario was really working against me here. I took a deep breath. "I wanted to apologize."

Keaton's eyebrow shot up. "Apologize for what? The lion? Because I've got to tell you that every time I close my eyes, I see that thing running toward me. You never told me that you had magic before, Bass. It was less than a meter away when it disappeared. I could see the whites of its eyes. That was just rude. Who summons a lion on a friend?" He jabbed a finger in the direction of the gauntlet on my wrist. "You're just lucky that I picked that up last week. Swapped one of my men for it."

"You... swapped one of your men."

Keaton nodded. "Yeah... useless bastard. I would have sold him as a slave, but he was far too lazy, and far too ugly for a pleasure slave. Chalia would have laughed in my face." He tilted his head to the side, curiosity sparking in his eyes. "So... this apology?"

Right. I was supposed to be apologizing. "I wanted to say sorry about the lion, of course, but I also wanted to apologize for..."

"For?"

"You know."

Keaton blinked. "No."

"For leaving without saying goodbye, and for accidentally taking your money."

It was a toss-up whose snort was loudest, Keaton's or Jack's. Keaton scowled. "You can't accidentally take someone's money. Oh no, look what's fallen into my pocket. I should return it, but I can't remember where I got it from." He gave me a challenging look.

I gave a shrug. "Anyway... I apologize. We all make mistakes occasionally, and that was one of mine and I'm a big enough man to admit it."

Jack cleared his throat in a "get on with it" way. He sure was keen for me to get my hands on Keaton. Where was I supposed to start? *Touch myself.* I flattened my hand to my chest and rubbed it seductively over my skin.

Keaton's eyebrows met in the middle. "Are you okay? Have you got chest pains? You're not having a heart attack, are you? That'll affect your price. Chalia can be a real bitch if I try and sell her defective goods."

That hadn't gone as well as I'd hoped. What else had Jack suggested? *Be nice.* What did that mean? I needed to compliment Keaton. "Your hair... it's very... brown. And your eyes are..." What were you supposed to say about eyes? If it was Jack, I'd tell him that they put emeralds to shame, that no precious jewel could even begin to compare to them, but Keaton's eyes weren't green. "They're brown too."

"Okaaaay." Keaton elongated the word as if he was confused about what was going on. His frown deepened, something suddenly seeming to occur to him. "What happened to your shirt?" His gaze dropped lower. "And you may want to..." He waved a finger at my crotch, at the pubic hair on display thanks to Jack's instructions. "You know, put the mouse back in the hole."

I braced a hand against one of the bars and leaned closer. "I lost my shirt."

Jack's voice piped up from the back of the cell. "Always the same with you, isn't it? You're *always* losing your shirt around *attractive* men. This, Sebastian... this is the reason I don't trust you. You're always enticing men with your chest, and your... shiny golden hair. But I know what the problem is now, don't I? You never got over Keaton, did you? You left that night because you could see you were about to embark on the love affair to end all love affairs, and you were scared, weren't you?"

He appeared out of the shadows to press a hand to his chest in the perfect parody of a spurned lover. "And you robbed him because you secretly hoped he would come after you. You think it's kismet that you met again in that forest. In fact, I bet you talked me into going in there because you were desperate to bump into him again. You've been planning this for weeks, haven't you? All so you could have a touching reunion with your long-lost lover."

"I did?" I coughed. "I mean... I did. I admit it."

Keaton's expression said he was having difficulty processing what was going on. That made two of us. "You said he was your traveling companion."

"Oh, that's what he tells everyone." Jack's voice was laced with a convincing amount of bitterness. "He just can't commit, because of the"—he waved a hand airily— "unrequited love thing. Well, do you know what?" He tossed his head in a dramatic fashion. "You can have him. He's all yours. Now that I've met you, I understand that I can't possibly compete. I don't dress all in black. I'm not edgy and dangerous. I don't prowl through the forest and lie in wait for unwitting travelers. I don't have a gang of savage men at my beck and call. I'm just a... farm boy."

Keaton blinked a few times. "You're in love with me?"

I stared at him. He wasn't bad looking, but without the benefit of a great deal of alcohol in my veins, he reminded me somewhat of a dog, all droopy and sad-eyed. "Er... yes." I hastened to add more, aware that Jack was doing a hell of a lot more to sell this than I was. "Madly and deeply."

"Why?"

"Why?" I put as much incredulity into the word as I could muster and drew it out in an effort to buy some time while I furiously tried to work out what I was supposed to say. I gave a little laugh for good measure as if the question had been quite ridiculous. "You may as well ask why the sun rises and sets every day, why the stars appear in the sky every night, and why the sea is blue. The answer is the same for all of those questions. It's because it simply is." Would he accept an answer that hadn't really been an answer? I'd assumed he'd prefer it to, you look like a dog, a brown-eyed dog.

There was a moment of silence. And then Keaton stood taller, his hand lifting to smooth back his hair in a self-conscious gesture. "Well, I have to say, Bass, that all of this has come a bit out of the blue. If only you'd stayed that night, instead of becoming overwhelmed by your feelings and running away."

He really had swallowed all of Jack's bullshit, hook, line, and sinker. Jack must be very pleased with himself, but I didn't dare look his way to confirm my suspicions lest it gave the game away. "I know. I'm a coward. It's not too late, though, is it?" I leaned conspiratorially close, Keaton taking the bait and leaning in too, our faces as close as they could get with the obstruction of the bars between us. "I'm here. You're here."

Keaton swallowed. "What are you suggesting?"

"That we... go somewhere private maybe." *Somewhere out of this cell and where no one will see me divesting you of the key.*

"Private?" Keaton said the word in a way that said it was of great import. His gaze darted left and right around the hideout, some of his fellow bandits having stopped what they were doing to stare at him. "What did you have in mind?"

"Erm..." It was difficult to get the words to come out. Especially when I had no intention of actually going through with it. I hadn't worked out how I was going to avoid it yet, but there had to be a way. Because If I did try and get physical with Keaton, my body was going to give away my lack of interest pretty quickly. Jack had far more faith in my physical prowess than I did if he hadn't foreseen that being a problem.

"You want to have sex with him, don't you? Right under my nose." Jack's screech would have put a banshee to shame. "Well, you do that. Don't think I care. You're dead to me, Sebastian. Dead."

Keaton's eyes widened, and then he was a flurry of motion, his hand plunging into his pocket to pull out the key to the cell. His fingers trembled slightly, and his tongue darted out to moisten his lips as he fitted the key in the lock. "We can do that."

Tugging me out of the cell, he closed the door and then locked it again, before sending the cell key in a high arc over to Pierce, who plucked it out of the air and pocketed it. That was unfortunate, but I'd deal with that later.

"Remember it's not just about you, Son, that you've got to please the other person as well."

They were the only words Efrain had spoken since this façade had begun. He didn't seem unduly bothered about his son being conned into believing something that wasn't true, but then, given his son had kept him locked up for years, I probably shouldn't have been overly surprised.

There was a lightness to Keaton's step as he led me over to the far corner of the room where a moth-eaten curtain hung. He wasted no time in pushing me through it, the curtain falling back into place in our wake to leave us in relative privacy, as long as you tuned out the muted conversation of the bandits in fairly close proximity. Behind the curtain was a bed, and not much else. I was unprepared for the hard shove that landed in the center of my chest. Losing my balance, I sprawled backwards on the bed, Keaton's weight immediately coming down on top of me. He propped himself up on his elbows, his heated gaze scouring my bare chest. "I am going to do so many things to you."

"Er... thanks. That's very kind of you." I had no idea where to put my hands so I left them sticking up in the air. Keaton seemed to have no such qualms, his fingers roaming across my chest before dropping lower. I was suddenly all too aware of my trousers being unfastened.

He smiled. "Listen to you. You sound all flustered. It's just me, and we've done this before."

I nodded. "We have. But..."

"But...?"

"It was different then."

His brow furrowed. "How?"

Well, that was a good question, wasn't it? How had it been different. Jack would no doubt have been able to think of something. A spark of inspiration came to me. "Because... I was in denial about my feelings then, but now I'm not."

Keaton's smile grew wider. "You say the sweetest things."

Lips started to descend toward mine and I panicked, covering Keaton's mouth with my hand before I could think better of it. "I can't."

He tried to say something, the indistinguishable words vibrating against my palm. I removed my hand. "What?"

"I said... why not? You love me. I love you."

I blinked at him. "You love me?"

He gave a one-shouldered shrug. "Yeah, why not."

"You were going to sell me to the highest bidder."

Fingers traced a path to my nipple. "It's like you said, we all make mistakes sometimes." He gave the nipple a tweak, and I tried to look pleased about it but suspected it came across more like constipation than pleasure. "But the important thing is that we learn from our mistakes, right?" His face glazed over with lust. "Now, I'm going to kiss you. Long and hard."

"Please don't. I mean... you can't."

Confusion dawned on his face. "But I want to. Why can't we kiss? We're two people in love. It's what people in love do." He waggled his eyebrows. "And a hell of a lot more."

"We can't kiss because... it would be a mistake before the wedding."

Keaton's eyes went so wide that it was a wonder they didn't pop out. "The wedding? You want to marry me?"

"Of course." I propped myself up on my elbows, the action forcing Keaton to have to sit up too if he didn't want to risk tumbling to the floor. "And we should save ourselves for that... to make the wedding night better."

"Even kissing?"

I nodded in a way that hopefully made it look as if I wasn't making everything up on the spot and desperately trying to get out of suffering even the merest physical contact with him. "Even kissing."

"But Jack said you wanted to have sex with me."

"Jack's jealous. And he's a victim to his base desires." *Oh, if only that were true.* "He doesn't realize that there are people in the world, *like us*, where relationships are about far more than just the physical." I maneuvered myself out from under Keaton and rolled him onto his side before wrapping myself around him from behind. "We should lie here for a while. We can think about the wedding." I slid my hand down his side until my fingers were mere inches from his right pocket. If the key to the gauntlet was in the other pocket, then I was screwed.

Keaton let out a little sigh of satisfaction. "This is nice. Sex would have been nicer, though. But I guess I can wait. When are we getting married?"

"Soon."

"Tomorrow?" There was a hopeful note in Keaton's voice.

"Probably not tomorrow."

Keaton shifted slightly, my fingers dropping lower to leave them tantalizingly close to being able to slide inside his pocket. "Actually, I'm quite busy tomorrow. I have to sell Jack. If I don't meet with Chalia tomorrow, he'll be hanging around for another month. I don't think I could take all that glowering jealousy for another week, let alone a month. Did you see the way he was looking at me?"

I made a sound of agreement, my mind elsewhere. I needed Keaton to go to sleep. Short of singing lullabies, how did you get someone to go to sleep when it wasn't even night? "I wouldn't take it personally. Jack looks at everybody that way."

Keaton squiggled backwards, his ass pressing against my very uninterested cock. It was the complete opposite of all the mornings I'd woken up so close to Jack. "So when can we get married?"

"Maybe next week."

"Next week!" There was a childish enthusiasm in his voice. "That sounds good. And then we can fuck for days on end."

Safe in the knowledge that he couldn't see my face, I grimaced. "Definitely. There will be much fucking once the vows have been exchanged."

Keaton let out a breathy sigh. "Tell me about my hair again."

"The brown-ness?"

"Yes."

"It's very brown. Like a... nut."

"Do you like nuts?"

I pulled a face at the weird question. "Very much so. They're one of my favorite things in the entire world. That's why I like your hair. It reminds me of one."

"What type of nut?"

"A... hazelnut."

"I like hazelnuts."

Keaton yawned and I had to stop myself from punching the air. I needed to keep him talking, and the more mundane the topic the better. "What else do you like?"

"Dogs." He went quiet for a moment. "Not lions."

"Dogs and lions are very different."

"They are. Imagine trying to take a lion for a walk."

I forced a laugh. "Imagine."

"You'll keep that gauntlet on while we're married, right?"

"If you want me to."

He shifted again. "I do. It's just... safer. You should have a pet name for me."

"Should I?"

He nodded. "Definitely. What are you going to call me?"

"My little... hazelnut?"

Another yawn. "I like that."

Well, that made one of us.

"And I'm going to call you..."

I waited, but nothing was forthcoming. "Keaton?" No response. I waited another minute. "Keaton, are you asleep?" Still no response." I began to inch my fingers toward his pocket, Keaton not stirring even when my fingers slid inside and began an exploration.

Empty.

I said a million obscenities in my head, each one more vehement than the last. I needed to get to the other pocket, but Keaton was currently lying on it. Inch by slow inch, I managed to extricate myself from him. Placing my fingers on his shoulder, I rolled him onto his back with infinite care. His eyes opened and he mumbled a few unintelligible words. I held my breath. Eventually, his eyes closed again, and I forced myself to count to fifty. Just breathing and counting, my body so still I may as well have been a statue. When he didn't stir, I kept one eye on his face while I went for his pocket. I kept my movements as slow as possible and my touch as light as I was able to.

The touch of metal beneath my fingertips was as close to nirvana as I'd ever experienced. Praying it was the right key, I carefully eased it out of his pocket. The action of fitting the key into the gauntlet was somewhat awkward given that the gauntlet was on my right hand, and I had to use my left. Keaton stirred again and I went still. The key was in the lock, but I hadn't turned it yet. He mumbled another string of nonsense and I waited until he was once more silent before turning the key. The first attempt didn't prove successful. Sweat broke out on my brow. I tried again, the lock cooperating this time. The gauntlet slid off my wrist, the rush of power back into my body almost dizzying in its intensity.

I took a moment to breathe, to test what reserves I had. I'd never been magically bound before. Therefore, there was a possibility that as well as blocking my magic, the gauntlet might have depleted the amount available to me, but it was all there, sparking and sizzling under my skin, desperate to be released.

Keaton suddenly sat up. "What's going on, baby?" His gaze searched my face for a moment before dropping to the discarded gauntlet on the bed. "What are you doing?"

I smiled at him, a genuine one this time, one that was probably full of smug triumph. "Getting out of here."

"But you love me."

"Erm… about that, kind of not so much."

"You lied?"

"Afraid so."

"But Jack said…"

I laughed. "Jack is a bigger liar than I am, apparently. Maybe don't lock people up if you want them to speak the truth."

Keaton opened his mouth, the look on his face saying that he was going to shout to his men. I held my hand up, gold sparks already dripping from my fingertips. "I wouldn't do that if I was you."

He shook his head, a look of fear on his face. "Not the lion."

I hadn't gotten to the point where I'd decided what it was going to be, but given how scared Keaton was of it, it seemed like as good a choice as any. I released the magic, the strands gradually curling around themselves and knitting together until they formed the head and body of a lion. And yes, perhaps it was a bit bigger than it needed to be. Keaton let out a strangled squeak, and I pressed a finger to my lips. "Shhhh. He doesn't like loud noises." I advanced the lion until it jumped on the bed to straddle Keaton, the bandit lying back in an attempt to get as far from it as he could. I grinned at the picture it made with its massive paws on either side of Keaton's thighs, and its shaggy mane hanging down to tickle his chest. He was completely pinned. "How are you doing there, my little hazelnut?"

"Please, Bass. It's looking at me. I'll do anything you want, just don't let it eat me."

"You can start by telling me what you did with mine and Jack's money? I'm assuming you haven't had a chance to spend it yet."

"Chest. Under the bed." Keaton's breath was coming out in short little pants and his forehead was sheened with sweat.

I dropped to my knees to look under the bed. There was indeed a chest there. I dragged it out and lifted the lid, spotting two familiar money pouches immediately. I pocketed them both and then rifled through the rest of what was there. A lot of it was junk, but at the bottom there was another money pouch. Figuring the other bandits would assume we were having sex and that we weren't about to be disturbed any time soon, I opened it up. It contained fifty gold coins. I pondered the decision for less than a second before pocketing that too. Keaton craned his neck over the side of the bed to see what I was doing. "You're robbing me again."

"Looks like." I finished going through the rest of the chest, smiling when I unearthed a pair of handcuffs with the key in the lock. "Well, that's opportune. You see, I need the lion to take care of the rest of your men." I fastened the handcuffs around Keaton's right wrist and attached him to the metal bedpost. The key went in my pocket with the rest of my bounty.

"You're making a big mistake."

I laughed. "Course I am. I should have just sat around and allowed myself to be sold." I picked up the gauntlet. "I'll take this too." I handled it gingerly, not sure whether even holding it would affect my magic, but the lion remained resolutely solid. It seemed the gauntlet only worked when it was closed. That was useful to know.

I made the lion climb off the bed and come to stand at my side, Keaton letting out a shaky breath. "Where's the key to the handcuffs?"

I patted my pocket. "I have it. It would be to my advantage if you were stuck here for a while."

"That's not fair."

I smiled at his weak protestations. About to pull the curtain back, I hesitated and

turned back to Keaton. "By the way, the lion has no reason to come back here... unless..."

He lifted his head off the bed to meet my gaze, his expression wary. "Unless what?"

"Unless I hear that you're still selling people. If I were you, I'd let Charia know that you're done with that particular game."

Keaton's nod couldn't have been more enthusiastic. "I will. I promise."

I studied him for a moment. "Just out of interest, what was your pet name for me going to be?"

Keaton's cheeks flamed. He cleared his throat. "I was thinking Muscles."

CHAPTER FIFTEEN

JACK

I paced from one side of the cell to the other, my eyes barely straying from the curtain on the far side of the room that Keaton and Sebastian had disappeared behind. Every now and again, I'd stop pacing to press myself against the bars and listen. "I can't hear anything."

"Like what?" There was a genuine note of confusion in Efrain's voice.

"Sex noises."

"Is Sebastian usually loud?"

"How would I know?" Realizing I'd snapped at him, I forced myself to take a deep breath. "Sorry." I ran a hand through my hair and resumed pacing. "I'm just a bit stressed about the whole thing. If this doesn't work, then I've got the whole slave thing to worry about."

"Oh, so it's the slave thing you're worried about? Not the fact that Sebastian is having sex with someone else."

I aimed a glare Efrain's way. "Sebastian can have sex with whoever he wants. I don't care either way." Even in the dimness of the cell, I could see Efrain's smirk. "I don't. You seem to be forgetting that I was the one who sent him to seduce Keaton."

"Doesn't mean you're happy with it."

I pressed myself against the bars again. Had the curtain just twitched? Apparently not. I sighed. Whatever was going on behind that curtain was definitely taking a while. I scanned the rest of the hideout. There was a card game going on by the door, most of the men apart from Pierce the Brute and Chadwick Scarface involved in it. A whoop went up, Toothless Damon seemingly having won big.

Efrain came to stand next to me. "He cheats, that one. He's got so many cards hidden around his person that it's a wonder he doesn't leave a trail when he walks."

And then the curtain did pull back, a lion erupting from the space with a loud roar. There was a moment of stunned silence, and then all hell broke loose, Jeffrey Threefingers pushing himself back from the table so violently that it tipped over, all of its contents crashing to the floor. Efrain leaned forward to peer through the bars. "Is that a...?"

I nodded proudly, my lips curving up into a smile. "That's a lion. Sebastian's lion."

All the men who'd been playing cards took one look at it and made the most of their close proximity to the exit by beating a hasty retreat, disappearing into the darkness. Chadwick Scarface and Pierce the Brute weren't so lucky, the lion between them and the way out. They settled for backing away instead. Of Keaton, there was no sign.

Sebastian appeared from behind the curtain, his hair a golden cloud as he stood with his hands on his hips and surveyed the room. Spying something in the corner, he went over to pick it up. It took me a moment to realize it was my bow and my quiver of arrows. His gaze found mine as the lion backed the two men into the opposite corner, any attempt from them to get past triggering the swipe of a huge paw in their direction, the pair of them cowering back. I squeezed my arm through the bars to gesture Sebastian over. "Give me my bow."

He sauntered over like he had all the time in the world, passing my bow and arrows through the bars once he reached me. I immediately felt better with them in my hands, which was somewhat ridiculous considering I was still locked in a cell. "Where's the key?"

Sebastian inclined his head toward the two men. "Pierce has it. Give me a minute."

The lion unleashed another mighty roar as Sebastian went over to join it, one hand resting on its back while he held out the other. "Give me the key to the cell."

Pierce stared at him. He was definitely the calmer of the two men, even if he was making sure to keep well away from the lion. "I don't have it."

Sebastian's mouth twisted. "I wouldn't start lying." He moved the lion closer, its gigantic paws eating up the ground easily and its tail twitching in a way that revealed its agitation.

Efrain's swallow next to me was loud. "Are lions normally that big?"

"I don't think so. I think Sebastian made it bigger."

"He can do that?"

"Sebastian can do many things. And a few of those things aren't irritating."

Pierce had given up on pretending he didn't have the key, apparently realizing it was a stand-off he had no way of winning. He produced it from his pocket and waved it at Sebastian, the lion following its motion like it had been offered a new toy to play with.

Sebastian inclined his head toward Chadwick. "Give it to him." He pointed a finger at Chadwick. "You're going to unlock the cell. Don't even think about trying anything. The lion can run a lot faster than you. And if you think the scar you already have is bad, it will be nothing compared to the damage those claws will do once it catches you."

Chadwick gave a shudder as he snatched the key. The lion let him pass and he ran straight over. His trembling fingers made the task appear far more difficult than it was as he struggled to turn the key in the lock, the pale waxiness of his skin making his scar stand out even more lividly than it usually did.

The door of the cell swung open, and I aimed the arrow I'd already notched at Chadwick. It might not be as big a threat as a lion, but it would suffice. He seemed to agree, immediately throwing both hands in the air in a gesture of surrender.

Sebastian glanced our way. "Let him go, Jack. He can run and find his friends."

I lowered the bow slowly, and Chadwick turned on his heel, sprinting away. He was in such a rush that he almost fell over three times on his way to the exit. I left the cell and went to stand next to Sebastian, Pierce still hemmed in by the lion. "Why are we keeping this one?"

"He hit you."

I lifted a hand to the bump on my forehead. "That's right."

Pierce's eyes went wide. "It was an accident. Well, not an accident, but you would have got away if I hadn't done it. I had no choice."

"You didn't have to hit me so hard."

"It wasn't hard." Pierce curled his hand into a fist and lifted it. He stared at it in a way that said he shouldn't be blamed for what his hands had done, as if it was a completely separate entity. "I have big hands."

Sebastian tipped his head to one side. "I'm not hearing an apology from you for hurting Jack, for being far rougher with him than you needed to be."

Pierce blinked owlishly at Sebastian. "What?"

The lion growled and Pierce suddenly couldn't get the words out fast enough. "Sorry. So sorry. I shouldn't have hit you. I'm too strong. I know that. It won't happen again."

Sebastian turned his attention to me. "I'm not really happy with letting this one roam free while we're making our getaway."

He made a good point. I cast about for a solution, my gaze alighting on the cell. "We can put him in the cell."

Pierce frowned. "I don't want to go in the—"

"Or..." I raised my voice over his. "We can let the lion kill him."

"I'll go in the cell. Call off your lion, and I'll go in the cell. I want to go in the cell. I like the cell. I've always liked the cell."

Sebastian made the lion back away a couple of steps, Pierce hurrying over to the cell. I gestured for Efrain to come out, the older man looking quite bemused as I picked the key up from where Chadwick had dropped it during his hasty retreat. I locked the door, Pierce staring sulkily out from behind the bars. That left Sebastian and me without any antagonists. We weren't out of the woods, but we were certainly in a much better position than we'd been previously. "Where's Keaton?"

Sebastian grinned. "Fastened to the bed." I raised an eyebrow, and he frowned. "Not like that."

With the lion trotting at his side, Sebastian walked over to the exit. I went to follow but stopped when I realized that Efrain wasn't following. "Come on, Efrain. We're getting out of here."

The old man took a seat by the fire, stretching his hands out toward the flames. "I'm staying."

"You're... But he had you locked up. He kept you prisoner for years."

Efrain smiled sheepishly and gave a shrug. "He's my boy. I need to keep an eye on him. If I don't do it, who will?"

Sebastian walked back over to join me. "Are you sure?" When Efrain gave an emphatic nod. Sebastian reached into his pocket and pulled out a small key. He held it out to Efrain. "You'll need this to set Keaton free." Efrain reached out to take it, but Sebastian drew it back an inch. "It would be extremely beneficial to both me and Jack if you could hang onto it for a while before admitting you have it. A few hours at least. And maybe you could use it to negotiate some better living conditions before you release him."

Efrain's lips curled up at the corners. "I like the way you think." He took the key and then gave a half-hearted salute. "I'm thinking maybe twenty-four hours. Keaton doesn't get enough rest. Being confined to bed would do him good. Plus…" His eyes twinkled. "He'll have missed his rendezvous with Chalia by that time."

"Ah, about that." Sebastian's lips twitched, his gaze straying over to the lion, who was washing his paw with a huge pink tongue. "I may have told Keaton that the lion would be back if he continued to sell people."

Efrain nodded. "Good. I'll be sure to remind him of that." He jerked his chin in the direction of the cell. "What about that key? I'm thinking I might lose that one for forty-eight hours."

"I heard that, Efrain! Don't forget who brings you food."

Efrain didn't seem at all bothered by the anger in Pierce's voice. He raised his own voice without turning around. "Maybe seventy-two hours if the prisoner is particularly unruly. Or maybe I'll bury the key near a tree. Trees are very confusing. They all look the same. It's very likely I'd never be able to locate the right place again."

Sebastian passed the cell key over as well, after Pierce had the good sense to fall silent.

Efrain glanced toward the exit. "You two better go. I don't how long it will be before they start crawling back, but I'd wager not that long. They know you can't keep the lion around forever."

Sebastian held out his hand and I took it, our fingers threading together in a way that felt right. With my other hand, I gave Efrain a wave. I felt guilty leaving him here, but I could tell from the obstinate jut of his chin that there was no changing his mind. Sometimes you just had to accept that people made choices you didn't agree with.

I'd been right about it being a cave, the tunnel to outside thankfully short with only one possible route to take. The sky was dark and overcast as we reached the cave entrance and broke into a run. Sebastian seemed to know where he was going, so I was happy to let him lead. There were trees in the distance, presumably the forest where we'd run into the bandits, Sebastian's route taking us in the opposite direction. The lion padded along beside us, occasionally letting out a little roar, its large amber eyes perusing our surroundings.

We kept running for a while, a state of affairs I was perfectly happy with.

The more distance we put between ourselves and the bandits, the happier I'd be. Eventually though, I was too out of breath to go on. I dropped Sebastian's hand to come to a stop, my hands braced on my thighs as I bent over and dragged oxygen into my lungs. A drop of rain splashed on my hand, the sky even darker as I looked up. Sebastian was staring at the sky too, the lion gone.

Feeling better, I straightened to see where we were. We were in the middle of a large field, beneath its only tree. "We forgot your shirt."

Sebastian looked down at himself and then shrugged. "I'll get a new one." He pulled a money pouch out of his pocket and shook it so the coins tinkled. It was a very familiar pouch. "Maybe you can buy me one."

I snatched the money pouch off him. "You can buy your own shirt. I'm assuming that if you got my money back, you got yours back too."

He lifted another money pouch. "Certainly did." He pulled out a third pouch. "And I found this."

I tried my best to look stern but failed miserably. "You robbed him?"

He nodded. "Figured he deserved it this time."

I couldn't really argue with that. Not when Keaton had been hellbent on selling me into a life of slavery. I held out my hand, and Sebastian raised an inquisitive eyebrow. "I assume I get a share. How much is in there? I'll take half."

"Half?" Raindrops were falling faster now. I moved closer to the trunk of the tree in an effort to escape the worst of them, Sebastian following. "Why half?"

"To..." I thought about it. "To compensate me for the time spent in a dirty and dank cell."

"That wasn't my fault."

Even I couldn't twist the narrative enough to claim that it had been Sebastian's fault, given that I'd been the one who'd insisted on taking that route despite his protestations to the contrary. "No... It was Keaton's fault. And that's Keaton's money. Therefore, it's only fair that he should provide me with compensation."

Sebastian's eyebrow arched an inch. "Technically, as soon as it left Keaton's possession, it became my money." I held his gaze without blinking and eventually he sighed, making a big production out of counting twenty gold coins into my hand.

I closed my fingers around them, concentrating on the action without lifting my head as I transferred them to my own pouch. "Speaking of Keaton, how far did you get with him?"

"How far?"

I toed at the ground, the rain starting to turn the soil to mud. "Yeah, how far? Kissing? Blow job? Penetration?"

"Does it matter?"

There was a twig on the ground. It had an interesting shape, almost like an arrowhead. I traced it with my eyes as I gave a shrug which hopefully came across far more casual than it had felt to perform it, my body seeming to forget what muscles were required to pull off the action. "Just... curious, that's all."

"There was no kissing."

"Uh-huh."

"No blow job either."

"Right."

"And definitely no fucking."

I jerked my head up to find Sebastian grinning at me evilly. I regarded him with a narrow-eyed stare. "How did you pull that one off?"

"Just sheer genius, Jack. Feel free to bow to my prowess."

I rolled my eyes. "I'll pass, thanks."

The rain was absolutely pelting it down now, the tree's foliage doing very little to shelter us from the inclement weather. Sebastian looked like a drowned rat as he turned to scan our surroundings. "We need to find shelter. By my calculations, Embercliff is only about half an hour away." He lifted his hand to point straight ahead. "That way."

He went to walk in that direction, and I grabbed his arm, the hair-roughened skin damp beneath my fingertips. "Wait!"

His brow creased. "For what?"

I stepped closer, my heart thudding so hard he could probably feel it as I pressed my damp chest to his bare one and slid my hands into that magnificent hair of his. And even though it was wet, it was still magnificent. "For this." It felt right as I slanted my lips over his. There was a fleeting moment where Sebastian went still, but from that point on he was only too eager to reciprocate as I teased the juncture of his mouth with my tongue. It wasn't the prettiest of kisses, our mouths moving in too much of a frenzy as our tongues met. But it was hot and wet. And oh, so good.

I was in no rush to end it, Sebastian seeming to feel the same way. His fingers curled around my back to plaster me to him. And we were—head to toe— the heat building between us completely at odds with the rain-soaked atmosphere.

When I finally drew back, I couldn't quite convince myself to let go, my hands still fastened on Sebastian's shoulders, the taut muscles bunching beneath my fingertips. Sebastian stared at me, surprise reflected in his blue eyes. "What was that for?"

"Does it have to be for anything? Can't it just... be?"

"I suppose so." One corner of his mouth tugged up into a crooked smile. "You're a good kisser, Jack Shaw."

I gave him a wink. "You may bow to my prowess."

He gave me a playful shove. "You first."

"Not gonna happen."

He cupped my cheek, the skin of his palm cool against my heated skin. "I'd like to spend more time kissing you."

I gave him a cheeky smile. "I bet you would. We'll have to see, won't we?" I wiped rain away from my face. Funny, I hadn't even noticed it while we'd been kissing. We started to walk in the direction Sebastian had indicated earlier. "By the way, your seduction techniques really need work."

Sebastian's gaze slid over to me. "What do you mean?"

I mimicked his accent, which was far posher than mine, a mystery I hadn't yet solved. "Your hair is so brown. Just like your eyes. Seriously, is that the best you could come up with?"

"When I don't actually like the person, yes."

"Yet, you slept with him."

"I was drunk, and it was a long time ago." Sebastian sounded genuinely offended.

"And there was I thinking you were some sort of lothario." I gave an exaggerated snort. "It couldn't have been further from the truth."

"How do I get you to shut up?"

"I don't know. You could try kissing me again. That would probably work."

Sebastian swung me round, barely a second passing before his lips were on mine once more. I smiled into the kiss and joined in just as enthusiastically as I had the first. As ways to stay warm went, it was pretty satisfying. Sebastian might be on his way to marry a prince, but for the next couple of days, he was mine. And I was definitely due some fun to celebrate my near miss with slavery.

Chapter Sixteen

Sebastian

My breath caught in my throat as Jack's naked body glowed in the light of the fire. Our time in Embercliff had passed with lots more kissing, but we hadn't gone any further than that. But now that we were in Steelmeadow, it seemed Jack had decided to up the stakes. It was hard to believe, as he stood there brazenly, making absolutely no effort to cover himself, that this was the same person who'd demanded I avert my gaze while he'd undressed to bathe only a couple of weeks ago.

Jack held his hands out to the side, my gaze drawn by the proud jut of his cock as it curved toward his abdomen. His chin lifted, green eyes flashing a warning as he spoke. "You're supposed to say something when someone strips for you."

I swallowed, the action difficult when my throat was suddenly so dry. "That's hard to do when someone takes your breath away."

Jack's lips twitched into a pleased smile. "That's more like it. Tell me more."

"You're so beautiful." He was. All hard planes and taut skin. He might not have big muscles, but there wasn't an ounce of fat on him. "Someone should immortalize you in a painting."

Jack crossed the room to stand in front of me, my position on the floor placing me at the perfect vantage point to admire the gorgeous swollen organ between his legs. "I take back what I said about your seduction techniques."

"Do I need to seduce you?" My voice was husky and tinged with need, my own cock pushing insistently against the front of my trousers.

Jack tipped his head to one side to study me, the smile still hovering on his lips. "It would be nice." He gave a slight toss of his head. "You should always make the effort."

Unable to resist the siren call of his cock for one second longer, I surged forward, desperate to touch it with my lips. A palm landed on my forehead to hold me at bay. "Ah! Not yet. You're wearing too many clothes."

I stood, the urge to simply rip my clothes off needing to be tempered. The shirt I wore was a new one purchased in Embercliff, the last one having been left in a forlorn pile on the floor of a cell. Pierce the Brute had probably used it as a handkerchief. I kept my eyes on Jack as I dealt with the annoyance of buttons and fastenings. Finally, after what seemed like an age, I stood as naked as Jack, his heated gaze traveling over every inch of my body. "You'll do, I suppose. At a push."

It was such a Jack statement that I laughed. "Very magnanimous of you." I swooped in, Jack getting no time to protest before I threw him over my shoulder, and from there onto the bed, his laughter echoing mine in a sweet symphony of joy. He lay back, his arms thrown wide, and his taut body laid out before me in the best sort of invitation.

I didn't hesitate on taking him up on it. With my elbows resting on the bed to keep most of my weight off him, I fitted my body to his. I'd once thought that Jack might be something of a prude, given his almost priggish attitude toward casual sex. Not that it had ever stopped me from wanting him. It might even have made me want him more. But as we kissed almost lazily, both of us content to spend time reminding the other of what we tasted like, there was nothing prudish about the way his hands roamed over my back and ass, and the way he lifted his legs to rest his feet on the back of my thighs. He was so open, so unguarded, that it shocked me to the core.

Burying my face in his neck, I breathed him in, that slight tang of sweat and musk that was Jack and Jack alone. "You drive me crazy, farm boy."

Fingers dug into my back, Jack making small movements with his hips to rub his hard cock over mine, enough to tease and torment, but nowhere near enough to provide satisfaction. "You're really going to call me that in bed." He didn't sound annoyed by it. Just slightly bemused.

"I am." I nosed his jawbone, the slight rasp of his stubble sharp against my skin. "You need a shave."

He shifted as if he was about to get up. "I'll go and do it."

"Don't you dare!"

He laughed, relaxing back on the pillow. For a moment, we just stared at each other, Jack eventually raising an eyebrow in a "now what?" inquiry.

"I'm just enjoying the moment. I didn't know if we'd ever get here."

Jack's sigh spoke of amused defeat. "I was determined that we wouldn't."

"I know."

"I'm obviously a weak man."

I leaned forward to drop a gentle kiss on his lips. "Never. There are many things I could call you, Jack Shaw, some of them pretty colorful, but weak isn't one of them."

His smile was slow and seductive. "So… how about showing me how much you appreciate me changing my mind."

"I can do that."

"Actions speak louder than words."

I shook my head ruefully. "Like I said, *very* bossy." I slid down his body until I was faced with that delectable cock, my fingers curling around his hip bones to hold him still. I admired him for a moment, my cock throbbing in time with my rapid pulse as I rode a dizzying wave of emotion and need.

Two groans echoed in unison as my lips made contact with Jack's cock. I allowed myself no more than a lick before drawing back to gauge his reaction, Jack's eyes squeezed tightly shut, the muscles of his abdomen taut. I went back in again, this time bringing my tongue into play and using it to explore every dip and hollow of the rigid flesh. Only when I'd mapped it to my satisfaction did I slide my lips over the head and take him deep, my mouth and throat deliciously full of Jack as I breathed through my nose.

I'd only taken a few sucks when Jack raised his head, lidded green eyes blazing with desire as he watched his cock disappear between my lips. "Turn around."

Lost as I was in a haze of lust, it took longer than it should have to realize his intention, the rush of elation in my chest once I had, almost incapacitating. Reluctantly relinquishing my stiff prize, I turned my body around. Straddling his thighs, I backed up until my cock was in line with his mouth. When gentle fingers wrapped themselves around me to steer my cock between his lips, it was all I could do not to come immediately. "Fuck!"

Jack's chuckle created an interesting vibration along the length of my spit-slicked shaft. Ducking my head between his thighs, I resumed my earlier intention to make Jack come apart in my hands. Except, given the strength of my arousal, and the effect Jack's talented mouth was having on me, it seemed the tables had been well and truly turned. I could already feel the first tendrils of orgasm start to creep across my skin, my balls growing tight as Jack rolled them in his palm, my cock pulsing as he swallowed me down.

I sucked harder. Took him deeper. In a last gasp attempt to make him come before me, I searched out the puckered flesh buried between his ass cheeks. I grazed it experimentally, Jack making no attempt to shift away from the intimate caress. I pushed a bit harder, my finger barely getting inside before Jack shuddered and came, my mouth filling with a hot, salty liquid I was only too happy to swallow. I gave in to my orgasm seconds later, Jack's mouth and tongue continuing to massage me through it until I was nothing but a boneless pile of euphoria and lassitude. Closing my eyes, I collapsed on the bed with a huge smile on my face.

"Hey?"

In lieu of a proper response, I made a grunting sound.

"Are you coming up here, or are you staying down there all night?"

I cracked open one eye, Jack's foot flexing in front of my face. "You have nice feet."

"My face is better."

It took a supreme amount of effort to flip myself around and crawl up the bed until my head was at the same point as Jack's was. Once I had, I collapsed again. "You're right. Your face is better."

He studied me with amusement, his features far more relaxed than I'd ever seen them before. If only I'd known that all he needed was a good orgasm. Although, it wasn't like I'd ever been unwilling to give him that from the first day we'd met. All the unwillingness to get naked and rub against each other had always been firmly on his side.

He smiled. "I'm relieved you think so." He levered himself up to drag the blankets over us and I snuggled closer, Jack settling on his side so that we faced each other. His eyes were intent on my face as he reached out, gentle fingers tracing the curve of my neck. "I was thinking…"

I captured his hand and kissed his fingers. "About what?"

"This will probably sound terrible."

"You? Sound terrible? Surely not. That would be far too shocking an event." He snatched his fingers back and I smiled.

"This… prince…"

"Prince Montgomery of Arrowgarde?"

He nodded and then went silent.

"What about him?"

"I was thinking… you know, given that he's already been stuck in that tower for months, that a few more days probably wouldn't hurt."

I propped myself up on my elbow and studied Jack's face. The slight blush on his cheeks was particularly charming given what we'd just gotten up to. "And… what are you suggesting we do for those few days instead?"

Jack gave a one-shouldered shrug that looked anything but casual. His face suddenly became animated in a way that said something had only just occurred to him, which I didn't buy for one second. "We could… stay here for a while."

"Here?" I gestured around the room. "Or…" I dropped my hand to indicate the bed. "Here?"

He sat up, the blankets dropping to his waist. "In bed. Or…" His gaze scoured the room. "Against the wall over there. Or in front of the fire on the rug. In the bath, maybe? Show a bit of imagination, Sebastian."

My spent cock still managed a twitch at the tableau of images he'd conjured up. "That would be…"

Jack's blush grew darker. "Terrible, I know. I told you it was. Forget I said anything. We should leave in the morning at first light. We can reach the tower by midday."

I pretended to give the idea some thought, even though I already knew what I was going to say. "I mean… you're right about him having been there for months. An extra couple of days really wouldn't make that much difference. I did already take a detour once. Not to mention the extra time spent rescuing you from bandits."

Jack cleared his throat. "And it's not like he'll know unless one of us tells him."

Gaze fixed on Jack's lips, I moved closer. Although Jack's cock had been a revelation, it felt like an age since I'd last kissed him. "I won't tell him."

His lips curved into a smile as he shook his head. "Neither will I."

I returned his smile. "Well, that's agreed then." And then there was just kissing, conversation not resuming for quite some time.

—ele—

Jack took a sip of his ale, his gaze finding mine over the top of the tankard. "We should probably leave for Knightshade tomorrow."

I gave a thoughtful nod. "Probably." We'd been having the same conversation for the last five days. Yet, when morning came, it invariably brought another day of kissing and orgasms, neither of us mentioning the elephant in the room until it was already too late to leave.

Jack sat back in his seat, his eyes heavy-lidded. "My parents must wonder where I am."

"Probably." I roused myself to say more, aware that I couldn't just keep repeating the same word over and over again. The problem was that most of my brain power was centered on how long it was before I could get Jack naked again. I liked him clothed, but I liked him naked more. He even lost that edge of cynicism after an orgasm. Not for long. But it certainly smoothed the rough edges for a short period of time. So far, we'd stuck to hand jobs and blow jobs, but it felt like it was only a matter of time before we built up to more. I was eager to sample Jack's ass, and only too happy to give mine over to him. Maybe we'd stay for another week. Towers were built to last, after all.

"Shit!"

My eyes shot to Jack as the curse slipped out. I followed his gaze across the room to what had prompted it. There was a big, green orc standing there. An all too familiar green orc whose fingers I fancied I could still feel around my neck. In a move that couldn't have been any more perfectly timed if we'd practiced it, Jack and I slid down our seats in unison, not stopping until we were under the table, the two of us effectively disappearing out of sight. We crouched there in the semi-darkness, staring at the pair of muscular legs across the room.

Jack's voice was a hiss in my ear. "What's he doing here?"

I shot him a glare. "How would I know? It's not like we're friends."

Jack let out a sigh. "Do you think he followed us?"

I considered the idea for a moment. "He can't have done."

"And what are you basing that on?"

I held his gaze. "Did you notice him on the ship? Oh, hang on, you spent most of the journey in the cabin feeling sorry for yourself. The king and queen of Cerensai could have been onboard, and you'd have been none the wiser."

Jack's glare was distinctly venomous. "I was ill."

I rolled my eyes. "And you were so much better once you went on deck, like I'd been telling you for days you would be. But did you listen? Of course, you didn't. Jack always knows best. Jack doesn't think he has to listen to the advice of other people."

"Jack is wondering why you're bringing this up when we've got far more important things to worry about." He grabbed my chin and turned my head back to the pair of legs. "We need to get out of here before he notices us. If he didn't follow us, then it's one hell of a coincidence, but that doesn't change the fact that Ulgan is intent on killing both of us." Jack went quiet for a moment. "Who's he talking to?"

I crept forward slowly on my hands and knees to peer out from beneath the table, the angle not great, but enough that I could just make it out. "The barmaid."

"Which one? The one who's been trying to get in your pants for days, or the one with the funny eye?"

I reversed until I was back beneath the relative safety of the table. "One of them has got a funny eye?"

Jack's mouth tightened. "You probably didn't notice. I don't think your eyes got any higher than her massive..." He stuck out his elbows and curled his hands into his chest to demonstrate what he was talking about.

"She's got a funny eye?"

Jack nodded. "One moves, but the other doesn't."

"Huh! I need to be more observant."

"Don't you just."

I risked another glance from under the table. "He doesn't look like he's going anywhere."

Jack made a frustrated noise. "Well, we can't stay here."

"Where are we going to go? To our room?"

Jack shook his head ruefully. "And then what happens if someone tells him that we're here? We're going to be trapped in our room with no means of escape. And it's way too high to jump out of the window. We need to leave."

He was right. "So we have to sleep rough tonight?" Jack's terse nod didn't give me the impression that he was any happier about it than I was. "Do you have everything you need?"

He patted his pockets before nodding. And then he grimaced. He shifted slightly, his hand reaching back to grope the seat where we'd previously been sitting. There was a look of triumph on his face as his hand reappeared holding his bow. "We need a distraction." He inclined his head to the left-hand side of the tavern, opposite the door to outside. "Something that happens over there. While everyone's looking that way, we run out of the door."

"Rat?"

Jack shook his head. "Too easy to catch or stamp on. Much as I hoped to live the rest of my live without seeing the damn thing again, I think it's going to have to be the monkey. The little fucker can climb. It's far nimbler."

I raised an eyebrow at Jack's character assassination of my monkey. "He likes you."

Jack's mouth twisted. "What does he do to people he doesn't like? Crap in their dinner?"

I opened my mouth to respond, but Jack grabbed my hand before I could. He shook it like he could make magic spill from it if he tried hard enough. "Come on, monkey up. As soon as everyone's focused on the monkey, crawl out from under the table and head for the door. I'll be right behind you."

"Why do I have to go first?"

"Fine. I'll go first. I just figured he hates you slightly more than he hates me. I thought you might want to put as much distance as you could between the two of you."

"I'll go first." I turned away before Jack's predictable eye roll could come into force.

I let the gold sparks spill from my fingertips, tendrils of magic combining together in the space of a few seconds to form the monkey. I patted it on the head before sending it out into the room. It leapt onto a table, plates and tankards going flying. From there it climbed a curtain. The screams and shouts started a moment later. Jack prodded me in the back, and I went, making my way to the door as quickly as I could when I was still on hands and knees. A startled man looked down as I took the quickest route, which happened to be between his legs. I glanced up at him. "Excuse me."

I could hear Jack right behind me. All we needed to do was make it to the door. Someone was trying to peel the monkey off the curtain, but it was resisting, its constant chattering making it clear how offensive it found their clumsy attempts to dislodge it from its new home. The door was about eight crawling steps away. It probably would have been quicker to walk upright, but I was committed now. And anyway, the door was right there.

"YOU!"

I froze as the bellow rang out across the tavern.

"AND YOU!"

I looked back over my shoulder to find Ulgan advancing on us, his nostrils flaring. His pointed teeth stretched his mouth obscenely as he smiled. At least I think it was a smile. To be honest, it was hard to tell. "I knew I'd get my hands on you eventually."

Jack let out a strangled squawk. "Sebastian, do something."

The monkey took a death-defying leap off the curtain, jumping from shoulder to shoulder to cross the room in record time. It darted across Ulgan's path just as he took a step. He tripped, a table splitting in half as he landed on it heavily. He let out a bellow of pure rage. I didn't wait to see him extricate himself from the broken wood and bits of food, some of which he was now wearing. Standing, I grabbed Jack's hand and dragged him out of the tavern. We didn't stop running until we were well away from Steelmeadow, both of us out of breath. We collapsed on the grass, a few minutes passing before I could breathe enough to speak. I rolled my head to the side to find Jack staring up at the night sky. I cleared my throat. "Well, that was a bit of a close shave."

Jack started to laugh, and after a few moments I joined in.

CHAPTER SEVENTEEN

JACK

The tower in the distance was quite something, its gray bulk dominating the horizon. "It's bigger than I thought it would be."

Sebastian tipped his head to the side as if he thought the new angle might make a difference to how it looked. "It is quite tall."

Quite was an understatement. "I'm assuming you factored that in when you came up with your plan to rescue the prince?"

A muscle in Sebastian's cheek twitched. "Plan?"

"You do have a plan?"

He shrugged. "Some of life's biggest successes come from improvisation."

I forced myself to breathe slowly, to not give in to the flare of indignant anger in my chest that Sebastian seemed to rouse so easily. "So that would be a no, then. What about when we were in Steelmeadow? You had plenty of time to think things through then."

"I was busy."

Heat stole into my cheeks at the memory of what being busy had entailed. Both of us had been insatiable. Once I'd dropped my inhibitions about having a fling, I'd certainly not held back. And neither had Sebastian. Passion had been all very well and good, but it left us standing in front of a tower with nothing but the vague intention to save a prince. "How many people have tried to rescue him before?"

"A fair few if tavern gossip is to be believed."

"And *they* probably had a plan."

Sebastian turned to face me. "I doubt it. They were all about the posturing. Nothing short of a frontal assault would have satisfied them. They probably walked right up to the door and announced that they'd come for the prince."

I eyed him warily. "And what are we about?"

Sebastian's grin was wide and unabashed. "We are about stealth. We are about being clever and sneaky."

I let out a breath. "Of course we are. We cheat to win money. We rob bandits." I had no idea when the "we" had crept in there. At some point Sebastian's criminal activities had become mine too. It was a worrying turn of events. Apparently, his cock was magic and made me take on all his sins.

Sebastian nodded proudly. "We do." He started walking and I fell into step beside him. "Besides, the prince might not be at the top of the tower."

I kept one eye on the tower as I considered his words. "I don't think that's very likely. It's the traditional place to keep people you don't want to be rescued. I hardly think we're going to find him waiting by the front door." We walked on in silence for a few minutes, the tower drawing ever closer. "Who are these people who took the prince anyway?" It was a question I probably should have asked a lot sooner. For all I knew, it was a gang of orcs or a fierce army of battle-scarred dwarves.

"The Cataclysmic Order."

I searched my memory for any recollection of who they might be but came up blank. "They sound nice. Who are they?"

"Dragon-shifting knights."

I stopped dead, Sebastian having to retrace his steps to return to my side, his eyes searching my face. "What's wrong?"

I stuck my finger in my ear and waggled it around. "My hearing apparently, because for one moment there I could have sworn you said we were walking headlong into a nest of dragon-shifting knights. But I must have been mistaken, because it would be nothing short of suicidal for the two of us to be facing those sorts of odds alone. Only a crazy person would do that. Someone who has a brain but doesn't actually stop to use it. Someone who may be pretty but hasn't been blessed with common sense."

Sebastian gave a one-shouldered shrug, and I had to rein in the urge to hit him. "They're just men. Well..." His brow creased. "They're not... they're men that can transform into dragons, but you get the gist."

He started walking again, but I didn't take so much as a step. "See you, Sebastian. Good luck."

He stopped, a few seconds passing before he eventually turned around, his expression wheedling. "Oh, come on, Jack. Where's your sense of adventure? You've faced orcs and bandits. What's a few dragons?"

"Orcs and bandits don't breathe fire. Dragons do."

Sebastian looked distinctly unimpressed. "Yeah, the big show-offs."

That was definitely a case of the pot calling the kettle black. "I would like to end the day not burnt to a crisp."

He smiled. It was the slow, sexy smile that over the last few days had usually culminated in sex. I had to take a moment to remind myself that we were outdoors rather than in the privacy of a room. "I would also like to end the day that way." Sebastian frowned. "With you not burnt to a crisp, that is. Anyway, it's not going to happen." I sat down with my back against a tree. Sebastian sighed but lowered himself into a cross-legged position opposite me. "I'm not going to let anything happen to you."

I raised an eyebrow. "And you can promise that, can you?" I pointed a finger at him. "You knew I didn't know what I was walking into. Did you not think to mention it? And"—my voice grew more strident—"do not shrug at me."

Sebastian's shoulders twitched but didn't move. Blue eyes caught and held mine. "What do you need from me, Jack?"

I sat up straighter. "For a start, I need to know who these people are. I've never heard of them."

Sebastian nodded. "Fair enough. The Cataclysmic Order hail from the kingdom of Nuviel. For hundreds of years, they were tasked with protecting the king, and did so with all the necessary zeal that such a role required. That, and Nuviel being an island left it almost impenetrable to people who might want to seize the crown."

"So what happened?"

Sebastian's expression turned pensive. "Nobody really knows, but there was some sort of stand-off, of which the upshot was that The Cataclysmic Order were banished from Nuviel."

I contemplated the information for a moment. "So... they were royal guards and now they go around kidnapping princes. That's quite the lifestyle change."

I guess"—Sebastian scratched his chin thoughtfully—"when you're used to the finer things in life, you try and find a way to hang onto them. Either that, or they just like stirring up trouble. Plus, they're dragons. Hoarding things is in their nature."

"There's a big difference between something shiny and a human being."

Sebastian inclined his head in recognition of my point. I still wasn't done asking questions. "And how does the shifter thing work?" The tilt of Sebastian's head said he didn't understand the question, forcing me to elaborate. "Are they in dragon form most of the time, or in human form? Do they need the light of the moon or something?" Heat raced to my cheeks when Sebastian gave me a look that clearly said I'd heard too many stories. "I'm not walking in there without an idea of what I'm dealing with. How many of them are there?"

"Five... six. One might have left and gone their own way."

"Might have?"

He nodded. "And as for your other questions. They're in human form most of the time. And they can shift at will. No"—his lips twitched—"moonlight or any other special conditions needed."

I stared at him. "Well, they sound like a marvelous group of people. Just the kind of people I wanted to bump into when I left Riverbrook."

Sebastian's gaze fastened on me for an uncomfortably long amount of time. Finally, he nodded. "You're right." He stood and dusted off his trousers. "You should stay here. I'll go and get the prince and we'll come up with a meeting place."

I stood too, a hundred thoughts racing chaotically through my brain. If I let him walk off now, would I ever see Sebastian again? The thought sat in my stomach like a lead weight, and I couldn't shake the feeling that if I did as he suggested, it would be a huge mistake. I shook my head. "Oh no, you don't. If you get yourself killed, it'll somehow be my fault. You're not pinning that on me."

"Jack!" There was a note of exasperation in Sebastian's voice.

I ignored him and set off toward the tower.

The tower didn't look any less foreboding up close. If anything, the fact that it was silent, with no signs of occupation, made it worse. I turned to Sebastian, keeping my voice to a low whisper. "Why isn't there anyone around?" He shook his head, his gaze not straying from the large wooden door set in the bottom of the tower. "And... if they can fly, why have they holed up here anyway? Why didn't they spirit Prince Montgomery away to a far-off kingdom? Why stay so close to Arrowgarde?"

"I assume so they can collect the ransom payments. The continued survival of the prince hinges on them being paid on time."

That made sense. I gave Sebastian a nudge. "Let's get started." We'd hashed out some sort of plan during the last couple of miles. It was far from foolproof, though, a lot of it relying on luck.

Sebastian's fingers twitched, the gold sparks transforming into a butterfly. There was nothing pretty about this one, the color of its wings designed to be as inconspicuous as possible, and to blend in with the dark stones of the tower. Even so, my heart was in my throat as I watched it flutter close to the tower, half expecting the door to fly open and a dragon to burst out of it demanding to know who dared set foot in his territory.

A hand reached for mine, and I gratefully threaded my fingers with Sebastian's, only too glad of the comfort. The butterfly found a window slit and flew in. I looked to Sebastian, but his eyes were closed, his forehead notched with concentration. "What can you see?"

"She's on the other side of the door. It's locked."

I guess it had been too much to hope that we might have been able to stroll right in. "What else?"

"Circular stairs. I'm taking the butterfly up them. There are rooms along the way, but most of them are empty."

"Keep talking. Tell me what you see."

"There's a room mid-way up the tower, on the right-hand side of the stairs. Two men in there."

"What are they doing?"

"I can't see. I can't risk taking the butterfly too close. They're busy, though, so we can probably sneak past them."

I rolled my eyes at the use of the word "probably." A lot of this was going to depend on probablys and what ifs.

Sebastian went silent for a while, and I tried to temper my impatience. "Any more men yet?"

"Not yet."

A spark of hope ignited in my chest. Two men were far better odds than five or six. Although, I had to remind myself that even one dragon would be one too many.

Sebastian grimaced. "Two more. Three-quarters of the way up the tower." He paused. "They're not close to the window. So far, no one will see us coming."

At least that was something. But there was still at least one man unaccounted for, possibly two, depending on whether what Sebastian had said about one of them having left was true.

Sebastian continued his commentary. "Room full of food. They can stay here for years with that amount of food. Plus, I assume they could fly off and get more if they needed to. Therefore, no one's starving them out. Nearly at the top."

"Any sign of the prince?"

He shook his head. It was hard to stay quiet and not keep hammering Sebastian with questions, but I knew he needed to concentrate.

"I'm at the top. It opens out into one big room."

I squeezed Sebastian's hand. "And?"

"The prince is there."

"Are you sure it's him? How can you tell?"

Sebastian smirked. "I just can."

I frowned. "Anyone else there?"

"No."

"So the prince isn't directly guarded?"

"No. I assume they think the locked door and the tower itself is enough of a deterrent."

I sighed. "Yeah, about that locked door."

Sebastian opened his eyes, the blue startling after not seeing it for so long. "I saw the keys. They were hanging on a hook in the first room I passed, the one with the two knights."

"That doesn't help us. We can't exactly knock on the door and say, would you mind lending us the keys so that we can come back later?"

"The monkey can get them."

"That's risky."

"Shhh... I need to concentrate for this."

I let go of Sebastian's hand and lowered myself to a crouch, my knee jigging up and down in time with the rapid thrum of my heartbeat. It felt like hours had passed before Sebastian made an announcement. "Got them."

I glanced up at him. "Yeah?"

"Yeah."

I let out a relieved breath. A couple of minutes went by before the monkey came skittering across the ground toward us, a bunch of keys hanging from his mouth. Sebastian grinned as he took them, shaking them in front of my face in a move that could only be described as triumphant. I batted his hand away. "Okay. Don't get cocky. That was the easy bit. What if one of them tries to leave? They're going to realize that the keys have disappeared from right under their nose."

"We move quick."

I waved a hand at the monkey. "Are we keeping the little fucker?"

Sebastian shook his head, the monkey shrinking until it transformed back into the butterfly. He threw a glance my way. "Last chance to stay here."

Despite the almost paralyzing fear attempting to claw its way up my throat, I stood taller and squared my shoulders. "No way. You'll fuck it up."

"Your trust in me is quite touching."

In lieu of a response, I gave him a hard look.

Sebastian sent the butterfly ahead and we moved toward the tower. I just hoped he had enough magic left for the final part of the plan. Because if not, we were both fucked. They wouldn't kill the prince. He was important to them. But Sebastian and I would have no such protection. The door loomed in front of us in no time at all, and Sebastian studied the keys, of which there were three. He chose the right one the first time, the door creaking as he pushed it open. We froze, and I imagined four knights all turning their heads in the direction of the door.

When no shouts rang out and there was no clatter of footsteps on the stairs, we stepped inside, Sebastian pulling the door closed behind us. Despite what I'd said only a few minutes before, there was nothing I could do but put my trust in Sebastian. He was the only one who could see through the eyes of the butterfly, and he was also the only one who knew where the knights were. Therefore, difficult as it would be for me—not to mention completely against my nature—I was going to have to listen to him if I wanted to make it out of here alive.

We moved slow, both of us focused on making as little noise as possible. One misstep could ruin everything and have four angry dragons bearing down on us. The fact that they wouldn't be able to shift in the tower without destroying it didn't have me feeling any better about the prospect. The stairs seemed endless as we traversed them, like a constant circling to infinity.

Sebastian threw out an arm to halt my progress and I froze, my heart beating so fast it was all I could do not to be sick. What was I doing? I was a farmer. How the hell had I found myself trying to stay out of sight of dragon shifters while climbing to the top of a tower?

Neither of us could speak, so all I could do was stare at Sebastian in the gloom of the stairway, the slitted windows letting very little light through. He held up a hand and I nodded. I assumed we'd reached the room where the first two knights were, and if we tried to pass at the moment, they would see us. I pressed my back against the wall and forced myself to breathe slowly.

Sebastian held his hand up with two fingers pointing down. He wiggled them energetically and I got it. He was telling me that when he gave me the signal, we needed to be fast. He placed a finger on his lips. Fast and quiet. Easy, right? It didn't feel easy. It felt like I was completely out of my depth. I dragged in a lungful of musty air, the interior of the tower none too fresh, and I kept my eyes on Sebastian.

He held up a hand again, all five fingers pointing up. After a second, he lowered one. A countdown. I readied myself. As soon as he lowered the last finger, I moved. I didn't look at the room as we passed it, too scared that if I caught sight of one of the knights I would freeze and not be able to get moving again.

Once we'd passed the room, we rounded the curve of the stairs and came to a stop. Again, I watched Sebastian's face, knowing he'd left the butterfly behind and would be able to tell if they'd seen or heard anything suspicious.

Seconds might as well have been hours as I waited for confirmation, Sebastian finally smiling and holding up a thumb to say we were good. The butterfly fluttered back into view, and we continued on our way, back to slow and quiet. We still had one more room to navigate. This time, the whole process happened much quicker, Sebastian immediately giving the signal to go. With the last possible obstacle navigated, there was nothing left to do except continue to the top of the tower. Even so, Sebastian kept the butterfly. It was better to be safe than sorry. There was always the possibility that he'd missed the presence of the other two knights.

And then we were at the top of the tower, the room the stairs led into far brighter than the stairway. At its center, sitting on a goddamn throne of all things, was a blond-haired man. He rose from it with a look of confusion on his face, and I took the opportunity to study him. He had pale blue eyes and golden skin. He was tall and willowy and extremely elegant in a way that only a prince could be. In short, he was so pretty that it hurt.

His voice when he spoke was light and cultured, every sound perfectly enunciated. "Are you here to rescue me?"

Sebastian placed a hand on his hip, the pose reminding me of when I'd first met him. "I certainly am."

I noticed the "we" had gone, the knowledge causing something dark to form in my chest. It grew exponentially larger as the prince flew across the room and launched himself into Sebastian's arms. "And you're so handsome too. I dreamed of someone handsome coming to rescue me, but you're even better than anything I could have conjured up." His hands roved all over Sebastian's back. "And you're strong too. All those muscles."

I cleared my throat. "Sebastian?"

But Sebastian, with his arms full of fawning prince, seemed to have forgotten I was even there.

The prince tipped his head back, his eyes shining. "You're so tall. I will have to wear heels when we get married. What's your name?"

Sebastian laughed in a way that said he found the prince quite charming. "My name's Bass."

I tried again, my tone more urgent this time. "Sebastian, we need to go. Now! Every second we hang around here, is a second we risk being discovered."

My words finally seemed to get through to him, Sebastian tearing his gaze away from the prince for long enough to glance my way. It lasted less than a second, though, before his gaze strayed back to where it had started. He detached himself from Prince Montgomery and performed a surprisingly polished bow, with one arm outstretched in front of him. "Your Highness, we must leave. Jack is quite right that at the moment we remain undetected. However, that is not a state of affairs that may remain for much longer."

The prince's golden brow wrinkled slightly. From the lack of lines on it, it wasn't an expression he pulled that frequently. "Jack?"

He'd said the word like it was a word derived from a language he'd never heard before.

Sebastian waved a hand in my direction. "Jack Shaw."

The prince's scrutiny started at my feet and took its time in traveling slowly upwards, each inch seeming to displease him more than the one before it. "What is... Jack?"

Not who. What. I got the deliberate snub loud and clear. I opened my mouth to tell him exactly what I was, and where he could stick his blue-blooded disdain, but Sebastian's hand was already on Prince Montgomery's lower back to steer him toward the large window on the opposite side of the room. "We need to escape this way, Your Highness."

The prince gave a musical laugh. Jeez! Even his laugh was pretty. I hadn't thought it was possible to hate him more than I already did, but apparently it was. I wondered what would happen if I pushed him out of the window. I gave myself a few seconds to enjoy the mental image of his arms and legs windmilling wildly before he hit the ground with a pronounced *splat*. But as I didn't have any plans to spend the rest of my life locked in a dungeon, it wasn't going to happen. Therefore, the only thing I could do was join them at the window just as the prince peered over the sill to the long descent below.

Prince Montgomery shook his head, his golden hair shifting slightly before falling back into perfect formation. "No, I'm afraid I cannot leave this way. You will have to make alternative arrangements."

I offered him a sweet smile. "That's quite understandable. We can leave you here instead. You can spend a few more years on your throne ruling nothing and nobody."

Sebastian threw me a hard glance. "The prince doesn't know the plan yet. He probably thinks we're expecting him to climb down the tower. And if he was capable of doing that, he would have done so already and rescued himself. Isn't that right, Your Highness?"

The prince blinked. He had very long eyelashes that gave the action a certain element of grace. Everything he did was so damn regal. Finally, he nodded. "That is right. I am very brave."

Sebastian nodded fervently. "I don't doubt it."

I did. I doubted the prince had ever been required to perform anything braver than eating an apple that might not be at peak ripeness. I threw a glance back at the stairs. "Sebastian, get on with it."

Gold sparks began to swirl from Sebastian's fingertips, the prince letting out a little gasp of surprise. He jumped up and down and clapped excitedly. "You have magic too. You are just so perfect."

As eyerolls went, the one I performed had to be one of my most energetic. It was unfortunate then that it was wasted, neither man looking my way. Sebastian, because he was busy forming the magic into a giant… well, I didn't know what sort of bird it was exactly, an eagle maybe, and Prince Montgomery because he couldn't take his eyes off Sebastian. It was clear that Sebastian could do no wrong in his eyes, and no doubt Sebastian would soak it up like the world's biggest sponge.

It was only when the bird flapped its huge wings, the draft buffeting all three of us that the prince looked that way. I saw the moment the truth dawned on him, his pretty features twisting in horror. He turned imploring eyes on Sebastian. "Bass, much as I adore you, and I can't wait for you to complete my rescue so that we may be married, I regret to inform you that as the heir to Arrowgarde, I simply cannot be carried by a giant bird. It is not the done thing for someone of my status."

I had a pithy reply to that hovering on my tongue, but I didn't get a chance to voice it, footsteps on the stairs a far more pressing matter to have to deal with. Sebastian had heard it too, the two of us exchanging glances. We didn't have any choice. There was no going down that way. Leaving via the window was the only option if we didn't want to get caught. Therefore, the only decision to make was whether to take the prince or leave him.

Tempting as it was to choose the latter, I suspected that should Sebastian be thwarted in this rescue attempt, he'd insist on trying again. Therefore, given that I had no intention of ever returning to this place again, it was better for all concerned—the prince included—if we left with him this time.

The eagle was as close as it could get to the tower, but with its sheer size and wingspan that wasn't very close. A jump would be required. A jump that would mean putting my trust in Sebastian completely. However, the likelihood of getting the prince to jump was slim to none, which left us with somewhat of a dilemma. Apparently, the prince's so-called bravery didn't extend to things that he deemed as being beneath him. With the footsteps growing increasingly louder, I came to a decision.

I grabbed the prince and threw him over my shoulder. He was surprisingly light. I'd lifted pigs that were heavier. They'd put up more of a fight as well, the fists that beat at my back doing very little damage and all too easy to ignore.

Saying a silent prayer, I climbed onto the sill with my armful of prince, closed my eyes, and then jumped. For a moment, there was nothing but the rush of air and I mentally prepared myself for the impact of the ground, and the knowledge that I would be forever immortalized as the man who'd forced a prince to plummet to his death.

And then I was being lifted, the sudden change in direction making my stomach lurch. Sharp talons dug into my back, but I wasn't about to complain about them when they were the only things preventing me from meeting my maker. Steeling myself, I opened my eyes, immediately wishing I hadn't, the ground below much too far away and rushing past at a dizzying speed. As ways to travel went, this had become my least favorite.

I turned my head, relieved to see Sebastian dangling from the other talon. The prince, meanwhile, was still struggling in my grasp. He didn't seem to care that the freedom he was striving for would mean certain death. I tightened my arm around him. "Keep still. If I drop you, you're dead."

"I will have you executed, Jack Shaw."

God, I wanted to let him go. It wasn't like the window. I could pretend it was an accident, that his weight had gotten to be too much for me. Even Sebastian wouldn't be able to prove it was a lie. I took in a breath and blew it out slowly. I wasn't a murderer, and if I was going to start, it was probably better to start with someone a little less important than a prince. "Great. I'll look forward to it. It will mean I don't have to listen to you whine ever again. You seem to keep forgetting, *your highness*..." I said it very differently from how Sebastian had said it. His address had held a great deal of respect, whereas mine made it sound more like an insult, like I didn't believe he'd earned such a title. "We're rescuing you. We're risking our lives to return you to the bosom of your family where you can go back to leading a pampered and privileged existence."

Prince Montgomery sniffed. "I don't like you."

At least he'd stopped struggling. "I assure you the feeling is quite mutual."

Realizing that Sebastian hadn't said a word, I turned to look at him. A bolt of alarm shot through me as I took in his closed eyes and the sheen of sweat on his brow. "Sebastian, what's wrong?"

"Not much magic left."

Ignoring the lurch of nausea it caused, I looked down. We were too high for me to make out where we were and how far we'd traveled from the tower. "Then set us down."

"We need to get as far as we can."

"We need to go down before the eagle disappears and we all fall to our deaths."

Sebastian didn't answer, his eyes still closed. "I can hold on a bit longer."

The load over my shoulder gave another wriggle. "What's going on? What are you discussing?"

"Nothing for you to worry about, *Prince*." To Sebastian, I said, "Save your magic. We might need it. Take us down."

He gave a curt nod, and I breathed a sigh of relief as the eagle went into a glide, the ground growing steadily closer. It deposited us on the ground with surprising gentleness, the feeling reminiscent of when I'd left the ship. I was definitely a land person. Not sea. Not air. I was going to do everything I could in the future to stay on land. And that was a promise.

As for the eagle, it had disappeared the moment we'd landed. Sebastian had his hands braced on his knees. He'd once told me that sustaining the magic for a long period of time took its toll on his physical state, but knowing that and seeing it first-hand were very different things. I touched his arm. Are you going to be okay?"

He nodded, lifting his head to force a smile. "I'll be fine. I just need a rest. How's Prince Montgomery?"

We both looked toward the prince. He was stood a few feet away, smoothing his hair back with his fingers and straightening his collar, as if he wasn't in the middle of nowhere and instead was about to face his people. I lowered my voice. "Your *fiancé* is a bit of a dick."

I'd used the word in the hope that Sebastian would laugh and tell me not to be silly, that a marriage wasn't going to happen. Instead, he merely looked pensive. "You have to remember that he's been under a lot of stress."

Great! He was sticking up for him. Absolutely fucking marvelous. It seemed that whatever we'd shared in the past few days was no match for someone who almost had hearts coming out of their eyes whenever they looked Sebastian's way, and I'd been stupid to ever think I could match up. He was a prince. I was a farmer. I had absolutely nothing to offer Sebastian apart from my body. And I'd already offered that to him.

Something caught my eye, and I grabbed Sebastian's arm, forcing him to face the same direction I was. "Please tell me, that's not what I think it is."

Sebastian's eyes went wide at the sight of two mounted figures in the distance, growing steadily larger as they galloped toward us. "Fuck!"

I shared that sentiment. It seemed we'd located the two missing knights, or rather, they'd located us. The order didn't really matter. What did matter was that they'd dismounted, their bodies shimmering as they transformed from men into dragons. Big dragons. Dragons that immediately took to the sky, their reason for shifting becoming abundantly clear as they gained on us much faster. Well, that and the fact that they'd now be able to breathe fire as an added bonus.

"Run!"

I wasn't about to ignore Sebastian's command. In fact, I'd been about to shout the same thing.

Prince Montgomery, who'd somehow remained oblivious of the impending threat up to now, shook his head. "I'm a prince. I don't—"

I threw him over my shoulder again and ran.

CHAPTER EIGHTEEN

SEBASTIAN

Nothing could overcome fatigue more than seeing two huge dragons bearing down on you. Seeing Jack had Prince Montgomery over his shoulder once more, I ran at Jack's side. Every now and again, I'd risk a glance back. They were much faster than us. Therefore, if we continued over open ground, they would be on us in no time. We needed cover, and we needed it quick. Luckily, we were running alongside a forest, the solution obvious. "This way, Jack."

I veered right, Jack following without argument, the prince's chin bouncing inelegantly off his back. Jack looked over at me. "Why... are we... heading... this way? Trees are... flammable. Fire... and wood... don't mix."

"Do you have a better idea?"

Taking his silence for acknowledgment that he didn't, I glanced back one final time before the trees swallowed us up. The dragons had gotten close enough that I could see the red of their eyes. They could easily have breathed fire, but I guessed burning the prince to a crisp wouldn't exactly further their plans.

We ran on for a few minutes before Jack slowed to a stop and lowered Prince Montgomery to the ground, the prince pulling himself up to his full height and fixing Jack with a withering stare. "I'm going to tell Mummy and Daddy about how you keep manhandling me."

Jack's lip curled. "You do that. Can you also tell them that no matter how tempting it was, I didn't abandon you so that the dragons could recapture you and stick you back in that tower." He cast a nervous glance back the way we'd come. "Speaking of which, we need to keep moving."

The prince muttered something but did fall into step beside us as we continued at a fast pace. Jack's jaw was set as I threw a look his way. "They'll have to shift back. That's why I headed this way." He nodded but didn't comment. "I'm sorry I dragged you into this." No response. His silence bothered me. Jack could be incredibly biting at times and extremely critical, but he was rarely silent. "Jack?"

He came to a sudden stop. "Shh... listen."

I listened. "I can't hear anything."

Jack gave a slow nod. "Exactly. They're not following. Which begs the question why not?"

I shrugged. "Perhaps they went back for their horses. If they can't be in their dragon form, they would be quicker on horseback than they are on foot."

Jack's brow furrowed. "Perhaps."

"So... we'd be better to keep moving." Jack nodded his assent and we started moving again. I contemplated another apology but decided against it. There was no guarantee that it would get any better a reception than the previous one. I'd save it for when we were somewhere safe, and we could laugh about everything that had happened.

The deeper we got into the forest, the darker it grew, the trees seeming to grow closer together, and the canopies above our head blocking out all but the merest glimmer of light. There was a sense of wrongness to the forest as well. Something I was struggling to put my finger on. It finally came to me. It was the silence. Forests were usually full of noise. This one wasn't. There was no birdsong. No scurry of animals. No rustle of leaves. There was nothing at all apart from the sound of our own footsteps.

"It's too quiet."

Jack had come to the same conclusion I had. Rather than agreeing with him—because let's be honest, I'd made it a policy never to do that—I faked a breezy optimism. "Quiet is good. Quiet means we don't have dragons in hot pursuit. Quiet means we're on our own. Quiet means—"

A hissing sound brought our little procession to a sudden and abrupt stop. I lowered my voice to a whisper. "What direction did that come from?"

All three of us pointed in a different direction. That wasn't good. That wasn't good at all. We'd automatically formed ourselves into a circle with our backs pressed together. There was another hiss, this one coming from a different direction than the first one I'd heard. Almost like we were surrounded. I hadn't liked the silence, but I liked this even less. It was possible I liked it even less than dragons.

Jack's shoulder shifted next to mine. "I'm going to ask you something, Sebastian, and I don't want you to give me any bullshit."

Even though it was difficult to know which direction to head in, we moved a few steps as a shuffling unit, like some sort of three-headed hydra. It seemed a better option than letting whatever was closing in on us call the shots. "Go on."

"You remember way back when we were discussing where the prince might have been taken?"

I made a noise of agreement as we took another few steps, more hisses filtering through the trees. "I remember."

"Well..." Jack's voice was tight. "It strikes me that the forest you mentioned, the one *you* said the abductors wouldn't possibly consider taking refuge in... In fact, *you* said you'd have to be an idiot to set foot in there, is most likely the same forest that we're currently in. Therefore, I just wanted to check as *you* led us in here, that you're fully comfortable with the title of idiot?"

I grimaced. "I wouldn't say fully comfortable. I'd say... that I would face it with a grudging acceptance and a healthy dose of regret."

"What's wrong with this forest?" The prince sounded confused.

Jack snorted. "All yours, Sebastian."

"Nothing for you to worry about, Your Highness." We edged a little farther, the hisses growing steadily louder. "It's just that we might not be alone in here. There might be a few... basilisks."

"Basilisks!" There was no hiding the horror in the prince's voice. "Are you telling me that this is The Dark Forest?"

"Aptly named," Jack muttered.

I ignored him. "I believe so."

There was a short silence while the prince took in the information. He gave a toss of his head. "In that case, I demand that you take me elsewhere. I am far too important to find myself at the mercy of basilisks."

I opened my mouth to speak, but Jack got in there first. "Trust us, we don't intend to hang around here any longer than we need to." To me, he said, "So what's the plan, Sebastian? We're surrounded by deadly creatures who by the sound of it are closing in on us. We can't go back the way we came because of the dragons." He gave a humorless laugh. "I guess at least we know now why they didn't follow. *They* had more sense. You're out of magic so you can't conjure up something a basilisk doesn't like. And I don't even know what that would be. Are they scared of anything?"

Something moved out of the corner of my eye, a dark shape, and I very nearly turned to look at it. I grabbed Jack's shoulder as he started to turn.

"Don't look at it. Whatever you do, don't look at it. One glance is fatal, but it only works if we look at it." More dark shapes appeared in the periphery of my vision. We moved in the only direction we could, the hissing now so loud I had to raise my voice to be heard above it. "Weasels."

"What about them?" Jack kept his gaze fixed on the ground, the prince doing the same.

Our shuffling walk had gotten faster, more polished, desperation forcing us to learn the skill of moving as one without separating or falling over pretty damn fast. "Basilisks don't like the odor of a weasel."

Jack let out a snort. "What a shame, then, that there aren't any around here. You can have that put on my tombstone. Here lies Jack Shaw. In his last few moments, all he wanted was a weasel. Oh, wait..." His voice was dripping with sarcasm. "You'll be dead too."

I couldn't help but smile. Even under the direst of circumstances, Jack never lost his spiky edge. "Well, at least my imminent death should make you feel better."

"It does a bit. I'd just rather not share your demise. I had plans."

"Crops to plant? Pigs to feed? Those sorts of plans? Goats to—?"

"Something like that." Jack came to a sudden halt, Prince Montgomery and I crashing into his back. He pointed at the ground. "What's that?"

I followed his gaze to a viscous substance that dripped from the leaves. "Basilisk poison, I assume. Don't touch it."

"Funnily enough, I had no plans to. Hence me not walking into it. So... we don't just have however many basilisks to contend with... which incidentally, how many of the fuckers are there? But we have to worry about coming into contact with their little slime trails that they've left behind."

"I don't know how many there are." That was the truth. What I did know was that their numbers seemed to be swelling by the minute. What concerned me more, though, was why there weren't any in the direction we were heading. It gave me the distinct impression we were being herded. If that was the case, the question was where, and for what purpose? Checking for poison first, I guided our little group behind the thick trunk of a tree. "We can't keep going where they want us to go."

Jack met my gaze. "So what do you suggest?"

"We need to go that way." Without looking, I lifted my hand to point in the opposite direction, knowing there were at least two or three basilisks in the way.

Jack laughed. "Easy. We'll just tell our hissing friends to stand aside. And while we're at it, we'll tell them that if they could kindly refrain from looking at us or spitting poison in our direction, we'd very much appreciate it."

"You should tell them that they must move by order of the kingdom of Arrowgarde." Prince Montgomery accompanied the decree with an aristocratic tilt of his head.

Jack threw him a scathing look. "I tell you what, why don't you try it? Sebastian and I will wait here, and you can let us know how it goes. Unless you're dead of course, and then you won't be able to tell us anything, but at least it will be quiet, so it's kind of a win-win for me."

"I'm going to have you executed in the most painful way possible."

Jack raised an eyebrow. "Yeah? What way is that then? Tell me more."

"It will be—"

I cut in, concerned that if I didn't bring a halt to the argument, Jack was likely to throw Prince Montgomery at the basilisks. And then all of this would have been for nothing. "Stop. Both of you. Now isn't the time. I think we can all agree that there's no reasoning with the basilisks, royal decree or no royal decree. For some reason, they want us to go this way. That's why they're waiting. That's why they haven't attacked. Maybe there's a king basilisk they want to deliver us to, or maybe they want to imprison us rather than kill us. I can't pretend to know. But what I do know is that we can't just allow ourselves to be shepherded, and that means working together."

I left a deliberate pause, and when neither man offered any argument, I continued. "I'm going to conjure a weasel. We're going to cover ourselves in its scent, and we're going to pray that's enough of a deterrent to get past them. I'll keep the weasel for as long as I can, but my magic reserves are already low, so we need to move fast. Agreed?"

Both men nodded, the prince seeming a little distracted like he hadn't actually been listening. A twig snapped to the right, Jack's head automatically jerking up to see what it was. I moved fast to put myself between him and the noise, the action ensuring that all he could see was me. "Concentrate, Jack." He let out a shaky breath and then nodded again.

I let the magic free, closing my eyes as I formed it into a weasel at least a hundred times bigger than the actual animals, the finished creature towering over us. I wasted no time in plunging my hands into its fur and rubbing them all over me, Jack following my lead and doing the same. The prince, however, just stood there. Jack and I both turned to look at him. He shook his head. "No. I most certainly will not soil myself with the foul odor of a woodland animal. Especially when said creature is of gargantuan proportions."

Jack sighed and then grabbed him, pushing the prince headfirst into the weasel's fur. There was a splutter of something about "all the thirteen kingdoms watching the execution" before Jack pushed him harder against the weasel and the prince lost the ability to talk. Once he was satisfied that the front of the prince was coated, he flipped him around, the prince's blue eyes wide with incredulity as Jack took no prisoners and rubbed the back of the prince against the weasel.

Prince Montgomery's shocked gaze found mine. "As my future husband to be, I demand that you stop this uncouth lout from treating me like this."

My lips twitched. "I'm afraid the uncouth lout is just trying to keep you safe from basilisks, Your Highness." I didn't wait for a response, my magic already waning. We moved as one again. Only this time we had a giant weasel as part of our circle. There was a lot to think about as we changed direction. Keep your eyes on the ground. Look out for venom. Stay close to the weasel. Don't go too fast or too slow. And on top of that, I had to control the weasel. If the volume of the hissing was anything to go by, the basilisks weren't at all happy about his appearance, which was good news.

"Can you look at them through the weasel's eyes, or...?"

Jack left the question unfinished, but the meaning was clear enough.

"I don't know. I haven't tried." If I could, it would make life a lot easier. Trying to navigate your way past something that you couldn't even look at was like trying to thread a needle without holding the needle.

"Maybe you shouldn't..."

But I was already lifting the weasel's head. There were a number of things that could happen. It could kill the weasel, which would leave us relying on just its odor to keep us safe. It could instantaneously kill both the weasel and myself, or... everything could be fine, my magic protecting me from the deadly effect of the basilisk's stare.

The weasel focused on the three basilisks that barred our path. And I was... fine. And the weasel was too.

"Sebastian?" There was genuine concern in Jack's voice, warmth settling in the pit of my stomach in response to it. "I'm okay."

"Yeah?"

"Yeah."

"What do they look like?"

"Gray and slimy. They're like a really muscly snake. Bigger than a snake, though. Very sharp teeth. Not at all friendly-looking."

"Are they moving out of the way?"

"Not yet." The larger of the three basilisks had its yellow slitted eyes trained on the weasel, its head moving slightly as it tracked it. "I'm going to run the weasel straight at it."

"Are you sure that's the best idea?"

I wasn't, but I did it anyway. We needed to know if the basilisk was scared of the weasel. Because if it wasn't, and we were heading straight for it, we may as well have signed our own death warrants. The basilisk let the weasel get to within five meters of it, and then it turned, slithering back into the undergrowth as fast as its over-muscled tail would carry it. I let out a whoop at the clear path it had left behind. Grabbing both Jack and the prince's hands, I pulled them along with me, using the weasel to cover our backs and trusting the fact that we stank of weasel to be enough to keep the rest at a safe distance.

We ran until our lungs were bursting, the prince seeming to have forgotten that he didn't run and matching us stride for stride. I kept the weasel around for as long as I could before relinquishing it, the rest of my energy needed to prevent myself from collapsing.

The sunlight as we broke out of the forest had to be the sweetest thing I'd ever experienced. The fact that there were no dragons lying in wait for us came a close second. I only had a moment to appreciate it before I was swept up into an embrace, my lips curling into a smile. Jack. Except, it wasn't Jack, it was Prince Montgomery, his face shining with a mixture of relief and gratitude. "Sebastian, you're such a clever thing. You deserve a reward for your efforts, and I have just the thing."

His lips were on mine before I could even consider what he was talking about. Long fingers delved into my hair to cup my skull, holding my head still in a surprisingly strong grip as his lips plundered mine. I tried to move back, to put some space between us, but he wasn't having any of it, his fingers tightening.

It was a closed-mouth kiss, but it was still a kiss. And when it should have ended, it carried on. It must have been at least a minute. Or did it just feel longer?

The prince smelt of weasel, but then I guess I did too, and it didn't seem to bother him in the slightest. I tried to say something, but with Prince Montgomery's lips suctioned to mine, it came out as nothing more than a strangled noise.

"Well, this is just marvelous, isn't it?" Jack's voice. I made another half-hearted attempt to free myself, but it proved just as fruitless as the first had. The prince apparently wasn't letting go until he deemed the kiss finished, which could be any time between the next minute and the end of the century. "Don't mind me. You two just carry on. I mean... it's not like there's any dragons around here, or basilisks. Perhaps you'd like to take your clothes off and get down and dirty on the grass while I watch. Or are you expecting me to turn my back and pretend I can't see anything? I'm afraid I'm not that amenable."

I flattened my palms against Prince Montgomery's chest and gave an experimental push. Nothing. He was certainly determined. I'd give him that. He reminded me of a limpet. A very amorous limpet. I was just starting to consider the possibility that he might never let go and I could be at risk of suffocation, when he pulled back with a huge smile on his face.

His cheeks were flushed, and his eyes were sparkling as he trailed a finger down my chest. "Well... wasn't that a beautiful first kiss. I probably should have waited." He fluttered his lashes. "I don't want you getting the wrong idea about me. I'm not normally so... forward, but... as my rescuer, we're engaged so it's okay. Right?"

All I could do was stare at him. He pouted prettily and then gave another flutter of his lashes. "You've gone shy. How utterly charming. You need to remember that I was locked up in that tower for a very long time." His gaze trailed slowly down my body, pausing at my crotch. "A *very* long time."

I swallowed and looked over at Jack. Jack would know what to say to rescue me from the prince's clutches. Except, there was no Jack. I turned in a slow circle. He was nowhere to be seen. I finally caught sight of him in the distance walking away. "JACK!"

He didn't turn. Prince Montgomery stepped in front of me, his hand on my arm. "Don't worry about him. He's probably trying to escape from execution."

I shook off his hand and went after Jack, the prince sighing and then following. "JACK!" He still didn't give any impression of having heard me. We caught up to him after a couple of minutes, Jack not turning his head as we fell into step beside him. "Where are you going?"

He lifted his face to squint at the sun. "East. That's where Lastwick is, right?"

I nodded. "Without me?" I wasn't able to keep the plaintive note out of my voice.

Jack gave a disdainful sniff. "You were busy. I decided that I wasn't happy to hang around on the edge of a forest full of basilisks. That it's a little presumptuous to assume that they wouldn't leave the forest. I'm naturally suspicious like that. Oh, and you know, there's also the small matter of the dragons who could quite easily fly *over* the forest." He lifted his head to the sky. "Thankfully, they seem to have given up." His gaze flicked across to the prince. "They're probably glad to be rid of him."

"Jack!" If he heard the note of warning in my voice, he didn't pay any heed to it. Luckily, the prince seemed oblivious to our conversation.

"Oh, and then"—Jack lowered his head to his chest with a baleful expression on his face—"there's the fact that I stink of weasel. I need a bath."

"You should be used to it, a farm boy like you."

"I don't farm weasels."

"Maybe you should. Maybe there's an untapped market for it. People could go on jaunts to The Dark Forest with a dozen weasels strapped to their chest."

My attempt to make Jack smile didn't elicit so much as a lip twitch, and I'd have had to have been a fool not to realize he was avoiding looking at me. "About the…" I cast a quick look across to the prince. I swore inwardly. I couldn't have the conversation I needed to have with the prince present.

"About the what?"

I let out a sigh. "Nothing. We'll talk later."

Jack raised an eyebrow but didn't say anything.

"Bass…" Prince Montgomery's voice was deliberately weak and reedy. "I cannot walk a step farther without assistance. It has been a rather trying day. Can you conjure me a horse, a white one? White complements my coloring beautifully."

We'd ground to a halt, Jack carrying on walking as if he hadn't heard the prince speak. "I'm afraid, Your Highness, that I cannot. I used up all my magic. I won't have more until I've eaten and rested."

"Huh!" The prince's expression was reminiscent of someone who had just chewed on a wasp and discovered that it didn't taste all that nice. "What are we to do, then?"

I watched Jack's disappearing back, biting down on the urge to tell the prince that perhaps if he pushed himself more, his legs might be made to last a little longer. Instead, I turned around and offered him my back. "It would be an honor to carry you."

Prince Montgomery blinked in astonishment. "I'm not sure that's seemly, but…" He turned his head to scan the surrounding countryside. "There's no one around, and I am very tired." *You and me both.*

It took a bit of maneuvering, but eventually we managed to get the prince settled on my back, his hands occasionally wandering to where they shouldn't as I took off in hot pursuit of Jack, who seemed to have sped up if the distance between us was any indication. A more sensitive man than I was might have started to think he'd rather be alone. I guessed I had a lot of making up to do later.

The prince had insisted on "dismounting" before we entered Lastwick. He'd dismissed a number of taverns as "not being up to standard" before finally settling on The Bronze Jellyfish as being "acceptable," the announcement accompanied by a slight wrinkling of his nose. Baths hadn't been able to wait. Not if we didn't want the rest of the tavern complaining. The chambermaid, for a bit of extra coin, had even seen to three separate baths and provided fresh clothes too. After bathing, we'd eaten a meal of thick, meaty soup and crusty bread, second helpings delivered without any of us having to ask.

And all the while, I'd watched Jack. He'd barely spoken since the forest, and on the brief occasion he'd met my gaze, it had skittered away almost immediately.

It wasn't just me. Prince Montgomery was also subjected to the same treatment.

We were all exhausted, the amount of energy expended and the bursts of furious activity combining in a lethal cocktail to leave us dead on our feet. Full stomachs only compounded the issue, retiring for the night not even needing to be discussed after eating. I led the way up the stairs, Jack bringing up the rear. It had been automatic to only ask for two rooms. Much as Jack had complained about it at times, we hadn't had separate rooms since the first night I'd met him. Despite the fatigue nibbling away at my limbs and my eyelids, I was looking forward to getting him alone.

I got as far as placing my hand on the door handle of mine and Jack's room before my name was called by Prince Montgomery. "Bass, sweetheart, what are you doing?"

I blinked at him blearily. "Going to bed."

Prince Montgomery's laughter was high and full of gentle amusement. "I can't possibly be left unattended. What if someone comes for me in the middle of the night? How do we know we haven't been followed? I would feel far better knowing that someone was watching over me."

"Jack and I could—"

Jack gave a snort. "Jack is not doing anything apart from going to bed. Jack is going to spend a few hours pretending that this whole day was nothing but a bad dream. Jack is…" He rubbed his face in a weary gesture. "Jack is talking about himself in the third person again, a state of affairs that never happened before he met you." At least he was looking at me again. It didn't last long, though before he broke eye contact and studied the door instead. "The prince is right. You should stay with him, just in case something happens. Let's not fool ourselves that nobody in the tavern recognized him. They might not have approached us and said as much, but there were definitely stares." His mouth twisted slightly. "And for once, they weren't looking at you. For all we know The Cataclysmic Order might have spies to feed information back to them here."

I lay my fingers on his arm and for a moment he just stared at them. I gave him a gentle shake. "We need to talk. In private."

He gave a nod, something in my chest easing. The feeling of relief was all too brief, his next words bringing me back to earth with a bump. "Not tonight, though. I'm far too tired."

Before I could argue, Jack had already slipped from my grasp, the door closing in his wake in a clear dismissal that couldn't be misconstrued. I pressed my hand to the door and sighed. There was nothing to stop me from opening it and demanding that Jack talk to me. Except for the fact that he didn't take kindly to anyone demanding anything. It would leave me facing a spitting and snarling Jack who no doubt wouldn't be prepared to listen to anything I had to say. Better to let him get some sleep and speak to him in the morning.

"Bass?"

I walked back over to the prince as he called my name. He lifted a hand, his fingers curling around my neck. "You can keep me warm tonight."

Gently peeling his fingers away from my skin, I kept hold of his hand, pressing it to my chest in a way that hopefully came across as less of a rejection. "Your Highness, while your offer is extremely flattering, we're in a tavern and people will talk. I'm not willing to do anything that would dishonor your name."

A slight wrinkle appeared on Prince Montgomery's brow. "I'm not a virgin."

I was way too tired for this conversation. I cast a quick glance along the length of the corridor, thankful that it was empty. "That's all well and good, and I'm very happy for you, but I'm sure some of the people in your kingdom like to imagine that you are. Therefore, it's in your best interests as heir to the throne, to keep any dalliances on the downlow." He blinked at me, and I was forced to elaborate. "Behind palace walls. Rather than in a tavern full of people."

"Oh."

I lifted his hand and pressed a kiss to the back of it before letting go of it. "Therefore, I'm going to bid you goodnight."

"Will I be safe? I really don't want to go back to that tower."

I gave him a reassuring smile. "I'm going to stay outside your room all night and guard you with my life."

Pale blue eyes caught and held mine. "Promise?"

"I promise." I opened his door and gave him a gentle push to get him inside before closing it behind him. I waited for a minute, half expecting the door to open again. When it stayed closed, I settled myself with my back against the door. It wasn't the comfiest of sleeping positions, but I'd endured worse. The corridor was relatively warm, and I was so tired that I fell asleep within minutes.

Chapter Nineteen

Jack

Arrowgarde was far more ostentatious than any other place I'd seen—all white marble walls with lattice works of perfumed flowers in every color you could name. Some buildings even had towers and spires. And they only seemed to grow more elaborate the closer we got to the palace, as if the people themselves had spilled out of it and set up home as close as they could.

The awe I felt at my surroundings wasn't enough to rid me of the large boulder that had taken up residence in my stomach. I was all too aware of what the next few hours would bring—a parting where I would bid farewell to Sebastian and he would go off to start a new life with the prince, who might be obnoxious but was also undeniably pretty, and apparently very eager if yesterday's kiss that I'd been forced to witness was anything to go by.

I'd learnt from previous mistakes and knew the difference between Sebastian kissing and Sebastian being kissed, but I wasn't fooling myself that Sebastian's reticence was anything other than a slight awkwardness at being with a new lover in front of the old one. And it wasn't as if he'd ever promised me anything. In fact, he'd always been up front about his intentions to marry the prince. I'd slept with him knowing that. That didn't mean it hurt any less, though.

Sebastian had continued insisting that we needed to talk this morning, but I'd fobbed him off. I didn't need him to let me down gently. I didn't need to be told that it had been fun while it lasted. Because then, I'd be forced to pretend I didn't care, when really, I did. I'd be forced to pretend that each word didn't feel like a knife in my gut. I could get through today. I had to.

Excited chatter had started from the moment we'd entered Arrowgarde, whispers of "Is that the prince?" and "I must be seeing things!" following in our wake. It only increased as we turned the final corner to see the palace laid out in front of us behind a heavily guarded wrought iron gate. And if I'd thought the rest of the buildings were impressive, they were nothing in comparison to the royal residence. It was white to match the rest of the buildings in Arrowgarde, or more likely they matched the palace. But it was also trimmed in gold with towers and turrets reaching up to the sky, the flag of Arrowgarde fluttering majestically in the breeze.

"Jack."

I turned my head to Prince Montgomery, surprised by the fact that he'd not only addressed me, but that he'd used my name. "Yes."

The prince gave a toss of his head, his blond hair reflecting the sunlight perfectly. They were going to be the perfect golden couple, a realization that made me feel sick to my stomach. They'd even match the damn palace. "I have decided that I'm not going to have you executed."

"Oh, that's very... kind of you."

The prince nodded sagely. "I had a talk with Bass this morning and he explained that you don't mix in the same cultured circles that we do, that you are far more used to behavior on a farm, so I shouldn't be insulted by your heavy-handed tactics."

"Do you mean when I threw you over my shoulder so we could escape from the tower? Or when I threw you over my shoulder so we could outrun the dragons?"

Prince Montgomery's lips thinned into a firm line. "I was thinking more of the weasel incident."

My lips twitched of their own accord, and I was forced to school my face into a suitably serious expression. I suspected that Sebastian would share my amusement if I looked his way, but I'd already decided not to do that. It was easier if I didn't look at him. "Ah, I see."

"Anyway"—the prince gave another toss of his head—"You are forgiven."

"Erm... thank you, I guess." I was saved from having to say more as the palace gates suddenly flew open, all hell breaking loose. There were people everywhere, our little group swallowed up within seconds, multiple conversations happening all around us, most of them centering on where the prince had come from and how he'd been rescued.

Voices grew higher and more excited, a woman who seemed to be a lady-in-waiting jostling me out of the way. The people surged back toward the palace, and, for a moment, I was swept along. I couldn't see Sebastian. Or the prince. Fighting against the surge of people, I came to a stop. I stood up on my tiptoes, straining to see above the crowd. There. A familiar blond head, the prince next to him, clinging onto his arm for dear life.

The crowd moved to enter the palace grounds as one huge entity, with Sebastian and the prince at its center. It was strangely reminiscent of the way we'd been forced to move through The Dark Forest, only instead of a giant weasel and basilisks, it was a group of people clad in silks, dripping in more jewels than I'd ever seen in my life.

Now that I'd located Sebastian, I went to follow, hurrying to catch up with the tail end of the procession as they made their way down the long path that led to the palace. A guard grabbed my arm, another swinging the gate shut before I could slip through it. I attempted to shrug him off, but he wasn't having any of it, his fingers digging into my arm. "Open it. I need to get in."

He regarded me with barely concealed disdain. "And who might you be?"

"Jack. Jack Shaw. I'm..." But what was I going to say, that I'd played just as big a part in rescuing the prince as Sebastian had? Sebastian might back me up, and it was a definite might, but the prince was far more likely, despite his words of forgiveness, to recall being manhandled and forcibly pushed into weasels. It was probably better if I didn't enter the palace.

Only, I'd expected something more between myself and Sebastian than just to watch him walk away. But then, whose fault was that? I had no one but myself to blame. He'd wanted to talk, and I'd wormed my way out of it, claiming tiredness, or being too busy, or simply ignoring him.

With one last glance at the disappearing crowd in all their finery, I turned and made my way back to the streets of Arrowgarde. Now what? There was only one possible answer. I needed to find a tavern a good sight less upmarket than the one in Lastwick we'd spent the previous night in, and I needed to get horribly drunk until I couldn't remember my own name, let alone Sebastian's.

I wandered for at least an hour until I found one to my liking, the hanging sign proclaiming it as The Lonely Harbor seeming particularly apt given my mood. Making my way over to the bar, I slapped two gold coins on its surface, the buxom barmaid raising her eyebrows. I pushed the coins closer to her. "Keep the drinks coming."

She scooped the coins off the bar and nodded before filling a tankard with foamy ale and pushing it my way. I drank it far faster than I usually would, the barmaid promptly replacing it with another. The fuzziness in my head felt good. It felt far better than thinking about Sebastian.

By the time I'd reached my third tankard, The Lonely Harbor had become a raucous hive of activity. I called the barmaid over. "What's going on?"

She smiled. "Haven't you heard? There are celebrations all over Arrowgarde. Against all the odds and after months of being incarcerated, Prince Montgomery has been returned. And..." She leaned forward. "His rescuer is apparently devilishly handsome." She pressed a hand to her chest, a dreamy expression settling on her face. "It's like some sort of fairytale. Not only do we have our future king back, but there's to be a royal wedding." My stomach turned over and I did my best not to vomit up all the ale I'd consumed. Oblivious to my inner turmoil, she continued. "They're talking about next week because apparently the prince is head over heels in love, which, why wouldn't you be when a tall, dashing stranger risks life and limb to save you? Prince Montgomery must have felt like he'd hit the jackpot. Not that he doesn't deserve it, the poor lamb. He must have been so brave."

I pointed at my tankard of ale. "I'm going to need another."

"Another!" She peered down at it. "But it's almost full."

I picked it up and drank most of it down in a series of rapid swallows. I banged the empty tankard on the bar. "No, it's not."

"I guess you're celebrating too."

"Something like that."

During the next hour, the conversation around me proved relentless. "I saw him. He's so handsome. That hair..." "The prince is so lucky." "I'd marry him in a heartbeat." "I don't need to marry him. Just give him to me for a night." That last comment was met by gusty, ribald laughter. "I wonder if they'll wear matching clothes. They need something that will complement their blue eyes." "I'm going to be at the wedding. I wouldn't miss it for the world." "Do you know where Sebastian comes from?" "I've heard a rumor that he has magic. Isn't that marvelous?"

My vision was starting to blur, and still the barrage of conversation continued, the inhabitants of Arrowgarde apparently having nothing better to talk about than the return of their prince, who was a wonderful man according to them, and his handsome, distinguished and very charming fiancé, who was apparently the most fabulous person in all of the thirteen kingdoms, even though no one had a clue who he was.

Someone nudged me, and I batted them away. I'd gotten used to the press of bodies against mine as the tavern filled up and people jostled to get to the bar. That didn't mean I liked it. Couldn't they see that all I wanted to do was get drunk in peace? I didn't want to talk to anyone. I didn't want to hear how wonderful the prince was, when I'd found him anything but, and I certainly didn't want to hear how charming the man who'd shared my bed for a week before he'd moved on to something better was.

The nudge came again, and I turned to give the person a piece of my mind. Except, there was no person. Just two monkeys, one of which kept tugging on my sleeve. No, not two monkeys. That was the ale, my vision eventually adjusting until there was only one. I stared at it. "You're not real. You're a product of my overactive imagination." It opened its mouth and made a familiar chattering sound. I pointed my finger at it. "Making noises doesn't prove anything." I lifted my finger to my temple and on the third attempt, one attempt almost culminating in me poking myself in my eye, I tapped my temple. "Imagination can make noises as well." I frowned. "At least I think so." I turned back to my ale, the bottom of the tankard rapidly approaching.

The barmaid appeared on the other side of the bar with a look of puzzlement on her face. "Is that your monkey?"

I shook my head. "There is no monkey."

She frowned. "But I can see it."

I let her announcement sink slowly in. "Shit!" I turned back to the monkey. "What do you want?" A few people threw me quizzical glances, one helpfully offering the piece of advice that monkeys can't talk so it wasn't going to answer me. Everyone seemed drunk enough not to find it strange that there was a monkey sitting in the tavern. The monkey tugged on my sleeve again. "I'm not going with you."

I gestured at my tankard, my flailing hand almost knocking it over. "Can't you see, I'm busy. And what are you doing here anyway? Well, not here, but"—I poked the monkey in the stomach, the animal shuffling back a few steps—"here. Shouldn't you be busy in the palace telling the prince how pretty he is?"

Alcohol had loosened my tongue, and now that I'd started, I couldn't stop. "Telling him how soft his hair is and how perfectly it falls back into place when he does that toss of his head that he loves doing so much." I sniggered. "He's quite the tosser if you ask me." I used an accompanying lewd hand gesture to illustrate the point, an elderly woman sitting at a table close by blinking at me in shock.

The monkey started chattering again. I stuck my fingers in my ears. "I can't hear you." I took my fingers out of my ears again. "Not that it matters when I can't speak monkey." Wrapping my hands around the tankard, which was still half full, I slumped over the bar. I needed to drink more until I could no longer see, and then there'd be no monkeys to worry about.

A surge of panic suddenly hit me, my hand shooting down to my pocket. I breathed a sigh of relief at the familiar bulge of my money pouch, which was thankfully on the opposite side to the monkey. "Hah! Not this time, you furry monster. Not unless you're going to wrestle me to the ground. And that's more the kind of thing that…" I trailed off, my mind assailed by images of Sebastian and me locked in a passionate embrace. "Never mind."

A woman screamed on the other side of a tavern, a high-pitched scream that made it sound like she was being murdered. "Oh my God, it's him, the prince's new fiancé. I thought they were lying when they said how handsome he is, but he really is."

Her voice was joined by a dozen others, all incredibly enthusiastic, all acting like the king himself had walked in. I glanced to my left to find the monkey gone. Good. I hated that damn thing and its clever little hands. And most of all, I hated the fact that it brought back memories of my first meeting with Sebastian. I kept my eyes fixed on the bar, refusing to look over to where I knew Sebastian was.

A few minutes passed, the cacophony of noise and excitement not having died down one little bit. It seemed to be working its way closer as well. And then fingers closed around my wrist, the grip firm and warm. I steeled myself before looking up into familiar blue eyes. Sebastian smiled, his eyes crinkling at the corners. "Hi."

I didn't say anything. I just blinked at him. And then Sebastian's newly acquired entourage swooped in with a barrage of questions. "What are you doing here?" "What's Prince Montgomery really like?" "Was it love at first sight?" "Did you love him before you rescued him? Is that why you were prepared to face death?" "Is he the love of your life?" "Did you see the dragons?" "Did they breathe fire?" "Did Prince Montgomery send you here to look at this as a possible wedding venue?" I almost laughed at that one, the idea so absurd. The prince had refused to set foot in nicer taverns than this, despite smelling of weasel and looking decidedly worse for wear. He was hardly going to be seen here in all his wedding finery.

The questions were never-ending, a tiny thread of sobriety starting to worm its way into my skull, and with it the beginnings of a headache. And despite the fact that the throng of people was thick enough to mostly block him from my view, Sebastian still hadn't let go of my wrist. Eyeing the gap that had opened up between myself and the door, I gave my wrist an experimental tug. His grip slackened, and I tugged harder, the promise of freedom almost in my grasp. And then his fingers tightened again. "Oh no, you don't! You're not getting away from me that easily."

He appeared at my side, his fingers intertwining with mine. And then Sebastian was the one heading toward the door, dragging me in his wake. The fresh air outside hit me like a physical slap in the face as I was pulled along without any idea where we were going, Sebastian's voice a constant buzz in my ear. "You see, that was exactly what I was trying to avoid by sending the monkey. I've become a huge celebrity in Arrowgarde, which is…" He paused. "Well, it's quite nice if I'm honest. Who doesn't like to be popular? Anyway, I digress…" I could hear the frown in his voice. "*You* were meant to follow the monkey so that we could talk in private."

He glanced back. "Now, we're being followed, and we have to lose them first." He accompanied his words with an increase in pace, and I was forced to jog to keep up with him, something my head and stomach really didn't appreciate. And still Sebastian was talking. "But of course, you wouldn't follow the monkey because it's you, and you're far too stubborn to ever do as you're told."

"I hate the monkey."

Sebastian took a sharp right, closely followed by a turn to the left. "You didn't need to forge a meaningful relationship with the monkey. The monkey was a message. One that I figured you'd understand."

"I understood it. I just chose to ignore it." I sounded sulky even to my own ears.

Another sharp left turn. "Of course, you did. You're Jack Shaw. You do what you want and to hell with everyone else."

There was a strange note in Sebastian's voice, one that had me trying to see his face. Only, we were moving too fast for that to be possible. "Where are we going?"

"Here."

Sebastian pulled me into a sweet-smelling alcove, the scent coming from a multitude of colorful flowers threaded into the metal latticework. It seemed to be some sort of gazebo. God knows how Sebastian had known it was here. Or perhaps he hadn't. Perhaps it had been nothing but blind luck. I hadn't been able to see the entrance, which meant anyone following us wouldn't be able to either. Therefore, we were alone. Just me and Sebastian. No monkeys. No Prince Montgomery. No lurking danger. Just us.

He steered me over to other side of the gazebo, his hands resting on my hips as his eyes searched my face. "What happened to you at the palace? Why did you disappear like that? One minute you were there, and the next you were gone! Why would you just leave?"

"Leave!" A bubbling fury threatened to rise up in me, and I was forced to push it down. "They wouldn't let me in. I was left standing at the gate, and *you* didn't even notice." The last bit came out far more accusatory than I'd intended it to.

Sebastian's features softened. "I did notice." I raised an eyebrow, and he grimaced. "Maybe not at that exact moment, but not long after." His fingers tightened on my hips, and it occurred to me that I really should be telling him to take his hands off me, that it wasn't appropriate for someone who was engaged to be touching someone other than their fiancé in such an intimate way. I didn't, though. I didn't say anything. "And then I couldn't come and look for you because I didn't think the king and queen would take too kindly to me telling them that their welcome reception had to wait."

"I bet they were happy to see their son again."

Sebastian smiled. "Ecstatic. And incredibly grateful."

A lump formed in my throat, and I had to cough to clear it. "So they've embraced you as their future son-in-law?" I was proud of myself for managing to say it without stumbling over the words.

Sebastian's head tipped to the side. "I'm not marrying the prince."

I contemplated his words for a moment. "They vetoed it."

He shook his head with a slight smile on his face. "Oh no, they were only too happy to join the two of us together in holy matrimony. There was already talk of who they were going to invite from the thirteen kingdoms, and the best candidate for the wedding suits. I had to explain to them, *and* Prince Montgomery, who was less than happy about it, incidentally, that despite the great honor they were bestowing on me that it wasn't going to happen, either now or in the future."

"But…?" The pounding in my head had grown more intense, and I wasn't entirely sure it had anything to do with the alcohol.

Sebastian moved closer, close enough that I could feel the heat of his body. "I was never going to marry the prince."

"Leofric said you wouldn't."

Sebastian gave a little laugh. "He knows me too well."

"So why did you say you were going to?"

Sebastian looked a little sheepish. "We didn't know each other very well, then. It was always the reward for rescuing him. Would you have believed me if I said I was doing it for purely altruistic reasons?"

I tipped my head back and stared at him. "How much did you ask for instead of his hand in marriage?"

Sebastian looked away. "I thought you were drunk, but your mind seems just as sharp as ever."

"I'm sobering up."

"We should pour another drink down you."

I grabbed his chin and forced his head back to center, so he had no choice but to meet my gaze. "How much?"

His lips twitched. "The next ransom payment."

I laughed. "Oh yeah, very altruistic." I thought about it for a moment. "Half of that should be mine."

He raised an eyebrow. "Half? Without me, there would have been no eagle to escape from the tower, and there would have been no weasel to get past the basilisks."

"Without me, the prince would never have gone anywhere near the eagle. Or the weasel."

Sebastian started to laugh, and I glared at him. "What's so funny?"

He shook his head. "I don't think I'll ever be able to rid myself of the image of you pushing a prince headfirst into a weasel. You were somewhat brutal."

I narrowed my eyes at him. "Just because, unlike some people, I didn't treat him like he was a precious flower."

"One of us needed to be nice to him. He would have run off, if not."

I poked him in the chest. "And while we're on the subject, I don't remember you informing the prince that you weren't going to marry him. In fact, I remember you going along with it just fine, especially the kissing part."

"He kissed me."

My jaw tightened. "Yeah, that seems to happen a lot, doesn't it? Cassemir. The prince."

Sebastian grinned. "Careful there, Jack. Or I might start thinking you're jealous."

"Jealous!" My laugh was nothing short of scornful. "Hardly. I just couldn't believe that you were spending time on that while danger lurked around every corner. And I don't think you should lead people on."

Sebastian's gaze scoured my face. "Who are we talking about here? Prince Montgomery or you?"

I lifted my chin. "Prince Montgomery. You let him believe that you were going to marry him. And you spent last night with him. I might not like the man, but that's hardly playing fair."

Sebastian blinked. "Hang on! Let's get one thing straight. I did *not* spend last night in the prince's room. I slept outside in the corridor, which was decidedly uncomfortable. He invited me to his room, but I turned him down.

I wanted to spend the night with you, but you closed the door in my face. Remember?"

I remembered, and I suddenly felt like a child. A jealous child. That didn't mean I was going to admit it, though. There were a lot of things that neither Sebastian nor I admitted. It was just the way we were. I held his gaze. "Now what?"

Sebastian moved even closer, his chest pressing against mine. "We find a tavern. We get a room." His nose brushed mine, his head tilting one way, mine automatically going the other. "And then we see what happens." His breath skating over my lips was like a caress all of its own.

I wound my hands in Sebastian's hair. His were still on my hips. "You'd rather sleep with me than a prince?" I was asking for a lot, but I needed to hear it.

Sebastian's smile was slow and lazy. "I guess so. I've always had strange tastes."

I blamed the alcohol in my veins for pushing it that bit further. "But Prince Montgomery was so pretty."

"You're pretty."

I moved even closer, only a whisker of space between our lips now. "His personality was rather objectionable, though."

"His personality *was* rather objectionable."

That was enough for me to close the space. I put everything I had into that kiss, Sebastian not holding back either until we were both hard and gasping for breath. And then we kissed some more, lips curving into a smile and hands grasping at clothes in search of bare skin.

It felt like coming home, like the world had clicked back into place and everything had returned to the way it should be. We were still on borrowed time. I wasn't fooling myself about that, but it seemed like I had a little more of it. And I planned to make the most of it.

CHAPTER TWENTY

SEBASTIAN

We headed to the most down-market tavern we could find on the very edge of Arrowgarde, the place so dingy and dark that it was difficult to make out what the décor consisted of, assuming it even had any. I didn't pay any attention to its name, or to the man behind the counter who allocated us a room, flicking a couple of gold coins his way that were probably enough to buy us a week under its roof in a place like this. If Jack's twitchiness was anything to go by, he was as eager as I was for the two of us to be alone.

Our reward for slumming it was that no one raised so much as an eyebrow at our presence. The clientele of this tavern weren't people interested in the latest gossip from the palace. And I doubted any of them gave a damn about the return of Prince Montgomery. That suited us just fine.

The door to our room had barely closed behind us before we were kissing again, Jack's mouth pleasingly eager beneath mine. It had hurt when I'd found him gone without so much as a farewell. The hours after that had been a blur of forced politeness where my mind had been on other things, or one thing in particular, to be exact: a green-eyed farm boy whose words were frequently as sharp as his mind. I'd downplayed the royal family's reaction to my refusal to marry Prince Montgomery. The king and queen had regarded me with abject confusion, as if my words were nothing but a string of nonsense they couldn't believe were coming out of my mouth.

Compared to Prince Montgomery himself, they'd taken it well. He'd acted like I'd already walked him to the altar before making an announcement to the assembled congregation that I couldn't marry him. His sulky countenance was reminiscent of a child who had lost its favorite toy. He'd only calmed down when his parents had pointed out that they couldn't force me to marry him, that when all was said and done, I had still rescued him.

In the end, Prince Montgomery had stopped muttering about execution—my name joining Jack's on the chopping block for a short period of time—and had flounced out, leaving me with a pair of royals clearly embarrassed by their son's actions, the king claiming that his son had been under a great deal of strain and wasn't usually like that. I wasn't entirely sure I believed him.

The monkey had made it easier to search for Jack, his nimble steps covering far more ground in half the time than I could have managed without him. Actually, given my new level of fame, and the people's belief that I was going to marry their prince, I probably wouldn't have made it out of the first tavern. The surprise had been finding Jack so deep in his cups, but then, that was Jack all over—infuriatingly and endearingly unpredictable.

And now here we were, tongues moving together in a sweet slide and bodies pressed so close I could feel every muscle of Jack's. I slid my hands down his back, the fabric bunching under my fingers beyond frustrating. I wanted skin. And I wanted it three seconds ago.

Jack lifted his mouth for a few seconds. "Naked."

It seemed that for once we were in perfect accord. I nodded. "Naked."

The next few minutes were a flurry of motion with clothes removed by any available hands, depending on who got there first and what assistance was needed when fingers didn't prove dexterous enough to complete the task in record time. It didn't matter as long as the end result was the same. It still took longer than it should have done, both of us pausing at regular intervals to kiss whenever lips came into close proximity.

Finally, we were both naked, arousal hanging between us like a curtain of intensity and anticipation. Jack's gaze lifted from his lengthy appraisal of my hard cock to meet mine, a mixture of lust and calculation in his eyes. "I want you to fuck me."

Oxygen froze in my chest, my lungs forgetting what they were supposed to do with it. We'd never gone that far. We'd sucked and we'd stroked each other to climax, but penetration had been off the table so far. I wanted it badly, but I did have one slight objection to it. "I want you to fuck *me*."

Jack let out a snort, his eyes creasing with mirth. "Seriously! Can we not agree on that either?"

I met his smile with one of my own. "It appears not. I think if we ever start agreeing, it would be a sign of the world coming to an end." A moment of inspiration came to me. "We could toss a coin." I didn't wait for Jack's response to the idea before going for my money pouch, the folds of my discarded trousers finally giving it up.

Seating myself on the floor cross-legged, I extracted a coin and held it up. Jack wasn't looking at the coin, which I might have been fine with if his attention had been on my cock, but it was on my money pouch, his expression somewhat speculative. "How much?"

I played dumb. "How much, what?"

He rolled his eyes, one hand lowering to give his cock an idle stroke. "How much did they give you?"

I gave him a slow smile. "You're obsessed with money."

"*I'm* obsessed with money. Says Mr. I don't do anything for free."

I regarded him with growing amusement. "How much money have *you* got left, Jack?"

His brow creased with a lack of understanding. "What's that got to do with anything?"

My smile grew wider. "Let me see, after the tournament you had twenty gold coins. I gave you ten gold coins in Brittleharbor under the mistaken assumption that you were leaving. You kept those gold coins." He opened his mouth to protest, and I carried on before he got the opportunity. "Then there was the twenty gold coins of Mad Dog's that I gave you."

The frown still hadn't shifted from Jack's face. He really didn't know where I was going with this. I was going to enjoy this. Even though I already knew the total, I raised a hand and pretended to count. "So that's fifty. I found you drinking the contents of a tavern… which must have cost you a couple of gold coins. Which… not to go off on a tangent, but you must have amazing alcohol tolerance because you've all but sobered up."

Jack shrugged. "Ale is stronger in Riverbrook. A lot stronger."

"So"—I waved a hand at his discarded clothes a few feet away—"I'd wager anything that you have forty-eight gold coins in there."

Jack kept a suspicious eye on me as he reached for his pouch and started to count the coins, my smile of triumph when he got to forty-eight matched in intensity by the force of his glower.

He gave another shrug. "So you can do a few calculations. So what? Am I meant to be impressed?"

"You? Impressed? That'll be the day. You've completely missed my point, haven't you?"

Jack gave a dramatic sigh. "Which I'm sure *eventually* you'll get to if I don't fall asleep first."

I leaned forward. "Apart from tonight, where you were forced to spend money because I wasn't around, you haven't spent a single penny this whole trip. I've paid for everything. Yet... you claim *I'm* the one obsessed with money. You hoard so much you'd put a dragon to shame."

"Not true."

I dropped my gaze to the coins still in Jack's hand. "Proven to be true." I watched with growing amusement as he placed all the coins back in his money pouch and knotted the drawstring tightly. "That's it, make sure none of them fall out. Did it hurt when you had to pay for drinks tonight?"

Jack made a monumental effort to keep a straight face. He was successful for a few seconds before giving up the fight, his lips curling into a smile. "Actually, yes, it did. Especially when I didn't get a chance to drink two gold coins' worth before you swaggered in—"

"Swaggered?"

Jack nodded. "Definitely a swagger." He deepened his voice. "Oh, look at me everyone! I rescued your prince single-handedly without any help whatsoever. You should bow down before me and worship the ground I walk on."

"I didn't ask them to treat me like a hero."

"You didn't ask them not to. And..." Jack held up a finger. "You could have stopped the adoration at any point by letting them know you weren't going to marry their prince after all."

"They probably would have thrown things at me for daring to turn their prince down."

"Exactly." Jack's grin was a study in triumph. "I would have enjoyed that."

"You'd probably have joined in."

"Undoubtedly. There were some good rocks outside that tavern. Very pointy. Very hard. A good size for throwing."

I tilted my chin up and turned my head to the side so he could see my profile. "Not my face, though. You'd ruin my good looks. You wouldn't want that, would you? Not when you're going to fuck me."

Jack shook his head. "You're going to fuck me."

And just like that we were back to where we'd started. I held the coin up again. "Heads, I fuck you. Tails, you fuck me."

I went to throw the coin up in the air, Jack holding his hand up to stall me. "Wait!"

I froze. "What?"

Jack curled his fingers inwards in a clear instruction to hand it over. "I want to check the coin first. You cheat."

"I do not!"

Jack snatched the coin from my fingers, subjecting it to a thorough examination which included biting it. "I know a certain orc who would dispute that in the strongest of terms."

While Jack was busy with the coin, I drank in the sight of his naked body, letting my gaze linger on his firm musculature and his pretty cock, which despite the delay hadn't flagged in the slightest. But then neither had mine. Which begged the question why we were talking instead of doing something far more interesting. Leaning forward, I captured Jack's lips in a searing kiss. He melted into it and while his eyes were closed, I stole the coin back. "Call it, farm boy, seeing as you're worried about me cheating."

Jack's eyes narrowed. "Heads, you fuck me. Tails, I fuck you."

"So exactly what I already said, then." I flipped the coin in the air, letting it land on the floor rather than catching it. We narrowly avoided banging heads as we both lurched forwards to peer at it. I pulled a face at the result. "Heads."

Jack let out a whoop, and I tried to summon disappointment that I'd lost. Except, as I watched him grab oil and position himself face down on the bed, it was hard to see that there was any loser in this situation. Not when I was about to experience the pleasure of doing all the dirty things to him that I'd dreamed about. For a moment, the surge of lust rendered me immobile, and all I could do was stare at him, the curves of his back and shoulders, and the gentle swell of his ass all illuminated by the lit fire in the hearth.

Green eyes found mine across the room as Jack turned his head to the side. "I hate to break it to you, Sebastian, but your cock's not that long. You're going to have to come a bit closer."

I got to my feet. "Oh sorry, I didn't realize we were on a time crunch. Have you got somewhere else you need to be? Another tavern to drink dry perhaps? Or did you meet a nice goat this afternoon, and I'm just the warm up act?" Climbing onto the bed, I straddled Jack's calves so that his body was laid out before me. "Which reminds me, it feels like an opportune time to revisit that statement you once made. What was it you said? Something about how you wouldn't sleep with me if I was the last man left, that you'd turn to farmyard animals first. Have I recalled that correctly?"

"Shut up." There was laughter in Jack's voice. "And we already had sex. Or have you forgotten about that? Am I that easy to forget?"

I pressed my palms against his back and trailed my fingers along the length of his spine, Jack shifting slightly under my touch. I rode the wave of anticipation that begged me to go further, to cup the twin mounds of delicious flesh in my palms. Not yet. We had all night and I intended to savor this. "You're not forgettable at all. Far from it. In fact, you might be the most unforgettable person I've ever met. And I've met a lot of people."

Jack went silent. So much so that I gave him a little shake. "Are you going to sleep?"

"No. Just thinking."

"About?"

"Things."

It was like trying to get blood out of a stone. "Maybe I can give you some more interesting things to think about."

"Maybe you can."

I lowered my lips to Jack's back and slowly kissed my way down his spine, his skin bearing a slightly salty tang that I couldn't get enough of. I paused before going where I wanted to go, riding that same wave of restraint. Instead, I kissed my way back up over the taut skin, continuing over his shoulder until I could capture his lips, my throbbing cock notching itself perfectly in the space between his ass cheeks. Jack writhed beneath me, the message about what he wanted only too clear.

"Bass!"

I stopped dead, my lips hovering by his ear. Despite me asking him to more times than I could recall, it was the first time he'd shortened my name. Now that he had, I was surprised to find I didn't like it. Not one little bit. "Call me Sebastian."

Jack's laugh was tinged with frustration. "Seriously?"

"Yeah. Everyone calls me Bass. You're the only one that calls me Sebastian."

"Sebastian." The name was said on a breathy release, tendrils of expectation and yearning curling around my cock.

I smiled, and I finally allowed my hands and lips to stray to Jack's delicious ass, worshipping it with every fiber of my being. For this moment in time, Jack's ass was my altar, and I was the all too willing acolyte who would make it my aim in life to revere it.

The first touch of my tongue on Jack's hole had him bucking off the bed. I dived in, the taste musky and tangy, but unmistakably Jack. I got him good and wet before covering my fingers with oil and using them in combination with my tongue. By the time I was satisfied he was ready, Jack was only capable of making little mews of pleasure, his hips lifting off the bed in a silent plea for more, and his body drenched in sweat. Well, he didn't need to worry. I was going to give him more, and I was going to give it to him straightaway, before I came without getting inside him like some sort of gauche teen that had never been with a man before.

It felt like entering heaven as I pushed my oiled cock inside him, Jack's hips tipped up at the perfect angle to facilitate entry. His body yielded easily to the pressure, and in no time at all, I was seated fully inside him, the two of us both quiet as we adjusted to the new experience. He was tight and hot, and most of all, this wasn't just anyone. It was Jack, a fact that made the whole thing more satisfying. Jack, who had told me he would never sleep with me. Jack, who had refused to even share a bed with me at first. Jack, who had nearly left and gone his own way at Brittleharbor. I took a deep breath. "Ready?"

"More than ready."

My thrusts were gentle at first, but I could only keep that up for so long, a tingle in my balls broadcasting that this wasn't going to be any slow and lazy fuck. I pulled out, Jack protesting in broken words that made little sense. "Turn over." I wanted to see his face. I wanted those green eyes on me when I spilled deep in his body.

"Why?"

I let out a strangled laugh. Of course, he wouldn't do as I asked. Why would Jack in the middle of sex be any different than Jack the rest of the time. Unable to find the words I needed to explain, I settled for tugging on his arm. "Please."

Jack turned over, his eyes on me—just as I'd wanted—as I lifted his thighs and pushed back into him. We moved together, Jack's hand wrapping around his cock and jerking himself off as our movements grew more frenzied, both of us hurtling toward an orgasm that neither of us could have avoided even if we'd wanted to. Jack's breath was coming in tiny little gasps now, sometimes interspersed with the occasional exhalation of "yes, Sebastian, just like that" and "don't stop."

I kissed him hard, my hips a piston to drive my cock deep inside his pliant body.

Jack's free hand roamed over my back before it curled around my ass to force me harder into him. Had I once thought he was a prude? Of course, I'd also thought he was very bossy. Perhaps in this instance, one heavily outweighed the other.

Jack was close, his hand moving faster and his body sucking me in even deeper. When he came, he threw his head back, his groan of satisfaction an erotic echo around the room. I managed three more thrusts before I gave in to the torrent of sensation that washed over me. It dragged me under like a wave bashing a ship against the rocks before finally setting me free to listen to my own ragged pants, Jack's fingers stroking over my skin. I closed my eyes as I buried my face in his neck and allowed myself the momentary fantasy that we could stay like this forever.

Jack was the first to stir, my weight probably becoming too much for him. My cock slipped free as I rolled to the side to prop myself up on one elbow, my eyes glued to his face. Post sex, he was even more gorgeous, all flushed and languorous, the sight bringing a self-satisfied smile to my face that I'd been the one to make him look like that.

His eyes narrowed on me. "And you can stop looking at me like that."

I tried. I really did. In the end, unable to wipe the smile off my face, I rolled onto my back and stared up at the ceiling, Jack doing the same next to me.

Minutes ticked by before Jack let out a little sigh. "I have to go home. Back to Riverbrook, I mean."

The words hit me like an actual physical blow. "When?"

"Tomorrow."

"You can't spend a few more days here?" I lifted an arm to gesture around the room. "Well, maybe not here as in this tavern, because both of us deserve better, but maybe in Lastwick."

I felt Jack's gaze on me, but kept my eyes trained on the ceiling. "You don't want to stay in Arrowgarde?"

I let out a snort. "Are you kidding? By tomorrow, I'll be the most unpopular man who ever walked the streets, once it gets around that I turned down the prince."

"From hero to zero in twenty-four hours."

I could hear the smile in Jack's voice. "Don't sound so pleased about it."

Jack chuckled. "Maybe I should marry him. I was heavily involved in his rescue, after all, no matter how much you might try and pretend it was all you."

I tried to imagine it for a moment and couldn't. "Yeah, I don't think Prince Montgomery will go for that somehow. He's more likely to remember that he threatened to execute you. Then I'll have to rescue you, and it will turn into this huge unnecessary thing, and then we'll both be fugitives."

"That's true." There was a momentary pause. "I do need to go home, though. I've been gone so long that my mother will be worried sick."

I rolled my head to the side to look at him. "We'll leave tomorrow."

"We?" There was a note of caution in Jack's voice.

I smiled. "Of course, we. I'm hardly going to let you make the journey alone, am I? You'd probably get yourself kidnapped by bandits again, or neck deep in some other sort of trouble that doesn't bear thinking about."

"So you're going to escort me back to Riverbrook?"

"I am."

"All the way?"

"All the way."

It was Jack's turn to prop himself up on one elbow, his gaze warm on my face. "I'm not going by ship. I'm never setting foot on a ship again if I can help it."

"No ship."

"You promise?"

I smiled at him but didn't say anything.

"Sebastian?" There was a note of warning in his voice.

I blinked at him innocently. "Yes, farm boy."

Something passed across Jack's face. "I can never work out if that's an insult or…?"

"Or?"

He looked slightly sheepish. "An endearment."

I leaned over to plant a kiss on his lips, my cock already starting to indicate that it would be up for another round before the night was over. "It's definitely an endearment."

"Oh!"

I laughed. "Is that all you've got to say about it?"

Jack closed his eyes. "Yes, because I'm asleep."

"You're talking in your sleep, then."

"I may as well. You do. What are you going to regale me with tonight? Orc sex? Memories of Leofric? Or something else?"

I gathered him to me and covered us both up. "I don't know, but I'm sure you'll let me know in the morning. It will of course be heavily embellished and possibly an outright lie, but I'm sure it will be entertaining nevertheless. It usually is."

Jack made a sound in his throat that disputed that, but the fact that he didn't bother to argue told me he was already half asleep. I kissed his neck. "Night, Jack."

"Night, Sebastian."

CHAPTER TWENTY-ONE

JACK

"So, this is Riverbrook?"

I nodded, my throat thick with so many different emotions that speech suddenly seemed like the most difficult thing in the world. We were standing at the top of a hill, the path leading straight down to Riverbrook. My home that I hadn't seen for weeks was laid out in front of me, every field, every house painfully familiar.

That wasn't the only thing getting to me, though. It had been six days since Sebastian had announced his intention to escort me back to Riverbrook. And I'd spent those six days refusing to think about this moment. But here it was, and there was no avoiding it any longer. Time was finally up, and we would go our separate ways.

I would go home and return to a predictable life of farming, and Sebastian would... well, do whatever Sebastian did. Probably embark on more hair-raising escapades that would almost get him killed. How did you say goodbye to the man who you'd started off hating, but who had gradually wormed his way into your affections and become both a friend and lover? How did you pretend that it didn't hurt? Maybe the answer was that I didn't, that for once I needed to be honest, no matter how difficult the words might be, and how vulnerable they would leave me. Maybe if I did that, Sebastian would come back and see me some time. I filled my lungs with air and released it slowly to muster up courage. "Sebastian, I just wanted to say—"

"Where's your farm?"

"What?"

Sebastian waved a hand at the vista spread out in front of us. "Which one is yours?"

I lifted a hand to point. "That one, over there. You can see the yellow of the wheat I planted. The building on the right-hand side is my house."

"Who's been looking after it for you?"

"My brother, Dillon. We farm it together. One of my other brothers will have helped out if need be while I was gone."

There was a faint smile on Sebastian's lips, but I had no idea what it was for. I tried again. "Sebastian...?"

"How many brothers do you have?"

"Three, and two sisters."

"Big family. Are they like you?"

That last question had been asked with a sly look sent my way which immediately made me bristle. "Depends what you mean by that?"

"Feisty. Opinionated. Able to stand up for themselves."

I couldn't decide whether Sebastian's description of me was meant as a compliment or an insult. Knowing him, there were probably elements of both.

Sebastian threw a glance toward the sky, the sun already low. "You should probably go."

The words were delivered so casually, and with so little inflection that something cold settled in my chest. That was it? After all these weeks, that was all I got? We'd spent the previous night in bed laughing and making love. How did we go from that to this... nothingness?

Well, if Sebastian could be so blasé about our parting, then so could I. I had no intention of letting him see that his casual dismissal bothered me. Not in the slightest. I pulled my shoulders back and refused to look anywhere but straight ahead. "Well, it's been..."

"Yeah, it has. Take care, Jack."

"You too."

I started walking, my heart thudding in my chest and my stomach roiling like I'd eaten something that had disagreed with me. What would I see if I looked back? Was Sebastian watching me? Or would he have already turned away, ready to get on with the rest of his life? Unable to face the possibility of the latter, I didn't look back. It was best not to know.

With early evening turning to dusk, Riverbrook was quiet, farming having finished for the day. Despite that, I took the long route. I wasn't ready to face the cheerful greetings of friends if I took the path that led past Riverbrook's one and only tavern. A lump settled in my throat as my parents' farmhouse came into view. It looked exactly as it had when I'd left, the painted wood bearing no evidence of my weeks away.

I stopped in front of the door, steeling myself for what was about to come before I pushed the door open to step straight into the kitchen. My mother turned from the stove, her green eyes so similar to my own going wide, and the pie she held in her hands slipping from her fingers to crash to the floor. Picking my way carefully over lumps of broken pie crust and shattered clay, I made my way toward her. "Hi, Mum. I'm home."

She finally broke free from her frozen stillness for long enough to wrap me up in a warm, rose-scented embrace that was so achingly familiar it brought tears to my eyes. By that time, more people had been summoned to the kitchen by the call of breaking crockery, and I was passed from person to person, each embrace more crushing than the one that had come before.

So many questions were thrown at me simultaneously that I didn't get a chance to answer them until much later, when we all finally sat down, and I relayed as much of my adventure as I could bear to tell. My mother shed a few tears when I reached the part about Annabelle setting sail. My father presented more of a stiff upper lip, but there was no hiding the sadness in his eyes.

None of us could make sense of why Annabelle had left to go to sea, or why she'd crept away without a word to anyone. Various theories were thrown around but none of them seemed like a good fit. We talked long into the night and when the sun started creeping over the horizon, I slept in the room I'd grown up in instead of returning home. I was in no rush to return to a cold, empty house. At least here, there was enough noise and commotion to stop me dwelling on things I didn't want to think about.

The days that followed were long as I threw myself back into farming. And maybe I did work myself even harder so that I could fall into bed with an exhaustion that meant I fell asleep straight away. For the most part, it worked. If I was busy, there was no time to think about a certain blond-haired, blue-eyed man whose teasing and constant digs had become as natural as breathing to me, and about how quiet life seemed without him around. I was still avoiding the tavern, knowing that there would be questions I didn't want to answer about my time away. I'd have to face them eventually, but for the time being, it was just me and the animals.

My brother, Dillon, came to stand next to me at the fence. "What's going on, Jack."

"What's going on?" I pointed to the field of wheat stretching as far as the eye could see, its ears swaying gently in the breeze. "The crop is healthy, and it will be ready to be harvested in a few weeks' time. The sheep are well, and lambs were plentiful this year. The chickens are laying more eggs than ever. And the goats…" There was a hitch in my voice I couldn't help as I said the word, a flood of memories assailing me at the mention of that specific animal. I shook my head, my train of thought completely gone. "You did a great job while I was gone."

Dillon let out a gusty sigh. "Thanks, but you know that wasn't what I was referring to."

"No?"

"No." He turned his head to study my face. "You're back, but it's like you're not really back, like you're just going through the motions. What else happened that you're not saying? Did you think we wouldn't notice that there were huge holes in your story? When do we get the old Jack back?"

Something solidified in my chest. The same something that I'd been working so hard to keep at bay for days. I didn't need Dillon waltzing in and undoing all my hard work. "I don't know what you mean. Nothing happened." Dillon stared at me, and I wilted slightly under the scrutiny. "I'm fine."

"Are you?"

I forced a smile. "Never been better." I picked up the basket full of eggs that I'd set down a few minutes before and backed away a couple of steps. "Mum needs these. I said I'd take them to her."

"I'm sure she can wait a few minutes. We should talk about…"

But I'd already turned away, my steps long and hurried to put as much distance as I could between myself and my brother's far too inquisitive questions.

My mum was in the kitchen when I arrived, her hands full of freshly baked bread rolls. She turned with a smile as I came in through the door. "Perfect timing, Jack… Can you pass me a plate? A big one."

I went over to the cupboard and opened the door, frowning when I couldn't see the one I was looking for. "Where's the blue one? Did you break it?" I passed over a white one instead. It would be a squeeze to get them all on, but it was the biggest one available so it would have to do.

My mother took the plate and started arranging the bread rolls carefully. "The blue one?" Her forehead creased, but it only lasted for a few seconds before comprehension dawned on her face. "Oh, I gave that one to Sebastian."

I blinked. Once. Twice. Three times. "Sebastian?"

My mother nodded without lifting her head. Her lips pursed as she ran out of room on the plate and was forced to start balancing the bread rolls on top of each other. "Yes, Sebastian."

"Who's Sebastian?"

She did lift her head, then, a little laugh escaping from her throat. "'Who's Sebastian?' He's *your* friend, sweetheart. It should be me asking you that, not the other way around."

Perhaps I was dreaming, and the day had never started. That was the only explanation I could think of that made sense.

My mother added the last bread roll to the plate and stood back with her hands on her hips to admire her handiwork. "There." She wiped her hands on her apron. "I'll make tea." She turned to the kettle, seemingly oblivious to how lost for words I was, the name Sebastian still ricocheting round in my head. Luckily, my mother had always been good at carrying on a one-sided conversation. "He's a lovely young man."

"Sebastian?"

"Yes, Sebastian." She placed the kettle on the stove. "I was so surprised when he came and introduced himself."

"He came and introduced himself?"

"Yes, the other day. Such a polite, young man. We had tea together. So modest as well. He really played down the way he came to your rescue several times."

"He came to my rescue?" In the absence of anything better to say, I'd taken to parroting my mother's words. Not that she seemed to have noticed.

"So brave."

"Sebastian?"

She turned with a slight frown. "Of course. Are you okay, Jack? You seem to be struggling with following the conversation today."

"I'm just..." I shook my head and let out a breath. "Tell me more about your conversation with Sebastian."

"Well... as soon as I discovered that he was staying in that dreadful place, I sorted out some things for him. It was the least I could do. Plates, cutlery, some food. I told him that he could stay here, but he wouldn't hear of it. I offered him your old room. He did take a look at it, but in the end, he said he was happy where he was. I was surprised you hadn't asked him to stay with you." She shot me a reproachful look. "I thought I'd brought you up better than that to let your friends struggle."

"Is that what he called himself, my friend?" My mother's lips twitched in a way that told me that Sebastian might have said that, but that she'd gotten the impression nevertheless that there was more than friendship between us. "Where's he staying exactly?"

She turned, finally seeming to pick up on my confusion. "You didn't know he was here?"

I shook my head.

"Oh!" She opened her mouth and then closed it again, a few seconds of silence stretching between us before she finally spoke. "He didn't mention that."

"He wouldn't."

"He's staying at the old Smith residence at the edge of the village."

I frowned. The house she was referring to had been abandoned for years and had long since fallen into a state of disrepair. There was constant talk of knocking it down and re-using the land, but nobody ever seemed to get round to it. While I'd never had any reason to venture inside, it certainly didn't look habitable from the outside. "That place only has half a roof."

My mother nodded sagely. "I know, the poor boy. He insists it's fine, though. He says he likes being able to lie in the living room and look at the stars."

I was only half listening to her, thoughts bouncing chaotically around in my head. Sebastian was here. In Riverbrook. And he'd been here all along. But he hadn't told me. What did that mean? I guess there was only one person who could answer that question, and I didn't intend to waste any time in asking him it. That, and quite a few other questions. And they couldn't wait while I drank tea and made polite conversation with my mother. "I have to go."

"Are you going to see Sebastian?"

"I certainly am." The words came out a lot curter than I'd intended them to.

My mother smiled. "Oh good. I bet he'll appreciate the company." She removed the eggs from the basket I'd brought her and replaced them with half of the bread rolls from the plate. "Take these for him and tell him that I'll bring him a nice hot meal tomorrow, and that extra blanket that we talked about."

Anger buzzed beneath my skin as I strode to the edge of the village, the basket banging against my thigh with every step. What the fuck did Sebastian think he was playing at? He'd set up home here. *Here,* of all places. Why? What did he hope to gain from it? I'd seen Sebastian in action. He was a traveler. He was a man who thrived on challenge, who was only happy if he was putting himself at risk in some way. He needed danger like he needed oxygen. The only danger in Riverbrook was the distinct possibility of dying of boredom. Was my life a game to him? Was that what this was?

I did my best to ignore the other emotion, the one that insisted on dampening the fury. Relief. There was no other word for it. I was going to get to see Sebastian again. I was going to get to look into those pretty blue eyes. I'd be able to talk to him, when I'd spent days resigning myself to the idea that the past few weeks had been nothing but an amusing and passionate aberration, and that our paths were unlikely to cross again. My feelings were fluctuating so wildly that I wasn't sure whether I was going to kiss him or kill him. Or kiss him and then kill him.

Smoke curling from the chimney as I got close was an indication that Sebastian had managed to get a fire going in the hearth. As for the man himself, he was outside with his back to me, the sight bringing me to a sudden halt. He had an axe in his hands, the muscles in his back and shoulders bunching as he brought it down time after time to split a tree trunk into logs. He paused for a moment, rolling his shoulders back and then lifting his arm to wipe the sweat off his brow. "Are you just going to stand and watch me?"

I jerked my head up, scouring the surrounding trees until I finally located it—a tiny bird sitting on a branch acting as Sebastian's lookout. Why he thought he needed one in Riverbrook, I had no idea. But then, I guess some habits were hard to break. I'd been caught out again, so busy admiring his physical attributes that I hadn't even thought to check.

Heat rose to my cheeks as I positioned myself in front of him, those familiar blue eyes fastening on my face, and the corner of his lips tilting up in a smirk I knew only too well. There was a brief tussle of emotions in my chest, and then anger won out, my words coming out clipped and imbued with a spark of fury that threatened to grow into an inferno if I let it. "What the fuck do you think you're doing?"

Sebastian's brow furrowed, his gaze dropping to the axe in his hand, and then to what was left of the log. "Chopping wood. I need it for the fire. It gets cold at night with the big hole in the roof."

"Chopping wood!" I stared at him. "I can see you're chopping wood. I have eyes in my head. I meant… what are you doing in Riverbrook? Why are you…?"

I cast around for the right word. "Why are you *worming* your way into my mother's good books? Why were you at the house sniffing around my old room? You're meant to be long gone. Yet"—I lifted a hand to wave it down the length of his body—"here you are." I jerked my head at the tiny house behind us that I was pretty sure was leaning drunkenly to one side, as if it might give up the fight and keel over at any given time. There were signs of missing planks having been patched up. Sebastian's handiwork, I presumed. "You can't possibly mean to stay here."

Sebastian turned to look at the house. "Why not? We've slept in worse places."

There was that word "we" again. It triggered something delicate and raw in my chest, something that fluttered and threatened to break free. Sebastian continued. "We slept out in the open, remember, several times."

"We didn't have any choice. *You've* got a choice." I glanced down, almost surprised to see the basket at my feet, even though I'd been the one to leave it there. "My mother sent you some bread fresh out of the oven."

"Did she? She's such a sweetheart."

I bent down and extracted a roll. Weighing it in my hand, I straightened, and then threw it straight at Sebastian. Taken by surprise, it hit him square in the forehead. His mouth dropped open. "Ow! I don't think she wanted you to throw it at me. Your mother is a lovely woman. I've never gotten the impression that she's prone to acts of violence, unlike her—"

Forced to duck as I threw another roll, he didn't get to finish his sentence. This one hit him on the cheek. He backed away a step as I went for a third. "You're throwing bread rolls at a man with an axe. Are you crazy?"

I didn't know what I was, but I knew that it was making me feel better, each missile releasing a bit of the tension that had built up in my chest as it left my hand. The third hit him in the stomach. I swore as the fourth skimmed his shoulder. And then Sebastian was on me, the axe abandoned on the ground as his fingers wrapped around my wrists to stop me from pulling more bread rolls from the basket. "Stop assaulting me with bread. Your mother will ask me what I thought of it. I don't want to have to lie to her. I suspect she'd see straight through it."

My lips twitched. "You'd be right about that."

Fingers still gripping my wrists, Sebastian started pulling me toward the house. "Let's go inside. We can talk in private."

I made an attempt to dig my heels in, but he was stronger. "Do I get any say in this?"

"No. And you know I'll throw you over my shoulder if I need to."

"Bully."

"I'm not the one who just used bread as a weapon. I guess I'm lucky you didn't bring your bow."

"You are. Incredibly lucky."

Once we were inside, Sebastian let go. I put some distance between us as I examined my surroundings. It was pretty bad. The house had an intact floor, but that was about all it had going for it. The walls hadn't fared quite so well, with numerous gaps that hadn't yet been patched up. And that was before you got to the roof, sky visible from at least half of the one-room building.

A pile of blankets lay in the corner closest to the fire where there was actually a roof. There was a wooden table and chairs, but no other furniture. I pulled one of the chairs over to the fire and sat on it. After a few seconds, Sebastian pulled the other one next to mine. We were both silent as we stared into the flames.

Sebastian was the first to speak. "Have you calmed down now?"

I gave him a sideways look. "You move into my village. You don't bother to tell me you're sticking around. You introduce yourself to my mother without me knowing. How did you expect me to react?"

"I thought..." I raised an eyebrow when Sebastian didn't immediately finish his sentence. "That is, I hoped you might be pleased to see me."

"I am." The admission was out before I could stop it.

Sebastian started laughing. It went on for some time before he eventually got himself back under control. "Wow! Your version of being pleased to see someone, Jack Shaw, is unlike anyone else's. Other people's pleasure tends to be expressed through hugs and smiles, not bread missiles and shouting."

I turned my head to the side and held his gaze. "Why are you here? You still haven't answered that question."

"You're here. Where else would I be?"

Only seven words but they packed quite a punch and for a moment, all I could do was stare at him. "I don't understand. If you're here because of me..." I was proud of myself for not sniggering when I said that. "Then why not tell me you were here? It's been days. I thought you'd left. I didn't think I'd ever see you again."

Sebastian turned back to the fire with a grimace. "I didn't tell you at first because... I didn't want to spoil your homecoming. I figured you needed some time alone with your family."

"And then?"

Sebastian let out a sigh. "And then I wanted to, but I thought you might ask me to leave, so I kept putting it off. Which was stupid, because of course you were going to find out from your mum eventually. Or Dillon."

"Dillon?"

"We had a few drinks at the tavern. He's not like you. He's…"

"Be very careful what you say next."

Sebastian smirked. "I was just going to say he's more easygoing, that's all. He's never thrown bread at me once."

I went back to staring at the flames. It felt like I was standing at a fork in the road. Only instead of choosing a direction with my feet, I needed to do it with words.

Sebastian's chair gave a creak as he turned it to face me. "I should tell you something."

That sounded ominous. "What?"

"That first day when we met, you weren't my target."

I frowned. "What do you mean?"

"Do you remember an elf in the tavern? He was quite short for an elf. Long white-blond hair."

I thought back. It was difficult when it seemed so long ago. "Vaguely."

"He was my target. He'd spent the previous night boasting about how he'd cheated a dwarf out of a hundred gold coins. I figured that anyone whose lips were that loose deserved to get robbed, and it wasn't his money anyway."

I turned my chair so that it was a mirror image of Sebastian's, the two of us now facing each other. "So why didn't you rob him? Why did I pull the short straw? Did your monkey go rogue or something?"

Sebastian shook his head. "Because I saw you."

"And you thought I looked like an easier target, is that it?"

"Not at all. You looked…" He reached out and took my hand, turning it palm up as his lips slowly curved into a smile. "Well, I'd be lying if I didn't say that the first thing I noticed about you was how attractive you were." My breath hitched as he continued. "But after that, I noticed how lost and alone you looked. You were sad."

I let out a snort. "And nothing cheers a person up like getting robbed."

Sebastian gave me a lopsided grin. "I didn't want to rob you. Not really. I just wanted you to follow the monkey so I could meet you. I wanted to put a smile on your face, and I'd like to think I did that eventually. Once or twice anyway."

"You did." I looked up at him through my lashes. "You do." I threaded my fingers with his. "What are we, Sebastian?"

He held my gaze. "Friends. Lovers. Maybe more."

My heart started to beat faster. "More?"

Sebastian's grin was wicked. "That's what I've been working on, but you're difficult. You're high maintenance. You're stubborn. You're contrary. You don't say what's on your mind. You walk away rather than admit your feelings. You—"

"You didn't give me a chance to admit my feelings. We reached Riverbrook and you were like, 'off you go then.'"

Sebastian pulled a face. "Maybe."

"Definitely. And... I think you might have listed enough of my character flaws for one day."

Sebastian grabbed the legs of my chair and pulled them forward, so that I came to rest between his thighs. "They're not character flaws. You wouldn't be you without them." He leaned closer. "And you're... well, not perfect... that would be going too far, but you'll do."

I blinked at him. "I'll do! They're your great romantic words. They're the words you've chosen to woo me with. I'll do."

I would have had more to say about it but Sebastian was kissing me, and I really didn't care about words anymore. They could wait.

CHAPTER TWENTY-TWO

JACK

I lay with my head on Sebastian's chest and my fingers resting on his abdomen, the two of us lounging on his makeshift bed in a satiated postcoital tangle of limbs. I turned my head slightly to drop a kiss just above his right nipple. "This is nice."

Sebastian's fingers stilled in my hair before continuing their rhythmic stroking. "It is." He paused. "So you're not mad at me anymore?"

It took a great amount of willpower to lever myself up onto one elbow, but I eventually managed it. I stared down at him, taking in everything from his flushed cheeks to how red his lips were from too much kissing. If there was such a thing as too much kissing. His hair was a tangled mess as well, and I felt absurdly pleased to be the cause of all of those things. "Oh, I'm still mad at you."

Sebastian let out a weary sigh. "Why do I feel like that's a permanent state of affairs that only occasionally wanes."

I raised an eyebrow. "Probably because you keep doing stupid things."

A crease appeared on Sebastian's brow. "Like what?"

"Like... letting other men kiss you. Like telling me you're going to marry a prince when you had no such intention of doing so. Like setting up home in my village without bothering to tell me you're here. Like befriending my mother and my brother behind my back." I met his gaze with a challenge. "Shall I go on?"

"Probably not necessary." He brushed my hair back from my brow. "If you'd been a little more open about things, I wouldn't have felt like I had to hide my feelings, though."

"What did I do?"

An incredulous expression settled on Sebastian's face. "What did *you* do?"

"That's what I asked."

Sebastian sat up. "Let's see. You told me you wouldn't sleep with me if I was the last man alive. How are the goats by the way?" I glared at him, and he continued with a smirk. "You said you just wanted to be friends."

"I meant it at the time. I was determined not to fall prey to your"—I trailed my gaze over his bare chest—"considerable charms."

"You sent me to seduce another man." He plastered a hand to his chest in a dramatic fashion. "That hurt."

"I didn't *want* you to seduce another man."

"No?"

"No, of course not. I wasn't happy about it at all. It was just a necessary evil if we wanted to get out of there. I didn't fancy spending the rest of my life as a slave."

Sebastian looked somewhat mollified, and I realized it really had bothered him. I cast an eye around the somewhat dubious surroundings. "Are you really going to stay here?"

"What's wrong with it?"

I laughed. "Are you serious? Where do I start?"

Sebastian lay back down again. "It'll be fine once I've fixed it up some. It just needs work."

"And you're really going to stay here, and do it?"

He rolled his head to the side to meet my gaze. "You think I'm going to take off, don't you? Once I get bored of Riverbrook."

Something fluttered in my gut. That was exactly what I thought. "I think… you think you'll stay, but a few weeks down the line, a few months maybe, you'll need something more. I can assure you that there's no adventure in Riverbrook. There's just farming and people going about their daily lives. And I don't think I'm going to be enough to make up for that." The words were difficult, but at least they were honest. Sebastian was right in saying that we'd spent a lot of time skirting around each other, neither of us saying what really mattered. I guess I'd guarded my heart a little too carefully. So carefully that I'd almost let Sebastian walk away just to save face.

Sebastian looked thoughtful. "You can teach me to farm."

"I'd like my crops to live."

"Oh, come on, it can't be that difficult." He lifted his hand, his fingers trailing gold sparks. "And I might have a few tricks up my sleeve to save time."

I doubted it. Sebastian's gift might be useful when it came to evading dragons and basilisks, but it was hard to see where it might aid something as mundane as farming. It did remind me of something, though. "By the way, I was thinking about Prince Montgomery."

"Should I be worried?"

I shot Sebastian a scathing glance. "Not like that. I'd rather—"

"Screw farm animals?" Sebastian blinked innocently. "And we all know what happened last time you said that." The point didn't need elaboration, but he waved a hand to indicate our mutual state of nakedness anyway.

I shook my head ruefully. "Shouldn't he have had magic? He's a prince. I thought all royals were capable of wielding magic."

Sebastian rolled onto his back. "He did have magic."

I frowned. "We spent two days with him. I saw nothing remotely magical unless it was the ability to have perfect hair. What could he do?"

Sebastian's lips quirked. "It wasn't something we needed to call upon."

"So it *was* the hair?"

He chuckled. "It wasn't the hair."

I leaned closer. "Well?"

"Would it make any difference if I told you he'd sworn me to secrecy?"

I didn't hesitate, even for a second. "No."

"Didn't think so." Sebastian leaned up on his elbows. "Prince Montgomery has the ability to locate water."

I stared at him. "Pretty useful if you're in a desert, or you're a farmer."

He nodded. His gaze dropped to my lips, his voice husky. "Come here. You're too far away, and I don't want to talk about Prince Montgomery."

Smiling, I shuffled forward. We sank into a kiss that quickly grew in heat and passion. It was hard to believe that Sebastian was not only here, but that he was apparently mine. If not forever, then at least for the next few weeks. And maybe if we fucked enough, I could keep him from getting bored for much longer than that.

I was kissing my way down his chest to his cock, the organ rising to meet me, when the knock on the door sounded. "Ignore it."

Sebastian let out a little moan as I slid my lips over the head of his cock. And then in the next second, there was no cock to suck on, Sebastian already on his feet and wrapping a blanket round his waist to preserve his modesty. He leaned down to drop a gentle kiss on my lips before making for the door. "It's probably your mother."

It took a moment for the words to sink in as I lay there naked and aroused. "What?" My voice came out high-pitched as I struggled to drag a blanket across my lap, the action seeming far more difficult than it should, as if my fingers had become nothing but useless appendages. "Then definitely don't answer the door."

But I was too late, Sebastian having already flung it open. There was a pause of a few seconds before he said "come in."

A man dressed in riding gear stepped inside, Sebastian closing the door behind him. "Good news. It's not your mother."

I stared at the man he'd ushered inside. "I can see that. My mother doesn't have a beard." The question, though, was who the hell was he? He wasn't from Riverbrook, not unless he'd arrived in my absence, and I didn't think that was the case. He had the slightly worn appearance of a man who'd ridden hard for at least a few hours. The man gave an awkward little bow to Sebastian. "My name is Frederick. I am a representative from the royal house of Chastershire in the neighboring kingdom of Osagezia. Poor fortune has befallen them, and your name reached the king and queen of Chastershire's ears after your daring rescue of Prince Montgomery. We have been trying to track you down for the last few days."

I squinted at the man, his upright posture making sense now that I knew he was a royal representative. They always looked like someone had stuck a stick up their ass. "How did you find him?"

Frederick turned to face me, his expression remaining carefully blank in spite of the fact that there was an awful lot of bare skin on display. But then, Sebastian wasn't much better, and he hadn't so much as batted an eyelid at that either. Frederick was obviously well-versed in the art of ignoring what he wasn't supposed to see. His gaze encompassed both of us as he answered the question. "One of our envoys spoke with Leofric. He told us that we were likely to find Mr. Beau here in Riverbrook. I came straightaway. The good people of Riverbrook were kind enough to point me in this direction. And here I am."

"Leofric!" I fastened my gaze on Sebastian. "How would he know you were here? I didn't even know you were here until today."

Sebastian grinned. "He knows me. Better than I know myself sometimes." He turned his attention to Frederick. "You better tell me what's going on."

Frederick gave another little bow. He gestured at one of the chairs. "May I?"

Sebastian pulled one over for him and Frederick sat down, Sebastian arranging the blanket carefully over his own lap as he took the other chair while I stayed on the floor. Frederick cleared his throat in a dramatic fashion before he started talking. "Two months ago, a precious artefact was stolen from the palace of Chastershire. It's an artefact that carries great religious significance to the people. It is required for any official function. Princess Surander was due to be married next month, but the ceremony cannot possibly go ahead in the artefact's absence."

Sebastian leaned forward, his biceps bunching. "Who stole it? And why?"

Frederick gave an expansive shrug. "We do not know who stole it, or what they wish to do with it. All we know is that the perpetrator or perpetrators have headed to Askophai, which makes it difficult to follow."

I looked to Sebastian, and he elaborated for me. "Askophai is to the north. Once you get past Osagezia, the climate becomes far colder, and a lot of the terrain is mountainous. It's an easy place to escape detection."

Frederick nodded. "Men have been sent, but they came back empty-handed. And the last group…" He looked momentarily uncomfortable. "They have not returned at all. It is feared they will never return, that something terrible has befallen them."

I interrupted. "This is a fascinating story, and I'm very sad for your kingdom that you've lost your, whatever it is, but what has this got to do with Sebastian? He didn't steal it." Realizing that it wasn't completely out of the question, I gave him a narrow-eyed look. "Did you? If so, you should give it back so the princess can get married."

Sebastian tapped his fingers on his thigh. "I didn't steal it." He gave a noisy exhale. "It sounds like a dangerous undertaking to get it back, especially given the lack of information you have about who has it." He waved his hand around the room. "And as you can see, I'm in the middle of extensive renovations that need to be completed before winter. And there are a few other things I need to do as well." His gaze strayed over to me, heat pooling in my stomach and a smile pulling at the corners of my mouth. Once he'd gotten rid of Frederick, we could get back to what we'd been doing, what I anticipated we'd spend the next few days doing.

Frederick coughed. "There is a quite sizeable reward of course."

The smile died on my lips. There was no sound in the room apart from the crackling of the fire.

Sebastian studied his fingernails. "How sizeable?"

"Six hundred gold coins."

Sebastian's whistle was long and low. "That is sizeable." Despite the fact that I was staring at him, he wouldn't meet my gaze. "You understand that this is not really what I do? I'm more of a…" He frowned like he couldn't think of a good way to end the sentence. It reminded me that apart from knowing he was a wanderer who seemed to know everything and everyone, I really didn't know much about him. Or anything, really, apart from where he came from.

Frederick gave a curt nod. "Of course, but we thought that maybe after the prince, that you..." He trailed off.

Sebastian looked thoughtful. "I'd have to give the proposition some careful consideration."

Frederick nodded again as he rose to his feet. "That's quite understandable. I will go and partake of the home comforts at the tavern. They will be most welcome after a day's riding. I will return for your answer in the morning."

Polite farewells were said as Frederick took his leave. I didn't listen, my mind churning with what I already knew was going to happen.

"Jack?" There was a slight note of frustration in Sebastian's voice, as if he'd already said my name a few times. I lifted my head to meet his gaze. "You're going to go." I couldn't help the slight note of bitterness in my voice. "I believed you when you said you were going to stay, but I saw it when he was talking, that look of excitement in your eyes. You wanted to do it even before he mentioned the reward."

"I didn't say yes." Sebastian's voice was quiet and laden with something that sounded like regret.

"But you will. Even if you could turn down an adventure, you're not turning down six hundred gold coins." I climbed to my feet, holding the blanket to me as I looked around for my clothes. Once I'd found them, I started to get dressed. I needed to get out of here. Once I was home, I'd be able to resume the mantle of cynical Jack, the man who'd been so determined that what he had with Sebastian was just a fling because he wasn't going to have his heart broken. It just went to show that cynical Jack had been right.

"Come with me."

I paused, the button on my shirt I'd been about to fasten slipping through my fingers. "What?"

Sebastian stepped forward, his eyes shining. "We're a team, you and I. Come with me. I'll probably get myself into all sorts of trouble if you're not there."

Something flared in my chest, something that felt very much like the excitement I'd accused Sebastian of feeling. "I can't just leave. There's the farm to think about. Harvest will be here in a couple of weeks. It's the busiest time of the year."

"Your brother can handle it."

It sounded so simple. Leave the farm for my brother to take care of, and just take off again. With Sebastian. Could I do that? Crazy as it was, the temptation was definitely there. "I don't have clothes suitable for the climate in the north."

Sebastian shrugged. "Neither do I. We'll get some in Osagezia." His fingers fastened around my shoulders. "We can keep each other warm."

"I'm not a blanket." My words sounded weak. I was wavering. I knew it, and Sebastian knew it. It would only take one more prod to send me careening over the precipice.

"Your sister might have sailed that way."

And there it was.

"We can carry on looking for her."

I exhaled slowly. "We could." I lifted my gaze to Sebastian. "We split the money half and half. Three hundred for me and three hundred for you."

He pulled a face. "That doesn't seem fair. They were looking for me, not you. You're more my... assistant."

I let out a choked laugh. "Assistant! In your dreams. Three hundred each or I'm not coming." I risked Sebastian turning me down flat, but then at least I'd know what mattered to him most. If I couldn't compete with money, then it was better to know that before I really got hurt. I spat on my palm and held it out. "Three hundred. Take it or leave it." I eyed him with a confidence I definitely wasn't feeling.

Sebastian's eyes narrowed. "You drive a hard bargain, Jack Shaw." He smiled before spitting on his palm and pressing it against mine. "Deal." We shook, his eyes twinkling. "What do you say to us hammering out the finer points of this deal in a slightly less traditional way. After all, we can't tell Frederick the good news until the morning."

I flattened my palm against his chest and pushed him against the wall, both of our blankets slipping to the floor to leave us naked. "The hammering sounds good. Who's going to be doing the hammering?"

Sebastian dragged his gaze languorously down the length of my body. "There's hours 'til morning. Why don't we start with you hammering me and then we'll see where we get to?"

"Or we could do it the other way round."

Sebastian let out a strangled groan. "Could you not agree with me just once, farm boy. Is this what it's going to be like in Askophai?"

I grinned at him, my chest filling with a peculiar sensation of lightness. "Undoubtedly. I hope you're ready for it."

Sebastian lowered his lips until they were so close to mine that I could feel the vibration when he spoke. "Oh, I'm ready for it. The question is whether the world is ready for us."

The End

Want to read Prince Montgomery's rescue from his point of view? You can download a bonus story by signing up to my newsletter here. The download link will be in the welcome email.

Jack and Sebastian will be back for another adventure in The Stubborn Accomplice. Pre-order it here.

THANKS

Thanks for reading this book. If you can take the time to leave a review, I would really appreciate it.

You can receive a number of FREE short stories and bonus chapters by signing up to my mailing list.

You'll also be informed about new releases and sales.

Want to see what I am working on before anyone else? Subscribe to my Patreon for WIP chapters and a version of A Temporary Situation written from Tristan's point of view. I'll also be writing bonus stories about established characters exclusive to my patrons.

Other places you can find me

Twitter. Bookbub Instagram Facebook. Website Days Den

MORE MM ROMANCE BOOKS BY H.L DAY

Romantic comedies

A Temporary Situation

A Christmas Situation

Temporary Insanity

Taking Love's Lead

Suspense

A Dance too Far

A Step too Far

Contemporary

Eager For You

Eager For More

Edge of Living

Kept in the Dark

Time for a Change

Christmas Riches

Not So Silent Night

Post-apocalyptic Sci-fi

Refuge

Rebellion

Exposed

Paranormal

The Beauty Within

The Longest Night

Read the blurb for these books through H.L Day's website or on H.L Day's Amazon
page.

Available In audio

Kept in the Dark

Edge of Living

A Dance too Far

A Step too Far

Exposed

The Beauty Within

If You Liked This Book, You May Also Like

A Temporary Situation

(Temporary; Tristan and Dom #1)

Personal assistant Dominic is a consummate professional. Funny then, that he harbors such unprofessional feelings toward Tristan Maxwell, the CEO of the company. No, not in that way. The man may be the walking epitome of gorgeousness dressed up in a designer suit. But, Dominic's immune. Unlike most of the workforce, he can see through the pretty facade to the arrogant, self-entitled asshole below. It's lucky then, that the man's easy enough to avoid.

Disaster strikes when Dominic finds himself having to work in close proximity as Tristan's P.A. The man is infuriatingly unflappable, infuriatingly good-humored, and infuriatingly unorthodox. In short, just infuriating. A late-night rescue leading to a drunken pass only complicates matters further, especially with the discovery that Tristan is both straight and engaged.

Hatred turns to tolerance, tolerance to friendship, and friendship to mutual passion. One thing's for sure, if Tristan sets his sights on Dominic, there's no way Dominic has the necessary armor or willpower to keep a force of nature like Tristan at bay for long, no matter how unprofessional a relationship with the boss might be. He may just have to revise everything he previously thought and believed in for a chance at love.

Buy now from Amazon

Not So Silent Night

One grumpy patient. One unconventional nurse. Twenty-two reindeer later.

Things aren't great for Xander Cole. It's Christmas, he's fractured his pelvis on a skiing trip he never wanted to go on, and his on/off boyfriend is most definitely off. No wonder he's not exactly full of festive cheer.

Ferris Night isn't having much luck either. His plan to take a break from work before starting a new job has been wrecked by a flooded flat. With nowhere to stay, he grabs the opportunity for a job as a live-in nurse with both hands. After all, how hard can it be?

Xander doesn't need a nurse. Especially one who's far too flirty, far too attractive, far too into Christmas, and far too good at getting his own way. But Ferris has never faced a challenge that couldn't be overcome with a bit of charm and perseverance. It doesn't matter how attractive Xander might be. He's immune. Maybe.

As banter and sparring between the two men turn into more, a nurse might not be needed, but both men could be in for a fresh start to the new year.

A low angst 63k romantic comedy, which features snarky banter, a slow burn relationship, two men who can give as good as they get, an annoying ex, and a Star Wars nativity scene.

Please note that this story was originally released as a single POV short story as part of the Winter Wonderland Prolific Works giveaway. The story has been revised and is now dual POV with over 40k of added content

Buy from Amazon

TEMPORARY INSANITY

(Temporary; Paul and Indy #1)

Sleeping with the enemy never felt so good.

When Paul Davenport comes face to face with the man he caught in bed with his boyfriend years before, it's hate at first sight. Well, second sight. Indy should be apologizing, not flirting. Except the gorgeous barman is completely oblivious to their paths ever having crossed before.

Despite his feelings, Paul's powerless to resist the full-on charm offensive that follows. It's fine though. It's just sex. No emotions. No getting to know each other. Just a bout of temporary insanity that's sure to run its course once the simmering passion starts to wear off.

Only what if it's not? Indy's nothing like the man Paul expected him to be from his past actions. What if they're perfect for each other and Paul's just too stubborn to see it? Forging a relationship with him would require an emotional U-turn Paul might not be capable of making.

There's a thin line between love and hate, and Paul's about to discover just how thin it really is. He can't possibly be falling for the man that ruined his life. Can he?

Warning: This book contains hate sex—sort of, lots of banter, and a pink elephant. No, really it does. Actually, two elephants.

Please note: Although this book is in the Temporary series, it occurs during the same timeline as A Temporary Situation. Therefore, both books can be read as standalones and in any order.

Buy from Amazon

TAKING LOVE'S LEAD

Sometimes you've got to stalk a man to win his heart

A whirlwind encounter has web designer Zachary Cole reassessing his life and what he wants from it. Knocked for six by a less than orthodox meeting with the sexy Edgar, he resolves to see him again. Even if it does involve hatching a plan using his heavily pregnant sister, her dalmatian, and a rather large dose of subterfuge.

Sick of being dumped, dog-walker Edgar's sworn off relationships. Zack might just happen to pop up wherever he goes, but that's not going to change anything. It's not like Zack would ever want anything more than a walk on the wild side with him anyway. They're just too different. He'll stick to his four-legged friends instead. They might get up to a lot of mischief but they never let him down.

Zack wants love. Edgar only wants friendship. Can the two men find common ground amid the chaos of Edgar's life? Or is Zack going to find that no matter what he does, he'll end up having to walk away?

A romantic comedy full of mad mishaps with dogs, ducks, and lakes. Oh, and two stubborn men as well who find it almost impossible to both be on the same page.

Buy from Amazon

Printed in Great Britain
by Amazon